MBA

DOUGLAS BOARD

Lightning
Books

Published in 2015 by
Lightning Books, an imprint of
EyeStorm Media Ltd
29 Barrow Street
Much Wenlock
Shropshire
TF13 6EN
www.lightning-books.com

ISBN: 978-1-785630-05-7

British Library Cataloguing in Publication Data.
A catalogue record for this book is available from the British Library.

Printed by CPI Group (UK) Ltd, Croydon CR0 4YY

In Praise of MBA

"A must read for anyone who enjoyed Franzen's Freedom or Eggers' The Circle. MBA challenges and amuses with equal measure and makes you wonder about the impact of the Anglo-American dream."

Felicity Wood, Deputy Features Editor, *The Bookseller*

"Given their role in shaping and propagating the ideas that govern all our working lives, business schools have for the most part unjustly escaped the attentions of fiction writers. All the more refreshing, then, to read Douglas Board's wonderfully enjoyable dissection of the swirling currents of ambition, dissembling, power and fortune that are all too often rationalised away in textbook accounts of 'leadership'. Witty and deeply informed, Board's rich satire is nearer the bone of business than a lot of people would want you to think.

Simon Caulkin, management writer in *Management Today, Financial Times Business Education* and at simoncaulkin.com

"This satirical novel is not just thought-provoking, it pokes your brain with a sharp pointed stick to get an explosive reaction. And the right reaction is laughter, constant chuckling coupled with a sheepish admission to self that MBAs are as full of bull as bureaucrats. Buy it, read it, then set a multiple answer exam on it. It's a hoot."

Peter Sullivan, former Group Editor-in-Chief of Independent Newspapers South Africa

"When the mindless, probably male, manager in your life puts you down, pick this up. Hilarious and spot on."
Sandra Burmeister, CEO Amrop Landelahni

"By focussing his farce on the business schools he knows so well, Board updates the campus novel and takes a big swing at the insincerities inherent in the ideology of neo-liberalism."
CM Taylor, author of *Premiership Psycho* and *Cloven*

"When, in the first chapter, Ben the CEO's executive assistant is asked to stand in for the CEO in the difficult task of firing Ben, I knew I had found a winning piece of writing. Board brings years of deep business experience and breathtaking wit to a La Cage aux Folles-like storyline where a cast of capricious characters comically converge in a crazed climax. MBA is a light, rompy read that never lets the reader go longer than a paragraph without a smile ... and more often, a guffaw."
John C Beck, author of *Good vs Good, Japan's Business Renaissance* and *The Attention Economy*

"A virtuoso plot and unrelieved bass-note of suspense whisk the reader through MBA with no time to fasten a seat-belt. Iconoclastic and LOL hilarious, this story unpicks the fabric of leadership and interrogates the murky motives of the über-'successful'. Irresistibly funny and deliciously uncomfortable, MBA is a seductive cocktail of politics, human relating, banking, feminism, the dangers of intelligent underwear and so many other unusual bed-fellows."
Rosemary Lain-Priestley, author of *Does My Soul Look Big In This?* and *Unwrapping The Sacred*

MBA

www.lol-mba.com
@lol_mba

FOREWORD
FOREWORD

(recorded at Hampton Management College three years later)

You're recording now? Jeez. Well, I guess so. Can I call you Doug? Since we've learned a bit about each other now.

I get it – a foreword from one of the characters. Some say *the* leading character. Speaking from the heart and telling it like it is: which is what leaders do. Feedback is, I'm pretty good at it. About two minutes' worth, you say? (*Pause.*)

None of us saw the banking crisis coming. Sure, I was ahead of most folks; I often am. But I've learned not to bullshit myself. Bullshitting yourself is a one-way trip; in God's good time you find out no one's selling returns. Remember the guy who made forty-six billion out of whatsmyname.com? Bill Szygenda. He bullshitted himself so much, he fooled the rest of us! But that's another story – one you can read in my book *Beyond Easy, Beyond Difficult.*

But look at it another way: the future is inevitable. It's staring us in the face. All we have to do is recognise it.

Hampton was zilch. Educationally, it was a trash can in the back street of a ghetto. For twenty years folks had dumped second-raters, third-raters and worse kinds of shit in it. But I saw a team hungry to be world-class. Starving. All they needed was leadership.

Today, the stars of the future know about Hampton. I mean – tomorrow's really bright kids in tomorrow's places, in Shanghai, in Togo, in Buenos Aires. Right here's where they want to study. Ahead of Harvard. Ahead of CEIBS. Read the surveys, do the math.

Why? Because today, Hampton is synonymous with telling the truth. And integrity is *the* key issue for business in the twenty-first century. Just get alignment around integrity – talking straight, thinking straight, feeling straight – and amazing things will happen.

This is the story of how we did that and how we hit a few home runs along the way. You know – doubled the number of doctors in the NHS and saved the world's banking system.

Here's the thing: those man-on-the-moon achievements depended on totally unseen people. This book will show you those unseen people. That's why I was tickled pink to become a Commander of the British Empire. What a neat idea – an empire you can't see to honour the people you can't see. Personally, as I told Her Majesty, it was a big enough honour just to spell 'honour' with a 'u'!

The bottom line? The only thing that will save us from the next crisis is what we've learned from this one. And what we've learned is, in the twenty-first century, leadership and learning are *the* key business issues.

Alongside integrity. And the environment.

Professor William C Gyro CBE
Deputy Governor of the Bank of England
Chairman of the United Nations Task Force on Leadership
and emeritus Dean, Hampton Management College

BOOK ONE

THE TOWER

MONDAY 11 JUNE (EVENING)
MONDAY 11 JUNE (EVENING)

London is being re-made. In 10 weeks the city's mop-topped mayor, a one-man Beatles revival with added bleach, will wave the Olympic flag in Beijing's stadium. Back home, the construction of a 21st-century stadium and velodrome has already begun. But the city's re-making is much more than this.

The first re-making is up. Skyscrapers are sprouting on the city's face like a fungus. Southwark Towers – 24 floors of offices next to the southeast rail terminus – is being demolished. In four years' time the 87 floors of the Shard will take its place. If you're going places in London, you're going up.

Ben Stillman is going up. He's barely 30 and he's chief of staff to a billionaire.

The city is being remade back towards its centre. In places like Johannesburg, after the rich moved outwards they sent removal vans back in to take their jobs with them. But most of the jobs that matter in London are still in the centre, and the people with money have come back to hug those jobs more closely. In London, the centre is the place to be.

Where Ben's at in his career could not be more central. He is the hub of 26,000 people labouring worldwide in everything from chemicals and agriculture to re-insurance. Ben is Alex Bakhtin's right hand.

The third reshaper of London is glass. All the new towers are glass from top to bottom. Welcome to a new kind of power, which sees all and displays all. It has no need to hide. Perhaps this power is modern and clean, democratic and accountable. But then a gust blows, a cable slips and a window cleaner's fingers get caught in the winching gear. As detergent and blood smear the glass, we glimpse something older. The cable that once suspended a human halfway between heaven and earth was the divine right of kings.

All-glass palaces: London's new way to tell passers-by that they count for shit. You're welcome to look in, because you're so lowly that what you see has no consequence.

A cloudless June evening was beginning as Ben's car crawled round London's traffic-choked concrete corset. Given the priceless treasure he was carrying, he had thought about arranging a police escort; Bakhtin Enterprises had that kind of clout. But how embarrassing to drive an Audi with state-of-the-art LED running lights at only 30 miles an hour, surrounded by flashing blues. Knowing his luck someone would see him and post the picture on YouTube.

YouTube – now that was a business! Founded when Ben had been in the final months of his MBA, and sold for

$1.6 billion 18 months later. What a time to be alive; what a time to be in business!

Of course, the other side of business was the gobbledygook that the bankers had produced for tomorrow's meeting in Paris. How complicated could borrowing 700 million be? Quite complicated, if the bankers had dreamt up that you should pay the interest on some Chilean mining equipment while the Chilean government paid the interest on your frozen orange juice.

After turning off the main artery from London, Ben's blood pressure rose. Not so much on the first part of the way to Hampton – small place, little traffic – as on the country road beyond. This snaked left and right and up and down. One unexpectedly sharp turn tapped the package in the back seat against a rear door, which made the driver anxious. This priceless package was a faux-Louis XIV chair made entirely of glass, one of Alex Bakhtin's wilder ideas for a present.

From the top of Pynbal's Ridge he headed down towards the lake and the college buildings of Hampton. Driving this way during his MBA, often the view had been cloaked in the dark of evening or winter. The valley's contents had eventually opened themselves to his gaze, modestly picturesque and unmemorable. But back then he had been driving a second-hand Mondeo that had made everything ordinary; now he was parting the forests of larch and silver birch in a sleek and alchemical beast.

The lake, narrow but with the evening sun glinting off its length, resembled a drawn sword. The dean's white house and the main two-level brick buildings were the handle, but now the handle was dwarfed by something new. A five-storey spore from outer space had landed, currently cloaked in scaffolding, hoardings and canvas wrappings. The new tower, presumably. The college had got a new dean and the new dean had got a new tower.

Looking back, Ben could not imagine how green he had been when he had started his MBA at the age of 25. Some of the teaching had been dire, but he had only paid thirty-five thousand to attend a second-division school. The main thing had been the business opportunities those three letters after someone's name could open up. The new dean imported from America was good news for Ben. Hampton was climbing the rankings and its alumni's careers were climbing with it.

Ben's mind wandered and the Audi wandered a little with it. So much so that he almost drove into a silver Lexus stopped around a bend. The air bed improvised behind Ben's seat did its job, cushioning 19 kilos of solid glass.

The rear window of the Lexus slid downwards. Above a green pashmina beamed the well-kept face of a woman who had been in her forties for perhaps 15 years. Her walnut hair, shoulder-length, was luxuriant to the point of deserving European environmental protection.

'You must be Ben,' she said. 'Hampton's golden boy returns. This is all my fault. I was telling Greg –'

She indicated the young man beside her. The driver was part blond, part jet-black, with gas-flame eyes, hair gel and an earring. He had about 20 years on the clock. An explanation of why Greg had stopped on the crown of the road looked as unlikely as an apology for escaping from a Hitler Youth boy band.

'– that we absolutely must be back for your speech. And we will. I hope the chair is all right.'

Ben glanced at the back seat. As far as he knew, only the dean at Hampton was aware of what he had been so gingerly ferrying from central London. So the woman now disappearing in his rear-view mirror must be Dianne Peach-Gyro, the dean's wife.

Ten minutes later, the mover and shaker himself came out of the front door of his house to welcome the college's returning hero. And why not? Bakhtin was gifting the college not just a glass chair but three million pounds, and Ben was his trusted courier. Gyro was an energetic 55 and over six feet tall, not counting the charcoal eyebrows that arched like a burger chain. Ben would pick him as a doubles tennis partner, no questions asked. A thick lacquer of superficiality might sit on top, but underneath Ben warmed to someone who so obviously got one hell of a lot done.

They shook hands. 'Safe trip?' Gyro asked.

'I was flashed a few times on the main road, but otherwise no problems at all.' Ben opened the Audi's rear door.

'You leave it right there, we'll take care of that baby.' Gyro ran one hand through his hair as if to stop it receding like the polar ice caps. 'You graduated here, when? Just before I arrived?'

'Yes, three years ago.'

'And now you're Alex's chief of staff. That's damn good. Hampton needs more of you and, you know what –' Gyro gestured at the scaffolding on the other side of the college building, 'if I have anything to do with it, Hampton's going to get them.' Gyro clapped Ben on the shoulder. 'What d'you say? A quick whisky, just a baby one, to steady the nerves?'

Ben smiled and shook his head. He wasn't nervous. He had stood in for Alex Bakhtin so many times that he could do it falling off a log. In fact, of the two Ben was the better speaker.

Of course with hindsight Ben should have been nervous. But come on, how could he have known what would shortly transpire?

Sixty minutes later the glass chair had been removed from the Audi and taken inside, where it radiated boldness to the 50 people in the room. Ben flipped the pages of Alex's speech notes but he wasn't looking at them. He was paid enough to know Bakhtin's life and leadership philosophy by heart.

The courtesies and apologies were complete. The dean had been thanked for his hospitality. The dean's secretary had been thanked, with the flowers that she had been told to organise for herself. The audience wanted to hear the thoughts of the charismatic entrepreneur Alex Bakhtin. They craved vowels that surged with the power of fortunes made, consonants that broke on the wreckage of lesser sums lost. Ben began:

'No less today than when I started, I teach my managers that the foundation of successful business is always people. Not any people, but those *selfless* people and their teamwork who create any business, any result, any human achievement whatsoever.

'On the farm where I was brought up, harvest time was hard. We rose at five and did not finish until midnight. Of course that was a business lesson – to work hard. But every farmer works hard. Yet not every farmer's child produces a business of international distinction.

'The difference lay in the workers we hired and how we treated them. Every harvest evening, my mother prepared food under the trees. Grilled fish or eggplants as big as houses – the ovens did not stop as long as our workers were still coming. Ten o'clock in the evening, eleven o'clock, still they were coming. The selfless workers. We ate with them, of course – another business lesson. And they ate their fill.

'I particularly remember the time when a son was born to one of our foremen. Without a word being said, my mother had already begun to roast a suckling pig. That foreman was a selfless worker. He worked the harvest the very day his son was born.

'Around midnight I would help my father clear the table. We fed the leftovers to the dogs. "Son," my father said to me one time, "have you seen any dogs better fed than ours?"

'"None, father!" I replied. "None in the whole world."

'"You are right!" he exclaimed. "But remember, they only feed after the selfless workers have had their fill."

'So this is what I teach my managers. Your shareholders have sharp teeth. I am one of them. We are dogs. We want to be the best-fed shareholders in the whole world. But only after your selfless workers have eaten their fill.'

Ben paused to let some of the eyes in his audience moisten. As he did so the crowd at the back of the room parted to admit the walnut-haired woman, still striking in a green pashmina, but now sparkling with diamonds.

'Distinguished professors and scholars of business, I fear that my working-man's philosophy is not worthy of you. But tonight I am so appreciative of the honour that you extend to me – and also to my tragically deceased wife – by establishing this new Chair of Selfless Leadership in her name.'

Ben pocketed the speech notes and continued, 'As Dean Gyro told you, Alex Bakhtin is so sorry that he cannot be here in person. As his chief of staff I know how deeply he had been looking forward to today, not only to meeting all of you but also to remembering his very dear Julia. But there is one task that Alex insists on handling personally, wherever in the company it may have to take place, even if there are other commitments that he has made. That task is downsizing. It is true – this year Bakhtin Enterprises will grow 27 percent. But the task of pruning for market fitness is never complete. He wants to be here, but the task of selfless leadership is sadly elsewhere tonight.'

There was a gratifying body to the applause that welled up around the room. The applause grew, listened to itself and decided what it wanted to do next. For a moment it waited respectfully. For the fallen, for the downsized, for the however many in whichever country with whom Alex Bakhtin had gone to be, this outpost of capitalism dipped its flag. But then glasses of champagne and canapé plates were downed, to enable the hands that had held them to come together more vigorously. Three million pounds of endowment were in the college coffers. And Ben had spoken well.

Gyro came forward and with the dean's help Ben unveiled the glass faux-Louis XIV chair – 'something to remind us of transparency in business, and a fitting accompaniment to the new tower'. Ben read out the engraving: 'Dedicated to selfless leaders by Alex Bakhtin'.

Delight surged around the room. It was a good night for Hampton – more money from a top business name – and a good night for Ben.

'I was told you could use this,' someone whispered in his ear. A glass of champagne was thrust into his hand. 'I'm the deputy dean, Dorothy Lines.'

Ben took a grateful gulp. 'Ben Stillman. A pleasure to meet you, Professor Lines. I guess getting an actual chair is a bit unusual?'

'Unusual and very witty, but what personally fascinates me is the legal aspect. Forgive me, my field is law.'

'Someone's got to do it,' Ben grinned.

'Very good of you to see it that way. The Julia Bakhtin Chair in Selfless Leadership will be the first endowed chair on either side of the Atlantic where the name will automatically change if our benefactor remarries.'

'How very practical.'

'Indeed. Now – my instructions were quite strict; everyone wants to meet our hero so you must circulate. But it's very nice to have a Hampton alumnus back in such distinguished circumstances.'

A woman stepped forward into Ben's path: half-Chinese, perhaps in her late thirties. 'May I?'

'Of course!' beamed the deputy dean. 'Connie Yung is the top student on the MSc programme we run for managers in the NHS. In fact, she's just agreed to join our board of governors. We wanted someone grown-up with recent student experience.'

Connie ignored Ben's offered hand. Her gaze ran up and down him like an airport scanner. She was wearing a light scent, something reminiscent of orchids and revenge. 'A bit of a slip, eh? The board of governors got me when they could have had you, Mr Hero.'

'Ah. We MBAs fail the grown-up part of the test.'

'Please tell your boss I'm gutted he couldn't make it, because I came to throw this drink over him. I'd been looking forward to it all day. He screwed a business I was in. Lots of my friends lost their jobs.'

Dorothy Lines' brow creased.

Ben's stomach jumped. 'Look, I'm sorry about that. Maybe there's another side to that story? Really I'm just a back-room boy. I wouldn't know.' Actually, her perfume was quite enticing, not cloying or insipid. 'Since you're joining the board of a business school, how about we call it quits and put it down to market forces?'

Connie smiled briefly. 'Oh, there was definitely an invisible hand, but it was your boss's.'

Ben wanted to say more, but Connie had turned away. Dorothy took his arm.

'So Connie's a doctor in the NHS?' In front of the deputy dean Ben wasn't going to fall into the trap of asking if she was a nurse.

'No, she's an HR director.'

He unsuccessfully tried to stifle a grimace. His only

experience in human resources had suggested to him that HR was glorified paper-shuffling.

A large, square-cut emerald ring with diamond acolytes surged into his view. The ring was attached to a left hand. The right hand brought a young man of Ben's age in tow, and a voice like a cello entered Ben between two of his lumbar vertebrae.

'*Bravissimo*, Mr Stillman! So I might have guessed; you are also an expert on our health system.' This time the warrior queen Dianne introduced herself. She was a psychologist as well as the dean's wife. Her younger male companion was Ed Lens, who worked in the Prime Minister's office. Ben gathered from Dianne that Ed was the mastermind behind Britain's world-leading health reforms. 'I am aghast,' Dianne continued, 'despite every effort, to have missed the first part of your talk. Although as a cheap shot in mitigation, I was there for more of it than Mr Bakhtin. Is it impertinent to ask whether any of those Bakhtin folk tales are true? We academics are impossible, I know – that unstoppable quest for facts.'

'All of it,' Ben replied, 'as far as I know. I've never met Alex's parents, but he does keep two dogs, Shareholder and Value. They salivate all over you, and then bite. They think it's a sign of affection.'

'Has Mr Bakhtin been to Number Ten?' inquired Lens. He had a climber's physique, though given his place of work his skill was probably climbing over bodies rather than rocks.

Ben tried to recall the photographs on Alex's wall. There was one at Number Ten, but with whom? Alex was not old enough for it to have been Thatcher, and Major had no glamour.

So probably it was the one who departed 12 months ago to spend more time with his international bank accounts, in which case best nothing mentioned. 'I don't think Mr Bakhtin has had the pleasure of meeting the Prime Minister. I'm sure he would consider the opportunity a great honour. The Prime Minister's recent book struck him very forcibly.' Well, it would strike him once Ben had written him a half-pager on it.

'Consider it done,' declared Dianne. Her hand settled on Ben's arm as if drawing a DNA sample for her personal database through his jacket and shirt. The two of them watched Lens depart. 'Ed has the most enormous influence. I wouldn't be at all surprised if the Prime Minister visited Hampton in the near future. So when were you a Hampton graduate? It must have been before our time. I couldn't have forgotten you if you had come to one of our student soirées.'

'I did the MBA three years back, part-time.'

'Were you working with Alex then?'

'No. After my first degree it was pretty tough to get a job, but I got in as a management trainee with the local water utility. It was dull as ditchwater …'

'Exquisitely appropriate!'

'… but they let me go down to four days a week and self-fund an MBA. Believe me, I had a stack of debt to pay off by the time I finished here.'

'Then Bakhtin Enterprises spotted you and you haven't looked back.'

'I guess.' For the past few minutes Ben felt that something inside him had been melting under Dianne's attention. He thought of the heat shield of a spacecraft being drawn into an atmosphere by a planet's gravity. Although guests twice Ben's age scampered around Dianne's periphery like mice, she had no eyes for them. 'An MBA is all very well but I had to prove myself first, running a real business – one of Bakhtin's smaller ones. But it must have gone OK because 10 months ago I became his chief of staff.'

With a start, Ben saw the time – 9.55pm. He made apologies. A text from Alex said 'Call', but the mobile's battery was dead. Free alcohol was still exerting its pull but the ranks of staff and guests had shrunk. Ben searched for a friendly face and was delighted to see Frank Jones, the only lecturer who could make the finance part of the MBA clear and funny. Frank's office was around the corner and yes, Ben could use his landline. The call clarity was excellent although, so far as Ben could quickly calculate, Alex was airborne over India.

The event had gone well and Ben said so. The glass chair had been much admired. There might be an invitation from Number Ten. There was every reason for Alex to be happy, but Ben's hormones had learned to put themselves into neutral until his boss's emotional state had been confirmed.

Things were fine. Alex had already received a gushingly complimentary text about both speech and chair. Dean Gyro knew how to gush fast, in six words or less.

'Ben, Ben, please no bullshit! You did it better than me! You read my mind perfectly!' Alex exclaimed. 'When I need you to be me, Ben, you never let me down.' There was a pause. Mind-reader or not, Ben had no clue as to where the conversation was headed. This was nothing new: part of the job description of genius was 'mystery'. In the background a cuckoo clock sounded the hour. A cuckoo clock in a private jet?

A meaningless question from Alex about whether it was now too late (when had that ever mattered in the Bakhtin empire?) led to a request. Could Ben 'be Alex' one more time that evening? This would be a very important time – much more important than three million pounds and some kilos of glass. Staff reductions were so tricky, and this one especially so. It was not news that would keep well. Would Ben do it? Would he promise? Did he understand? Or would he rather wait until Alex was back in three days to do it personally?

When Ben did grasp what Alex intended, having for two long minutes mustered every atom of reflex and memory accumulated over the past year to help him decode his boss's messages, he replied slowly that, yes, he would do it, that he did promise, that he understood, and that he would rather not wait.

Bakhtin had asked Ben to downsize himself. Which was how Frank came to be dragged out of the party with no explanation, ordered to bring two (no, three) glasses of champagne and marched to his office, where he sat at his square meeting table like a Wimbledon umpire. Ben fired up Frank's computer and printer, downloaded two copies of a document from Bakhtin Enterprises' intranet, and took one of the empty seats.

'Ben,' Ben began, looking at the empty chair facing him across the table. In truth what Ben was about to do, namely give himself a farewell speech, he would do better than Alex, who would have forgotten half of what Ben had done for the company. Forgotten as if he had never known. And (Alex's point), hadn't Ben earned the right for his contribution to the corporate cause to be remembered properly, and to be thanked for it to the best of Bakhtin Enterprises' ability to do it? And without doubt, the person who could do the best job was Ben.

So, Ben continued, this could be no easy conversation. Ben's record was beyond reproach. Ben had joined Bakhtin Enterprises from Hampton on an accelerated management traineeship, first in personnel (torture!) and then in marketing. In his second year he had progressed to his first role in general management, within the EFI division.

What a debut! He had taken a dull manufacturing business with an ageing plant, few advantages and no ambition, and he had stuffed the competition. Permanently stuffed them. Doubled EFI's market share. Quintupled profits – which continue to this day. Sustained profits. That was commercial promise for you, without a doubt. When 10 months ago the role of chief of staff to Alex himself had become vacant, Ben had been the obvious choice for it.

Here, at the centre of the group, how greatly he had contributed. How fully he had exemplified selflessness. How much he would be missed not only by Alex, but by so many executives around the world for whom he had been Alex (or better than Alex) when the demands of selfless leadership made his boss unavailable. As they did now.

To these hundreds of daily encounters, from six (or sometimes five or even four) in the morning till gone midnight, Ben had brought so much more than the diligence of a good-tempered amanuensis. Or even a clairvoyant one. Ben had brought – he pressed these points because he very much wanted Ben to hear them and to take them in – a gentle kindness and a renewing optimism which were not in Alex's gift. Often Ben had demonstrated that kindness could not be separated from attention to detail; details that could be overlooked so easily in a leader's sweeping focus on the big picture.

Such details needed to be dispatched here. At this point Ben put crosses in a few boxes on the documents he had printed. They were neither more nor less than the crosses that Alex would have put, had someone like Ben prompted Alex to think of them. Four months' pay in lieu of notice instead of three (selfless workers must eat their fill). Continued benefits, car, retirement contribution and health plan for that time. Access to the group's outplacement assistance within the limits set out in the schedule.

And how helpful of the annex to recall in English rather than legalese the restrictions on confidentiality and working for competitors which would continue for rather more than six months. Had writing them comprehensibly (while keeping the lawyers calm) not been one of Ben's first projects on joining the group? Ben recalled that it had.

Frank was impressed. Bemused, but certainly impressed.

And then with the benefit of much practice from many other goodbyes, the finely honed managerial sentiments leapt from caterpillar to butterfly, from dutiful appreciation of the past to excitement about the future ('your hopes, your dreams'). Ben scrawled his name, original and copy, in the two places provided for the corporation's signature, and swallowed a mouthful of champagne. He then moved to the other side of the table and scrawled the same name twice more in the places provided for the exiting executive. Swallowing a larger mouthful of champagne, he passed both documents to Frank to witness.

A few minutes later the two of them were pacing outside in the dark. Frank's cigarette, now glowing, now quiescent, moved like a lapping wave along the front of the main building. In all his 45 years, said Frank, he had never seen anything like what he had just witnessed. Ben said, well that was business for you. In removing Ben, Alex was in effect taking out a layer of management. The commercial reasons to do so were not pressing, but that was Alex's business genius – he was always ahead of the game, reading economies and markets before they moved. Ben didn't doubt that within six months, chopping Ben's job would seem prescient.

'How do you feel?' asked Frank.

Ben was not sure how he felt. 'Stunned, I guess. Numb.'

'But why you, his right-hand man and one of his best?' pressed Frank, still mystified by the turn and pace of events. You could build a cathedral (including getting planning permission for an underground car park) in the time it took to get rid of an academic in a university.

'Selfless leadership. Sharing the pain. A bad mistake if he had left his own team untouched.' Ben paused, reflecting. 'And he's right.'

'What about tomorrow?'

'I've no idea. I was meant to have been meeting some bankers in Paris, but right now I'm on gardening leave.'

'Someone waiting for you at home?'

'No, I've been living on planes since I left here. So any ideas for tomorrow would be welcome …' Ben broke off and pointed as they turned the corner of the administration building. 'What is *that*?'

The scaffolding-clad new tower had vanished and reappeared. Red construction lights hung in a giant circle in the sky four floors above them, like the marks of a laser pointer. Ben's eyes adjusted. He could make out the rim of a darkened flying saucer, perched on top of a column of scaffolding like a ball on a golf tee.

But Frank wasn't there. He was off, running with surprising agility back to the fading embers of the drinks party. The continued presence of alcohol meant that Dean Gyro had not yet exhausted his enthusiasm for the beauty of the college's new all-glass chair. 'Come on!' Frank called to Ben, pointing to the flying saucer. '*That* has given me an idea.'

MONDAY 11 JUNE (NIGHT)
MONDAY 11 JUNE (NIGHT)

The imam and the two others went upstairs. They entered the imam's office and all three complied with their religion's demands concerning shoes. The imam wore hand-stitched calf leather, polished brown brogues and the 30-year-old wore scuffed black Oxfords but both pairs cost over £300. Yet the mass-production slip-ons of the third member of the group were no less revealing. The capitalist religion requires consumption to be conspicuous and to demarcate wealth or salary. The imam had wealth; until minutes before the 30-year-old had had a six-figure salary; while the senior lecturer was – well, what need one say? A senior lecturer in a second-rate business school.

While Frank and Gyro huddled, Ben had a few minutes to look around. The dean's office had moved since his time as a student. He recalled two meetings involving cheap sherry, faded armchairs and a matching sofa. The sofa had been half-covered in research questionnaires and had been in the dean's house. In his first week as dean Gyro had moved the office out of the house and into the first floor, front and centre, of the main college building. The governors had paid top dollar for an American to come and do a job. Part of that job was to wake up anyone who was mistaking Hampton for the suburbs.

For what, in appointing Gyro, Hampton aspired to be was an internationally ranked business school – a *madrassa* of capitalism. Capitalism's *madrassas* were needed for exactly the same reason as those of any other self-respecting religion. The human population was exploding, young and global. Therefore any religion worthy of the name – even a religion aiming only to stand still, and the doctrine of shareholder value demanded much more than that – needed to attract ever larger numbers of the young and equip them for their role in the cause. Therefore *madrassas* were many, and each had their imams, but they were not equal.

A leading *madrassa* attracted ambitious minds from all over the world, and scattered them back to the world equipped not only with knowledge but fervour. William C Gyro had never put his job in those terms, but had the description been offered in a scriptural text such as the *Harvard Business Review*, he would have concurred immediately.

Everything in Gyro's office sent a message. Fluorescent lighting, pine shelves and tubular metal chairs upholstered in Smartie-pack colours matched the rest of the building. But together with the large desk (clear except for a state-of-the-art widescreen laptop), they expressed the first message: the new dean was a hard-working business executive, frugal but willing to make investments in new technology. This message was for the school's corporate clients: heads of 'talent' or 'learning' and other human-resource professionals in large businesses who spent seven-figure budgets on education. The second message – that this was the boss's office – was carried by the spacious acreage of ankle-deep carpet and the floor-to-ceiling windows that overlooked the lake.

A third message was conveyed by four layers of shelving running the length of the longest wall, and by the coat-stand near the door. The shelves bore books and journals and the coat-stand bore the crimson robes of Gyro's Harvard doctorate from 25 years ago. Most of the books and some of the journals had been read, as many as half by Gyro himself.

The third message did not fool the college's full-time academics (the church of reason was also the church of scepticism) but they did not need to be fooled. The message of the shelves and the gown was that the business-minded dean was flattering them rather than treating them with contempt. As scholars they well understood that to be the head of a business school is to try to unify two religions: rationality and money. No wonder the system's highest intellectual flowering was man as rational wealth-seeker, *homo economicus*.

The opposite wall gave pride of place to photographs – two triumphs on the football field at Jersey City; three platinum sales achievements at a global management consultancy ('Building The Future' awards in 1993, 1995 and 1996); two publishers' awards for books, and a White House dinner with George W Bush. The largest photograph was only 15 months old – Dean Gyro with Wilson Pinnacle Junior, the 72-year-old founder's son and CEO of Virtual Savings and Trust, at the groundbreaking ceremony for Hampton's new tower.

The fourth message was for donors: Gyro's a good guy, a winner and a money magnet.

'Well, Frank, this is a surprise and no mistake.' The cadaverous reflections of Gyro, Frank and Ben moved in the window. Gyro turned towards Frank, his quizzical expression disappearing. 'This young man isn't just a solution, he's a brainwave. And I thought you only brought me problems.'

Frank coughed. 'Questions, perhaps.'

Gyro turned his smile on Ben. 'Frank supplies the conscience of the school and I wouldn't have it any other way. Just occasionally, though, I have to remind him that the supply of ethics is also subject to the law of demand.'

Frank's brainwave was that for the next two weeks Ben should slide effortlessly from having been Bakhtin's right-hand man to becoming Gyro's. The role of dean's assistant had been vacated abruptly a few days earlier, just as preparations for the tower opening were reaching fever pitch.

'What do you say?' Gyro placed a hand on Ben's shoulder. 'The base salary you were on as a daily rate, plus accommodation and expenses? We'll work it out. I'm sure Alex paid you eye-wateringly well, but with luck a two-week dose won't bankrupt the school. In ten days – no, less – this place is going to be swarming with the very top names in global business. Including –' he jabbed at the photograph on the wall '– him. The tower opening is the culmination of Wilson Pinnacle Junior putting thirty million dollars into the college.'

'Thirty million!'

'Exactly. Hampton has never played in that league before, but as of June twenty-first, we do. On June twenty-first one hundred years ago, Pinnacle Senior founded the Virtual Savings Corporation of Delaware. That became Virtual Savings and Trust – which is huge. The Pinnacle Leadership Tower will be dedicated to him. Wilson has invited all his closest enemies and friends, billionaires the lot of them. And they are coming. Do this job for two weeks and you'll get to meet them all.' Gyro pressed his point. 'When I was your age I would have killed to get introductions like that.'

'Billionaires are pains in the arse,' Ben said.

'That's an essential fact. VIP handling 101. But how do you know? Because you've already been Alex's right-hand guy. You've done the job already. You'll eat them up like candy. For two weeks, that's it. Get the tower open, and help me tickle their fat tummies so they all give Hampton a little something.'

'Be the arse for them to be pains in, you mean,' Ben summarised. What the hell? One thing was clear: he did not need to consult his own diary for the next two weeks. Doing the Bakhtin job had rendered his private diary permanently blank.

'A Hampton arse, Ben. A master of the universe in the making, talent-spotted right here at Hampton.'

'What happened to the previous guy?' Ben imagined that Gyro could blow up a temper if he chose.

'Family circumstances,' said Gyro. 'Sudden and sad. Regardless of which, Richard couldn't hack it. Couldn't multi-task.' Gyro's brow furrowed. 'The elevator announcements were getting him down. Or the lift, if you prefer. Are you planning on getting beaten by lift announcements?'

Ben shook his head, perplexed but persuaded. Gyro went for the closing handclasp. 'If you haven't got your passport, Greg can go and get it: you need to grab some sleep. Frank will show you where. You'll be getting your briefing from me. Tomorrow. Early.'

Working for Bakhtin meant Ben never went anywhere without his passport, but he was surprised to need it again so soon after being fired. At reception Frank helped him collect emergency toiletries and a keycard for one of the vacant student rooms. Frank also lent Ben a couple of bits of clothing. By the time he had taken Ben to the residential block it had gone eleven.

After refurbishment, the student rooms were smart but they were still pastel cubicles for human laboratory animals. The swivel chair was now height-adjustable, the fluorescent tubes had been replaced with energy-efficient lighting and the window no longer opened. Air-conditioning, electronic doorlocks, ethernet cable and the power showers were all new: products of some of Pinnacle's thirty million, presumably.

Ben was agitated. In less than three hours he had gone from rising star to redundant, and the shock was wearing off. Connie Yung floated into his mind; at least she had clarity about Bakhtin. She might even have been right. He needed time to think about his situation. Then again, maybe he didn't; maybe he could just move on?

The room was hot, and he remembered that his passport was still in the Audi's glove compartment. However, the air-conditioning only kept running if the keycard stayed in its wall slot. Ben's wing seemed deserted, so he left his keycard in its slot and used the wastebasket to prop his room door ajar. A telephone directory did the same for the door into the car park.

Patchy clouds were moving in the sky, propelled by a night breeze. The breeze rippled the lake and was starting to cool the valley. The Audi was in a car park surrounded on three sides by the student residential block. In half a dozen windows lights or computer screens glimmered behind curtains, but otherwise the block was dark. Ben stuffed his passport and phone charger into his pocket and wandered over to the giant structure on the opposite side of the road. Since the tower was going to be his focus for the next two weeks, he wanted a closer look.

His eyes adjusted to the dark. The flying saucer that he had seen previously was perched on top of a four-storey square scaffolding tower. Assuming that the flying saucer was some kind of observation platform, Ben guessed that it might have a capacity for perhaps 150 people – but what could so many people want to look at?

Red lights ran around the scaffolding at ground and fourth-floor levels, as well as on the flying saucer itself, which was covered in tarpaulins and rope. The scaffolding supported wooden boards painted with the valley landscape on the ground, first and second floors and a sky scene for the upper floors – a kind of camouflage. There was no artist's impression of the tower itself.

At ground level a notice listed a sizeable army of architects, engineers and specialist consultants, some of whom were based in Los Angeles and Tokyo. The logo of Virtual Savings and Trust was everywhere, a giant V-tick in orange and gold.

As the clouds gave way to larger and larger patches of moonlight, the tower's design seemed to Ben a seductive tease. Presumably the 'flying saucer' was accessed via a central support column behind the scaffolding, but how? Ben knew the tower had a lot of glass – the chair he had delivered had been designed to match it – but how many millions could anyone want to spend on a glass toadstool? Still, a speck of Pinnacle's thirty mil was now going to end up in Ben's back pocket. There couldn't be any harm in that.

When Ben got back to his room he found the boy-band member beside his desk. Ben had left the door open, but thought the document case with his speech notes had been zipped up: now it was unzipped. The directions that Greg passed on were for Ben to turn up, with passport, at the dean's house at 7.30am sharp. Greg would drive them to Heathrow where they would both catch a flight to Hong Kong.

'I'm going with the dean to Hong Kong?' Ben repeated (yes). He asked when the cafeteria started breakfast (6.30am) and when he would be back (no idea). Greg dispensed answers with the warm personal touch of a motel ice-maker. He seemed to enjoy Ben's discomfort.

Ben tried a different tack. He held out his hand. 'We'll be working together for two weeks, so why don't we say hello? Ben Stillman.'

Greg didn't move. 'Is it not Dr Jones you'll be working with, Mr Stillman? Since your being here seems to be his doing.'

'He taught on my MBA, yes. But then so did lots of other people.'

'Hmm.' Greg shrugged, and melted fractionally; for a moment he seemed to want to help. 'Check out what happened to the bloke before you. And watch out for the tower opening. Security and all that. Lots of VIPs. Possible terrorist target.'

Was that half-a-dozen warnings or one? Ben said, 'You're joking. Hampton, a terrorist target?' But the driver had gone. In its high-rolling, jet-setting confusion Hampton was turning out to be bizarrely like the Bakhtin world that he had just exited.

By now the room was agreeably cool. Frank had lent him a shirt and some socks but hadn't offered underpants (Ben hadn't asked), so that was one item on the shopping list for tomorrow. The power shower and emergency toiletries did their jobs. With the reassuring glow of his phone on charge and his passport beside his bed, Ben felt the illusion of being in charge of his life start to return. He was happy about that.

So why had he been let go? For the past 10 months he had been Alex Bakhtin's chief of staff. He had shared Alex's outer office and every secret of the business with Tahmina, Alex's personal assistant. No one whom Alex regarded as merely adequate or mediocre would be dreamt of for such a role. He had landed it, a big promotion, because of a stunning track record as a business performer. Had he failed to make the grade in the new job? No. Six weeks ago Alex had awarded him an ahead-of-plan bonus.

More than that, in the cut-and-thrust of all his roles in Bakhtin's world, Ben had done some growing up. He had learned what real achievement was, and he had really achieved. In their telephone conversation three hours ago, he had put the question to Alex directly. For goodness' sake, Alex chewed up underperformers and spat them out often enough; Ben generally swept up the wreckage. If Ben had been underperforming, Alex would not only have said it, he would have growled it, shouted it, yelled it. Yet according to Alex, Ben had been performing flawlessly.

Put it down to personal chemistry? Was Ben too unlike Alex, or too much like him in some way? But he had done so many sensitive and personal things for his boss, such as tonight's speech in memory of Alex's late wife.

So Ben was left with nothing more than the unsatisfying mixture of reasons that he had offered Frank: a combination of cost-saving and market savvy, with the added twist that a business leader whose public credo was selfless leadership might see a necessity in chopping off his own right hand at a time when he was calling for sacrifices from others. It was the only logical answer, but it didn't feel to Ben like the answer. He felt as if he was lying on crisply ironed sheets holding a Rubik's cube, which was not the recommended recipe for sleep.

Ben turned out the light and pondered the stars by which he had navigated his career so far. Hampton had been the first star. Before Hampton, Ben had not aimed high; indeed he had not aimed at all. Through high school and a mediocre first degree he had floated on tides, happily and amiably, a creature of rockpools governed by the wind and the moon rather than by the stars.

But even a crab in a rockpool, gazing familiarly at the moon, might one night look to the fiery, distant and compelling stars beyond and wonder whether it had a future among them. Since the stars are so many, might there be one a little closer than the others, a bit more accessible, a bit less daunting, to which it might not be indescribably silly to hitch one's fate? An Alpha Centauri, so to speak; or in Ben's case, a Hampton MBA. And so he had persuaded his employers to cut him loose for a day a week and he had self-funded to join a *madrassa*.

ƎNNՐ ƐႽ ⅄⩑ⅆꙄƎNⅆƎM Ⴘ ƎNNՐ ႽႽ ⅄⩑ⅆꙄƎՈⱢ

Grapefruit, crayfish and chilli omelette is a brave combination, and the Sea Horse was the bravest attempt so far to bring fine dining to the Alderley shopping centre. But its chances were not good. Despite being by the entrance and having 'outdoors indoors' space (tables under umbrellas inside an atrium), none of the last three food establishments on the site had lasted more than 12 months. Alderley, the nearest town to Hampton, simply wasn't big enough. By contrast, McDonalds was always packed with people, most of whom supposedly never ate there. 'Bakhtin is bad news.' Connie had skipped the Sea Horse's curated omelette selection and stuck with *pain au chocolat*. 'I wish the college hadn't taken his money.'

'I wish *we* hadn't taken his money,' corrected Dorothy Lines. 'Don't forget you're a governor now.' The deputy dean was secretary to the board of governors. In theory the board governed everything the college did.

Dorothy had booked Connie for an induction breakfast as soon as her appointment had been confirmed. 'What did he do?' she asked. 'The usual crummy big-ego things, I suppose.'

'More than that. Do you remember the food-packaging scare about eighteen months ago?'

'Of course. I went round to my mother's to make sure she took stuff back to the supermarket. Six months later they said it was a false alarm – which was just as well. I'd forgotten she had an old freezer in the garage.'

'Bakhtin pushed our business off the road. I was the head of HR and had to make four hundred and twenty people redundant. Friends and myself included. It pushed several people over the edge, including one who committed suicide. It was then that I abandoned the private sector and started applying to the NHS, charities, that sort of thing.'

'A suicide – that's shocking!'

'No, it's what happens when you kick the jobs out from under a rural area. What was shocking was the way Bakhtin did it. We were the competition to one of his packaging businesses. Someone fed the press a scare story about a chemical we used to make plastic food wrap.'

'I remember.' The deputy dean frowned.

'The business died in Month Two. It was always going to take six months to get the all-clear – there's no quick way to prove something doesn't cause something else. We stopped production and tried to switch for a few months to the same chemical that Bakhtin used. But funnily enough he'd bought up the entire production of it just a few weeks before.' Remembering it made Connie feel bitter.

Lines left her poached egg on wholegrain alone. 'He locked the exit doors and lit a match.'

'Is that what business schools – sorry we – teach?'

'Absolutely not. Not in a million years. That's pure Bakhtin.'

Ben recalled a line that really was pure Alex Bakhtin: 'I travel in the back of a plane, no exceptions. It usually arrives within a minute or two of the front.' Alex omitted the punch line, which was that his back seat was normally a settee in a specially kitted Dassault Falcon 2000.

The 'selfless' leader's logic was faultless: private jets allowed confidential meetings and telephone calls. While in first and business class there might be fewer neighbours, there was also more chance that they could be interested in what you were discussing. When staff travelled without him, they flew economy.

So while private jets had become home turf to Ben, the first-class lounge at Heathrow Terminal 5 was a strange magic carpet. By nine o'clock in the morning he had already passed on the two offers of vintage champagne that Gyro had knocked back. He was still struggling with the idea of flying first class to Hong Kong, only to return as soon as the plane had refuelled. This nonsense was the product of Gyro's capacious business mind.

Ben was needed back at Hampton to trouble-shoot the tower opening while Gyro schmoozed Chinese big-wigs. Since Ben's predecessor was *hors de combat*, the only chance for Ben to get up to speed was to be closeted with Gyro on a 14-hour flight.

The two of them had set off from Hampton at 7.30am. Ben granted that Greg's handling of the Lexus was top notch even if he had only scored him three out of ten for smiling. Still, Greg had spared him any more auguries of disaster. Once Gyro had caught up with the news on the TV in the back of Greg's seat, Ben had peppered him with questions on the challenges that would make or break his next 10 days. He had spent an hour scribbling answers in a notebook.

Seated in the lounge scanning the results, Ben felt optimistic. The 10 days and nights would be long and he would be rushed off his feet, but the challenges were manageable. They could be boiled down to four:

First, the Pinnacle family. Wilson Pinnacle Junior had bought into the idea of the tower as a monument to his family's achievements, so egos were all over it. For example, Junior kept inviting new guests even though he had maxed out the tower's capacity three weeks earlier. Typical tycoonitis, which needed polite but firm management.

Second, Pinnacle's corporate executives. Short answer: tell them everything in triplicate and make them look good to their boss.

Third, the invited VIPs. These split into two groups. Those who had given money to the college already, like Bakhtin, needed to feel the college had not gone starry-eyed over someone else's bigger bucks. But at the same time the earth needed to move for those who had yet to give.

That was not an ideal metaphor. The fourth and last cluster of challenges was the tower itself. There would be snagging –

the usual things on a new building. But Ben could see that a lot of the job would involve sitting on the necks of the contractors day and night. Everywhere in the world contractors thought time and budgets were moveable feasts. Given that a significant portion of the world's personal wealth was due to jet in on 21 June, opening a week from Thursday was less moveable than the Great Wall of China.

Outlandish terrorist threats had not figured in Gyro's description of the problem, which suited Ben fine. With luck, he could turn some attention to how best to capitalise on the personal networking possibilities of this short stint. It was dawning on Ben that these might be as amazing as Gyro had promised. For example Gyro had just spotted the chairman of First Improvident, 'his bank'. The phrase meant the bank from which Gyro collected £60,000 a year as a non-executive director. The two were absorbed in conversation on the other side of the lounge.

As Ben stood guard over Gyro's briefcase and scattered papers, he realised that the next step for him was to judge the right timing and pretext to join the grown-ups' conversation. What was abundantly clear was that slipping out to the airside shops to look for new underpants was not the opportunity for which he was looking.

'Your background in human resources struck us as just the ticket. Of course you've only just joined, but the governors wonder if you would take on a little mission.' Dorothy Lines added hastily, 'It's not an investigation or anything like that – just finding out in your own time if we've learned all the lessons for the future.'

'Lessons about what?' Connie had never imagined becoming a student governor. The more she had seen of high places in organisations the less she had liked them. On the other hand, if the price of joining a board was accepting collective responsibility for its decisions, then she wanted her skills and values to make a difference.

Dorothy Lines explained. 'Richard Vanish was the dean's executive assistant until two weeks ago. I was the one Richard called on the Tuesday after the Monday holiday. He hadn't slept over the weekend, due partly to the stress of the job and partly to bad news about his mother's health. As the tower opening approached the job was just getting worse. So he asked if he could take his accumulated leave and not come back.'

'He called you, rather than the dean?'

'The answer would have been the same in either case, but one of us would have shouted and yelled. It's OK, we've dealt with Richard and we will manage the opening. But the question for the governors is, is there anything about the job that is a longer-term risk factor? Is the normal, day-to-day pressure on the dean's staff reasonable?' Lines pursed her lips. 'Not an inquiry, more of a second opinion. But a very valuable one from someone with your broad human resources perspective. In academia, we become insular very quickly.'

Connie thought that going to a senior manager in the NHS for a second opinion was hilarious, since the health service bred overwork and stress like flies. Perhaps that was the governors' sense of humour. Still, better to be breakfasted and given something to do than placed on the mantelpiece as a diversity token. 'A second opinion's no problem. But my final MSc classes are next week so there's a limit as to what I can do before then. '

'Of course. In any case everyone will be very tied up before the opening.'

'Not Richard, presumably.'

'No. But would talking to him be necessary? I promised we wouldn't harass him. We were colleagues for many years.'

Of course it would be necessary, Connie thought. There was no point in being a dumb torpedo fired at the dean by an unknown clique on the board. Besides, Vanish might be a total fruitcake. The waiter came past and refilled their coffees. She took the opportunity to change the subject. 'Speaking of the tower opening, the guest list is amazing. How did we pull it off?'

Lines nodded. 'At first, like many on the board I wasn't convinced. Would we simply end up with a glass toadstool – even become a laughing-stock? Those questions have been answered. The tower will be an extraordinary teaching space and put Hampton on the global map.'

'So all of the board are behind Gyro.'

'Most of us. Some questions haven't yet been answered. But everything Gyro has promised, he has delivered. His contacts are amazing.'

'So he's good news.'

'Definitely.'

Ben and Gyro were flying close to the nose of the 747. The good news for Ben was a six-foot-six sedan chair with walnut trim that folded flat. He relaxed as Eric the steward laid the tablecloths and cutlery for lunch. Because of the time-zone change, in 12 hours the final meal on the flight would be breakfast.

'Would that be your mediocrity research?' Ben had remembered in the nick of time this morning to look Gyro up on Wikipedia.

Gyro's expression confirmed that Ben had just scored some points. 'Old stuff, Ben, at the start of the eighties. You were just born. I hadn't planned to do a doctorate, but Harvard offered me a place, with funding. It was the chance of a lifetime, but I had to find a research idea. So there I was, drowning in people twice as smart, all scrabbling for something that hadn't already been studied to death. Excellent companies? Tom Peters was just about to hit the big time with them.

'Seriously crap companies that crash and burn? For years academics had been rubbernecking the wrecks on the corporate highway. And then one day I realised that there would always be thousands and thousands more mediocre companies than excellent or crap ones. All I had to do was figure out how to turn that into publishable research. And money.'

Ben was puzzled. 'I don't get it,' he said. 'Companies paid Tom Peters to teach them to be excellent. And they paid to avoid disaster. Why would they pay to be mediocre?'

Gyro reached across a generation to grip his companion's hand. Nothing in Gyro's life, before or since, had matched that moment of insight when he had seen the world differently and figured out how to put the difference into his bank account. 'Wherever you are in the world, whoever you are, you are surrounded by mediocrity.

'Maybe you're excellent or maybe you're average, but you've got mediocre competitors. You've got mediocre suppliers. You've got mediocre customers. You've got mediocre colleagues. Understand them, really understand them, take their mediocrity seriously and they can become your lunch. So I became a consultant and did a lot of lunch.'

Two thoughts passed through Ben's mind like a bullet and its shock wave. Thought one: this was either genius or purest bullshit. Thought two: was there a difference?

They both ordered Bloody Marys as they picked at duck terrine. So this was why Gyro was building the tower. From being a well-paid consultant, Gyro was returning to the land of high academic ideas with a multi-storey idea of his own.

'Every important concept of contemporary leadership is reflected in the tower's design. The auditorium is all glass. You look up? Everywhere you see the sky. What will students at the college learn? The sky's the limit. It's all glass. So you look down – straight down, between your feet. You see the ground. Nearly everywhere in the auditorium you see the ground. What do you learn?'

Don't be a leader if you get sick easily, thought Ben.

'However high you go as a leader, make sure you can see

the ground. Then, the walls are all glass. A perfect circle. Which means – ?' Gyro looked at Ben expectantly.

'Scan the horizon?' said Ben tentatively.

'Exactly!'

Gyro's eyes were glowing, and Ben was getting infected. The concept of the tower was uncanny, even mind-bending.

'Normally the acoustics of a glass circle would be terrible,' Gyro continued. 'All boom and echo, no clarity – just like leadership in most organisations. But using nanotechnology to modify the glass panels, we will have the perfect acoustic for the human voice and the human ear. Speaking in a natural way, without amplification, and hearing the contribution of everyone in the organisation, wherever they are sitting. That's another fundamental aspect of leadership. That's how leadership should be all the time. And we will teach this at Hampton.'

Gyro put on a pair of eyeshades, took a sleeping pill and tucked himself in for the night.

Ben got it, for a few minutes at least: in 10 days he would help open the Sistine Chapel of leadership. However the relentless, fragranced, air-conditioned cleanliness of the eastern-bound airplane led him to realise something else. His suit would travel a large fraction of the planet's circumference crumpled but serviceable. His shirt and socks, borrowed from Frank, had been clean this morning. But it had felt presumptuous to ask for the loan of a pair of underpants, and he had never made it out of the lounge to the shops at Heathrow.

He was wearing navy boxers with the word 'Tangiers' stitched down one side. These pants had already clocked up

18 hours on Monday. Another 36 hours were now in view, since Ben would turn round in Hong Kong without leaving airside or touching Chinese soil. He could do without trying to think about Sistine chapels while feeling dirty down below.

A thought came to him. A cornucopia of complimentary items for personal comfort had already come his way. Eric the steward had insisted that Ben ask for anything that might make his flight more comfortable. Arguably Eric's ingratiating tone was over the top, but at £6,000 a seat one can do over the top and then some. What if, contra Bakhtin, the airlines had got first-class travel right?

Six thousand pounds which removed a top man's trifling discomfort was nothing at all, if the greater greatness of the thoughts consequently thought – for example, beating malaria by giving away mosquito nets for free in Africa – could save millions from deadly peril. But how good was this first-class service, really? He should experiment.

Dorothy Lines saw Frank just as she signalled The Sea Horse waiter for the bill. 'Come and say hello to our new student governor! Do the two of you know each other? Dr Frank Jones, Connie Yung.'

'Congratulations. Trust Dorothy to sink her claws in right away. Now help me – I'm sure I've taught you but what was the class?' Frank perched the two shopping bags he was carrying on the table.

'Finance 2 on the MSc? I was one of the NHS students. It was the only finance module which made the least sense, even if you did predict that healthcare would bankrupt the country by 2020.'

Lines smiled. 'Frank does like to scare everybody witless.'

'I salute your courage, Connie, in joining the board of an about-to-be-bankrupt college. You realise the whole thing's a house of cards, financially speaking? It's never a dull moment with our dean, as long as you realise it's all bullshit of the most glorified kind.'

Lines hesitated. 'We do speak our mind in academia, Connie. It may take you a few months to adjust.' She tapped her code into the waiter's machine. 'Frank, if we might be practical for one moment? Practical and discreet.' Dorothy explained the task that the governors had asked Connie to take on. 'I thought that it might be useful if she spoke to Ben, whom you introduced into the dean's office last night. He'll experience the pressures of the role but won't have an axe to grind.'

Connie choked on her last mouthful of coffee. 'That man from Bakhtin is running the dean's office? Surely we haven't taken him on.'

Frank was surprised. 'Bakhtin's a hatchet man, but Ben's a good lad. He got fired himself, you know, after the speech. Well, the speech was drivelling hypocrisy, but since it was pure Bakhtin we all knew it was going to be. Definitely talk to Ben: he's only doing it for two weeks, so Gyro can't threaten him and we might all discover what's really going on.' Frank swung round to face the deputy dean. 'This is Gyro's third trip to the

Far East in six months, with no tangible benefit for the college. None at all. You can't deny it.'

Dorothy eyed him sharply. 'That's cheap, Frank. You're the first to bang on about how tip-toe cautious we should be about getting involved with business schools outside Europe.'

'But we don't even know which schools he's talking to!'

'Who in their right mind would share sensitive discussions about alliances with you? Anyway, there's one thing you can't deny,' Lines concluded, picking up two canisters of hair dye in Halloween orange and lurid purple which had fallen out of Frank's shopping. 'Whoever you bought these for, it isn't you.' Frank's scalp was as pale and smooth as a golf ball.

Ben's experiment with first-class service had gone like this. He had pressed the call button. Gyro was asleep but with other passengers in the cabin awake, Ben had drawn confidentially close to Eric before speaking. He had needed to strike a note of experienced confidence in what first-class service could provide. 'Eric, by any chance do you have clean underpants on board?' had looked like it would do the trick.

While most of the words had made it out of Ben's mouth unharmed, the last had died still-born. So what Ben had said was, 'Eric, by any chance do you have clean underpants on?' After an appositely brief locking of eyes, Eric had murmured, 'Let me see what I can do.'

Half an hour later, he had gestured Ben towards the galley and placed his hands lightly on Ben's waist. Ben had explained his predicament. Eric had the situation sized up: Ben's waist was 33. Now, after breakfast, Eric was coming through the cabin with Hong Kong landing cards. Instead of one of these, he passed Ben a note with a message and a scribbled UK mobile number. 'Mark is crew on the return flight. I've radioed him to get you a pair. This is my number if you want something else. Eric.'

The sun was fully up with only the lightest tropical haze as the 747 circled Hong Kong's outlying islands. The harbour was turquoise and shrinking; shrinking because no-one in Hong Kong had been told that land was supposed to be a found resource rather than a manufactured product. The crumpled turquoise handkerchief was criss-crossed with the wakes of innumerable container ships, passenger liners, barges, fishing boats and hydrofoils.

At 8am on Wednesday Hong Kong time (Tuesday midnight in London) these myriad vessels already moved with the busyness of an evangelical ant-colony moments before the Second Coming. Finally the sea vanished in favour of a protrusion and profusion of 30-, 40- and 50-floor honeycombs of apartments, a vertical mould spreading unstoppably over steep, rocky hills.

The return flight left on schedule at noon. Mark was working in premium economy but he found Ben and gave him two silver-coated packets. Two pairs of pants, 33-34 inch waist, one in London Lilac and one in Chicago Crimson. The twenty-pound note folded in Ben's top jacket pocket did not feel nearly enough but Mark's grin, as wide as a shark at playtime, covered any insult.

Desperate would have looked uncool, so he tucked one packet into his briefcase and waited five minutes. Then he went for a date with Chicago Crimson in the privacy of the first-class washroom. The cut and the colour struck him as more showtime in Las Vegas than pizza base in Chicago but the clean, out-of-the-packet fragrance was wonderful. The effect was like first communion and first date rolled into one. As a consequence Ben almost missed the instruction card with six national flags and microscopically printed texts in assorted languages.

How absurd! He had managed to put the underpants on; what warnings or other instructions could he conceivably need? 'Danger of suffocation', 'Dispose of this product in an environmentally friendly way' or – a particularly likely candidate – 'May contain nuts'? He put the card in his briefcase.

Four hours later, book-less and unable to sleep, Ben's body was on strike because of the crazy time-zone changes. Sarah Jessica Parker in the newly released *Sex and the City* movie was doing nothing for him, so he reclaimed the instruction card and read the English text.

WEARABLE COMPUTING BY LEADERSOFT

it began, revealing that the world's largest manufacturer of software for personal computers had extended its leading-edge offerings to undergarments.

We want you to enjoy SmartPants for Men in perfect condition. SmartPants uses only the most luxuriously soft, ultra-washable, bio-memory fabrics. Cutting-edge information processing capabilities remember your body shape, adjust the thickness of the air layer trapped by microscopic threads and cocoon your most sensitive parts at optimum temperature and humidity.

WARNING. This wearable processor is activated and energised by natural secretions. For your safety and protection, as well as to benefit from the latest software updates, register your garment on our website using the unique identifier printed below within one week of first use. Thank you! 63TQ8-G9GFZ-1CR52-773UA-L4EWX.

Surreptitiously Ben folded back his belt and the top of his trousers to see what his SmartPants might be up to. Were they twinkling with LED or fibre-optic displays? No. If he shifted in his seat in a way that required his underpants to change their shape, would they refuse – or perhaps emit an alarmingly loud and instantly recognisable jingle? Apparently not. Frankly, did they feel any different from those slightly tight, daringly-cut underpants which he had first bought as a teenager bereft of any clue as to what might constitute sartorial taste in the groin department? Not really.

Part of him winced at this onward, relentless ripping-off of consumers, manipulated into buying ever more ridiculous 'solutions' for hitherto unknown needs. This was another face of global capitalism. For a second time Ben nearly discarded the SmartPants instructions. Then he realised that a bottom-feeding data pirate masquerading as an aircraft cleaner might find his code and sell it to hackers who specialised in wearable computing. He had not the slightest wish for the physics of his sensitive parts to end up on the web. He tucked the card into his wallet and waited to land back at Heathrow early on Wednesday evening.

'What's physics envy?' Connie asked. The two women were climbing into Dorothy's brand new Fiat 500 for the drive back to the college.

Dorothy laughed. 'It's particularly appropriate for Frank, because he was a physicist originally. Did you know that his doctorate was in molecular hyper-magnetics? He showed me once but I couldn't understand a word of it. Physics envy is what we suffer from in the social sciences. It describes our lust for all the stuff, testable theories and hard results, that you can get in physics. The whole thing's a fantasy, of course; you can never measure human truth in the way you can measure weight or temperature or things like that. In any case, I find a good antidote to physics envy is ten minutes of advanced mathematics.'

The car eased onto the main road and picked up speed. 'When I first came to Hampton and got to know Frank,' she continued, 'I know physics envy drove him mad. He wanted to study human organisations because he'd come to see that they are the most interesting "things" there are, but he hated never being able to pin down "truth" in a black-and-white way.

'That's why he took to finance. It's the most objective of the management disciplines and he found the equations child's play. But you know, I think it's also why he's such an outstanding teacher: he really believes there are important insights that he is trying to pass on.'

'Is he right to be so rude about the dean?'

'In my book, it's never right to be rude. What do you achieve? Frank has good questions, but he doesn't handle well the fact that the dean doesn't have to answer to him. One time Frank stood for election to the board of governors, and he got trampled on. But like it or lump it, look at the tower, or the brand-new lecture theatres: they've been built with real money which the dean brought in. We haven't borrowed at all.

'I agree we don't quite know what the dean is up to in Asia, but he's always brought home the bacon far beyond anything his predecessors did. I wish Frank would give him more credit for that.'

WEDNESDAY 13 JUNE

Any life-form in any realm – mineral, vegetable, animal or human – can be said to undergo 'enlightenment'.
ECKHART TOLLE[1]

Habit 1 – Be Proactive. Being proactive is more than taking initiative. It is recognizing that we are responsible for our own choices and have the freedom to choose based on principles and values rather than on moods or conditions. Proactive people are agents of change and choose not to be victims, to be reactive, or to blame others.
STEPHEN COVEY[2]

Wednesday, mid-morning. The Lexus was parked diagonally across a lay-by off the Alderley by-pass with the passenger door open. Since the boss had flown the coop yesterday, a remix of 'I wish I was black and gay in 1985' was giving the car's six speakers a workout, covering the lay-by in surround sound. The driver's own workout earlier in the morning had been 85 lengths of the college pool rather than the usual 50. However, his gelled hair (blond with a comma of black over his right forehead) showed no sign of disarray.

---

[1] *A New Earth: Awakening To Your Life's Purpose*, Penguin, London (2006)
[2] *The 8th Habit: From Effectiveness to Greatness*, Simon and Schuster, London (2004)

The afternoon would be spent with the son of a Yankee billionaire (the son would be a wanker but the helicopter tour of the college would be interesting), then collecting Ben from Heathrow at 6pm this evening. So the driver had a free morning, and hence the chance of this meeting in a lay-by, for which he was early. Being early was no problem, because Greg Martin had a talent for waiting. That is why he had chosen his current occupation and why his current occupation had chosen him. He lit a stick of incense.

Considering how much waiting children do ('Are we there yet?'), the rarity of Greg's insight was surprising. By the age of eight he had noticed that waiting was an overlooked activity, despite there being quite a lot of it in life, even for adults and royalty: Prince Charles could not escape his share.

However, most people dealt with waiting with remarkable stupidity. They resorted to a particularly ineffectual combination of denial ('I'm not planning to do any waiting today') and surprised victim ('Why now? Why me? Just when I'm in a rush'). This approach was not for Greg. It flew in the face of the principles of self-improvement, of which Greg had read many – from Eckhart Tolle to the latest Stephen Covey.

Breathing, patience, persistence, grace: waiting was like swimming. Greg had taught himself to like it and to do it well. To be fair, waiting had not become an obsession or an out-of-control condition. He was no waiting abuser: he had never queued for hours outside a club because, according to a rumour on MySpace, the service inside was particularly s-l-o-w.

Like everything else, waiting and action needed to be in balance. He intended that this morning's meeting would lead to action. He spotted the white Corolla in plenty of time to snuff out his incense and kill the beats.

'You're looking very fine.' Amelia Henderson gave Greg a peck on the cheek and a clasp. 'So I trust you're coping with the boredom.'

Amelia poured tea from a Thermos into plastic cups while they sat side by side on a picnic bench. The need to overcome boredom had become as familiar as the Welsh border rain during Greg's training for undercover police work: your first assignment will last between six and 18 months, during which nothing will happen. Nothing. You will learn your identity. You will build and inhabit your cover – in his case, a new identity as Greg Martin.

'Well enough. It's waiting. I can do that. How are my mates doing?' Six months on it still felt a shock to have gone from the 24/7 intimacy of selection and training to a blank void. Given the types that Amelia's department selected, Greg's experience of training as the only time in his life when the walls of being a loner had really crumbled, was a common occurrence. From that they went on to not knowing what any of their undercover classmates were doing, or who they were becoming.

'They're all fine.' Amelia smiled. 'Charlotte's fine. You and she were the top of the class.'

As well as an item for the final three months, Greg reflected. His boss had known it as soon as the two of them knew it. The bedrooms as well as the grounds of the training establishment were observed; that this was so had been spelled out before any of them had applied. Anyone who could not cope with continuous observation of night-time habits was unsuited to the work.

'But I think you will be the first into action,' Amelia continued. Reading his mind she added, 'No, I don't say that to all the boys.' She crumpled her empty cup and put it in her handbag. 'So why this meeting?'

'I think something's going down where I am. At the college.'

'I know you think that. I also know you're keen as anything and bored silly – as you were warned in training.'

'You picked me because I'm good at this, didn't you? Well, look. Here's a copy of the VIP acceptances for Thursday week. The college is going to have billionaires coming out of its ears. These guys are so rich, this afternoon I've got to go play helicopters with one of their sons.'

Amelia scanned the list that Greg handed her. Her eyebrows moved fractionally. 'Fine. You've documented a terrorist opportunity. But there's no credible threat.'

'People this rich have enemies.'

'Yes, but they also have security. There's nothing to tie a particular threat to the college.'

'There is – Frank Jones. He's up to something.'

'So you said before, but you're wrong. Frank Jones has no record, no suspicious associations. What's more, which is a stroke of luck, in his final year at university he applied to the Civil Service. He didn't take up a place, but we found a psychological assessment of him – an idealist, harmless, into non-violence. Yes, that was thirty years ago but it tells us about his character and there's no evidence of any traumatic episode since. The reality is, Frank Jones is cleaner than you.'

'What about the rabbit he pulled out of his hat two nights ago? His name's Ben Stillman, someone Jones taught recently. Out of nowhere he's gone into the dean's office to mastermind the tower opening. Is that a coincidence? I've asked for him to be checked out.'

'I saw that on the file.' The 45-year-old from Inverness stood up and adjusted her hair in the reflection of the Lexus's windscreen. 'Greg, we picked you because you could become good at this, not because you already are. You'll have to earn your grey hairs like the rest of us.'

'But I can keep my eyes open.'

'Keep your eyes open but your head screwed on. This isn't about scoring on a first date.' Amelia swivelled to pierce Greg with her gaze. 'Believe me, I'll fail you for active service just like that, if you give me cause. The department's expectations of you are high, you know that; but you need to live up to them. We have plans.

'Let me remind you of our suspicions of Alex Bakhtin and his companies: a lot that's legit but terrific cover for money-laundering, arms, who knows what. We're guessing he's the main man; but we're just guessing. So one day this autumn we'll do Bakhtin's driver for driving under the influence. You'll be suggested as his replacement. What Bakhtin will do next is check you out with the dean of the college to which he has just given several million pounds and a glass chair. You need to pass that test with flying colours.'

All of which made sense, and Amelia had stroked his

competitive ego – top of the class, early into active service – but the result of the meeting was not the action for which Greg had hoped. He climbed into the Lexus, hit the sound system and shot off.

Some say 'house' came from the Warehouse in Chicago in the 1980s, some say not. Regardless, house music soon copied Mr Heinz and spawned 57 varieties – acid, progressive, hard, tribal, electro and all the others. Everything that could change did change, except for one thing – the beat. House music did not just have a beat, it was led by its beat – the heartbeat of a bionic man, a metronomic 120, 130 or 140 times a minute.

Greg loved the house beat. It changed time. With no beat, the passing minutes were placid and friendly accountants who had boring jobs in clocks; 24 hours later Greg would meet all of them again. With the house beat, time passing could dissolve the world in quite different ways. Seconds became like fugitive sleepers beneath the trans-Siberian express, drops of blood falling onto a piano keyboard or iron bars in the world's longest prison. Seconds flew past, not 60 but 120, 130 or 140 times each minute.

Greg had been the fifth-best advanced police driver in his year, and by the time he reached down twisty country lanes to the private airfield near Maidenhead, according to the on-board computer he had covered 52 miles in as many minutes.

At the airfield, Casey Pinnacle was not hard to spot. For one thing, only four years earlier his face (then 25-years-old) had been splattered across the cover of *Fortune*, the *Financial Times* and *The Economist*. Besides, apart from the desultory fluttering of the airfield's windsock, the only other life to be seen was a slightly older woman standing, like Casey, beside an aquamarine Lamborghini Reventón.

The coupé was parked as if it owned the place. Greg parked the Lexus more circumspectly and got out to take a better look. With a 6.5 litre engine and 3D longitudinal and transverse accelerometer, the Lamborghini was better equipped for flying than half of the parked aircraft.

Greg identified himself as Dean Gyro's driver. Casey was wearing chinos and a monogrammed shirt with the collar unbuttoned. White gold cufflinks flickered with blue light. The woman was in a plain white-and-navy outfit. Her dark glasses struck Greg as too expensive for a chauffeur. Not the mother, not the girlfriend and probably not the secretary. Actually, who could suffer the embarrassment of owning a Lamborghini and needing a chauffeur to drive it? So perhaps she was the bodyguard.

'Cool,' said Casey. 'This is Hilary. She's going to take us up in the helicopter.' To Greg's surprise, he reached out to shake hands.

Greg could now see the blue light from Casey's cufflinks more clearly. It showed digits which changed every few seconds. Greg remembered reading about them in the *Financial Times*.

In the classic rags-to-riches-to-rags family trajectory, Casey was overdue as the generation that would blow the lot. Casey's grandfather, Wilson Pinnacle Senior, was the entrepreneur who had emigrated to America as a teenager in 1903, in time to be inspired by the first powered flight by the Wright brothers in December of that year.

Having spent a few years contemplating the matter, one midsummer's day Wilson Senior had founded a bank, Virtual Savings of Delaware. Banking (Wilson Senior had concluded) would become to financial gravity as heavier-than-air flight was becoming to Newton's discovery: an industry in which fortunes could be made by doing miracles safely everyday. The opening of Hampton's glass tower on 21 June would mark the centenary of the doors of Wilson Senior's dream first opening to the American public.

Casey's father, Wilson Junior, was an accountant with an MBA from Wharton. Junior's dream night out was to curl up with some financial spreadsheets and be interrupted at 11.30pm with half-time refreshments (ideally some lightly grilled sea bass and a green salad). He was a business genius, or else very lucky.

By the time he was 30 he had taken Virtual Savings and Trust (as the bank had been renamed) to a pan-American business worth in excess of one billion dollars. Through the next 30 years he topped this with a dazzling display of entries and exits into new countries, riding the crest of globalisation. Today, Virtual Savings and Trust was one of the world's 50 largest banks – and the Pinnacle family still owned it all.

Enter stage left Casey, the solitary heir coming up to his 30th birthday later this summer. Presumably he was the disastrous wastrel or incompetent who in slow or quick time would smash the family fortune into smithereens? Not quite;

or at least not yet. Junior had spotted this risk and moved to outflank it.

Prudently, Junior had settled an allowance on Casey – something modest, like the GDP of one or two small African states – but he had locked most of the family inheritance up in tax-efficient irrevocable trusts. So long as Junior with his healthy eating and abstemious habits stayed alive, Casey would only come into any really big money before he was 45 if he earned it with his own hands.

But Casey had inherited his family's taste for financial wizardry and then some, although not their taste for hard work. Also he had come of age at the turn of the millennium, when the fashionable age to become shockingly rich dropped to below the age he was now. How could he solve this riddle without doing too much work?

Ordinary people regard stock exchanges as rather complicated, but rich people realise that they are basically ATMs where you put certain numbers in (you put them in prospectuses and similar documents) and cash comes out. The crucial advantage of stock exchanges over ATMs is that it is other people's cash that comes out. Casey had mulled over what numbers he could put in.

The key to freedom came when he realised the significance of Bowie bonds. David Bowie had collected huge amounts of cash from strangers in return for promising them the future royalties from particular music, and many other artists followed. Like mortgaging your house it was cash now and pay back later, with the important difference that if your future income tanked, it was the suckers who had bought the bonds who got stuffed.

And so, coming up to his 21st birthday, in between attending a few classes at Harvard, Casey briefly became a poster-child of financial capitalism. He was the first human being to float 49 percent of himself on a stock exchange. By legally forswearing the possibility of marrying or having children (what 21-year-old thinks this a hardship?), by promising to hire professional managers for his investments and finally by pledging to pay out 49 percent of his wealth and savings (including by then his inheritance) on his 46th birthday to his shareholders, he turned the wealth which Junior had tried to lock away in the future into cash now.

Had the landing of $1.6 billion in his bank account on his 21st birthday given him as much pleasure as outsmarting his dad's prudence? It was hard to tell. As the *Financial Times* had reported, the blue lights in his wireless cufflinks told him his stock market value minute by minute. They showed $4.0 billion as Hilary piloted Casey and Greg into the air.

Casey sat in the co-pilot's seat while Greg sat behind. The helicopter flew to Hampton back the way Greg had driven. Junior had negotiated with Gyro for Casey to celebrate his 30th with a war-gaming party in the college grounds at the end of July – upmarket paintballing, Gyro had called it. Reaching the head of the valley they flew over the student block, the new tower, the main administration and teaching block and the dean's house, and then down the length of the lake. Seeing the college – including the new glass tower – from above even Greg found mesmerising.

'Hilary, could we check out the glass tower again?' Casey's lips moved silently while a metallic rendition of his voice crackled out of Greg's headphones. The helicopter dipped, turned and hovered over the top of the flying saucer. They looked through the glass roof and the glass floor to the scaffolding and the ground. 'Dad will so like it! OK, so what's over there?'

Hilary pointed the helicopter in the desired direction while Greg explained what was beneath them. That was why he was here. They headed towards two small outbuildings like miniature matchboxes at the far end of the lake, one of them a wooden boathouse. Then they came back along Pynbal's Ridge, with its snaking road to Hampton, civilisation and London. Casey was busy using a GPS position-fixer to populate his Google Earth picture of the college with sites for articles for his 30th birthday war – 'arms caches', 'minefields', hideouts and ambushes.

They turned once more and flew along the less-used side of the valley. They skimmed Crassock hill, over grass meadows by the lakeside, three pairs of semi-detached staff houses and, near the top of the hill, the lovers' lookout.

'Zap those co-ordinates for mission control,' purred Casey, his fingers flickering over the position-finder. 'Great view of the valley. What's on the other side?' They flew over. 'Oh wow, just imagine a tank hiding down there and then coming over the hill with no warning!'

Greg's expression slipped briefly. His eyebrows and cheek muscles were saying 'Pillock!' but Casey mistook the expression for technical interest – boys' stuff. 'Maybe one of your old Brit tanks, a Chieftain or something, or an Israeli one like a Merkava 3. You can pretty much get them on eBay. I'd refit them with a searchlight and water-cannon. Then you need a water bowser as well, but that's where the lake comes in real handy.'

The wooden boathouse – the one that Frank Jones rented. Greg suddenly realised that they needed to hover over it while he took a few pictures on his phone. Casey had no objection; the college were thinking of constructing a new path, Greg improvised, and the chance to get an aerial view was a lucky break.

For a few minutes the three of them hung as if by a thread, silent in their own thoughts while the circular ripples beat outwards the grass and the lake. Greg snapped away. He had seen from the ground the faint wheeled tracks which led to the boathouse, but what he had not seen before were three irregularly spaced circular patches (one or two feet in diameter, he estimated) where the grass was slightly discoloured, or at least a different shade of green.

When they climbed out of the helicopter, Casey's digital cufflinks showed he was now worth $20 million more than when they had taken off.

Greg found it a relief to drive to an airport big enough to make even Casey's ego dwindle towards human. Terminal 5 had only opened earlier in the year, and approaching from an unfamiliar direction he needed to concentrate on his route more than usual. Ben had no luggage to collect but his aircraft got caught in Heathrow's aerial traffic jam, so it was 6.45pm when the Lexus broke free from the airport. They headed to a shopping centre which Ben could raid for clothes and toiletries. Forty minutes later he returned with a tired grin and his arms full of bags and a suit-carrier. He'd bought a dark suit and a summery suit – the college was paying – and some casual shirts and jeans, a change of shoes, plenty of socks and – of course – pants.

Ben asked about Greg's day. A few highlights from the helicopter trip were enough for Ben to thank his lucky stars that he would have moved on from his job at Hampton before Casey Pinnacle and his friends arrived to re-enact *Apocalypse Now*.

Greg flew a kite, airing some unanswered questions about Frank's use of the boathouse. Disused previously, for the past couple of years Frank had rented it from the college. He kept it heavily padlocked, yet never rowed or sailed. Three times in recent months Greg had found tracks by the hut, as if wheeled equipment had been brought in or out. But Frank had never moved anything boat-like along the college roads.

In sharing these thoughts, Greg took a calculated risk: time was short if he was to find the evidence Amelia would need to take action on the tower opening, and Ben might turn out to be a friend. If Ben was in fact Frank's plant, little would be lost. Frank already knew Greg was suspicious of him.

The kite crashed. Ben was so tired that his reaction to winning the Euro-lottery would have been non-committal, much less unanswered trifles about a boathouse, and for the remainder of the journey to the college the two travelled in silence.

After dropping Ben off, Greg parked the Lexus. He let the sound system play while he gave the leather upholstery its nightly wipe-down with spray foam and a cloth, but the house music it played now irritated him. He switched to the radio which flickered between unfamiliar stations, stopping at rock. 'American Girl' – a raw, lyric-led Tom Petty and the Heartbreakers song from maybe 1978 – leapt out at him. It sounded like a man shaving in the dark in front of a smoky campfire, using a cut-throat razor dipped in whisky. At any moment half his face might catch alight.

Greg was ready to catch alight. Even if others could not or chose not to see it, he was right to worry about the boathouse – seeing it from the air had been unexpected confirmation of that. Proactivity was Habit Number One for highly effective people, Greg recalled. Tomorrow he would not only check out the grass patches but buy a circular-hole saw. Then he could look inside the boathouse. The balance of waiting needed to shift towards action – so much so that with the rest of Ben's clutter, Greg almost threw away a silver packet marked 'London Lilac' that had slipped under the driver's seat.

When he got home he tried the pants on. They were an outrageously priced brand that Greg had never heard of, the equivalent of £50 in Hong Kong dollars for the pair, albeit with a 'buy one, get one free' sticker. Anyone stupid enough to pay that money for underpants could pay out for another pair. They were slightly loose on Greg's lanky swimmer's thighs – at least when he went to bed – but in the morning they fitted perfectly.

THURSDAY 14 JUNE

Shortly before 7am, Ben walked through the dean's outer office and let himself into Gyro's inner sanctum. For the next few days he had decided to use Gyro's office as his own. With one week left until the tower opening, he had no time to waste on college staff and contractors second-guessing whether to pay him any attention.

Ben reckoned the best chair to sit in to make clear that he was no junior underling was Gyro's. A quick look at his predecessor's base decided the matter – a broom cupboard on the ground floor, as far away from the action as it was possible to get: 'I'm hiding, I don't know anything, don't bother me'. The college might as well have booked an ambulance for Richard Vanish when they had given him the job, mused Ben. Besides, from the dean's office the view down the lake was spectacular.

Vanessa, Gyro's secretary, was a gem. She had fielded the messages that Ben had left from Hong Kong on her voicemail without complaint or, so far, error. For example, his identity and password had been set up on the college computer system with access to the correct computer drives. Hours could so easily have been wasted through unthinking sloppiness. He took a minute to register his SmartPants online – ridiculous, but who was the consumer to argue with capitalism?

Vanessa was on his side and Ben wanted to keep it that way. He knew enough about the power of secretaries. He hoped that giving her the afternoon off would be a pleasant surprise and set the tone for their relationship. He would not mention yet that on Monday he would need her not to be too precious about the position of her desk, her filing cabinets or the adjoining coffee machine and photocopier. It would just be for four days, but when Gyro returned Ben needed to share the outer office with her. He made a note on his pad – phone, another desk and computer network access needed by Monday.

He had two hours of quiet before someone plugged in the world and it started advancing towards him. He needed the time to read files, starting with the tower construction. He positioned himself in front of the widescreen laptop that Gyro used as his desk computer. The desk and computer formed the short bar of a T, with the long bar taken up by a meeting table. By the time he talked to Gyro on the phone there were many things still unread, but he had already formed a clear impression of how Vanish had handled things. It was mid-afternoon in Hong Kong.

'I started with the lift files. Talk about passing the buck! Between the architects, the builders and the lift engineers, never mind the announcement company, we're being pissed on from a great height. Vanish's idea of managing the situation seems to have been to buy an umbrella.'

'Exactly.' In the background Ben could hear Hong Kong's frenetic harbourside.

'I'm calling an emergency site meeting for ten o'clock this morning. From now we'll have site meetings every twelve hours, 10am and 10pm.'

'That's a top plan. I like it.'

'There's a meeting with PC Plod about security and traffic for the opening; I'll put that back to tomorrow. It's not a Day One priority. Greg can help with that, he knows the college grounds and any traffic issues better than anyone.'

'Good idea. Greg'll appreciate being involved.'

'How's it going with the China big-wigs?'

'I hate to say it in case it spooks things, but as of this morning pretty well. It's been heavy lifting but I think we're going to see some serious money move pretty soon. I damn well hope so, after the amount of eel and snake I've eaten.' Gyro always sounded confident, but the confidence was infectious – Ben could feel it stirring inside him. The lift, the tower, the opening – it was all manageable. None of it was rocket science.

'Vanessa has left a note about a 3.30pm meeting today? It was fixed months ago. Apparently you were going to dump it on Vanish. Her note says the meeting is 'GSG'.'

Gyro snorted. 'Oh, the Gender Strategy Group. It's nothing, a routine meeting. Just listen to a bunch of women say things and make them feel important. Thirty minutes, if that. Apology for absence – change of personnel – screw-up

– no higher priority for the dean than gender. You know, just like you did when you gave Alex's speech on Monday night.'

Ben was getting into his stride. Sure, by 3.30pm he could have read the minutes of the last two GSG meetings. But Gyro's reference to Ben having done the equivalent job for Bakhtin was on the money; Ben had learned to look further ahead. 'What latitude do I have to agree things?'

'Whatever you like,' was Gyro's reaction.

'So, women get sixty percent of all faculty promotions next year?'

'Don't be a dumb ass. All right. But I can't do anything right now, I'm just heading into a meeting on the HSBC yacht.'

'If you could email me a few thoughts anytime up to 10pm?' That would be 2pm at Hampton.

'Yes, sir,' Gyro conceded with a laugh. Ben's spirits crept up another notch. Giving your boss orders was one of the trickiest bits of being a chief of staff.

Vanessa arrived at a few minutes before nine, all mumsy and sensible. Ben's surprise offer of the afternoon off bowled her over. Clearly she hadn't experienced any considerate management for a long time.

'But will you cope? On your first day?' she protested. But in no time she acknowledged that with things building up towards the opening, and then Richard Vanish not coping, she had been doing pretty much double jobs with no time off since January.

'I'll be fine. I'll screw some things up but we'll fix it. Take the half-day now; next week will just be worse.' Ben was beaming. Now he had a team in place.

It was 9.10am. Oh yes, someone had plugged in the world.

'Cardew McCarthy.'

Ben recalled that McCarthy was ex-military, the main staff contact with VST and the Pinnacles. The voice on the telephone fitted: flat and precise. Ben introduced himself.

'We can do introductions next Thursday, Mr Stillman. I sure look forward to that. I'm glad someone's in charge. If I may say so between friends, about time. Meantime, we've got an issue come up. Item, the environmental impact of the tower. Given the internal and external coverage we are aiming for, including VST customers and staff, Mr Junior has identified that the new tower needs to be, I quote, "a model of environmental leadership".'

Ben's mind raced through everything on the tower which he had read on the plane or in the files this morning. While the design specification had covered every other imaginable symbolism of leadership, he had read nothing about its environmental impact.

'Well,' said Ben. 'It is a very high-quality project and I'm sure everything has been done in an environmentally thoughtful way. Perhaps I have got this wrong, but I don't think there ever were environmental leadership parameters in the tower specification.'

'Agreed.'

'And now would be a little late in the day to be changing anything that has not previously been thought of.'

'Agreed.'

'So, ah –' Ben paused. What had Gyro said about Cardew? Make the man look good to his boss. 'So how about I let you have a note showing, um, how the decisions already taken on the tower are very environmentally friendly ones.'

'I think we'll do good business, Mr Stillman. If you could ETA that note to me in the next five hours then Mr Junior will be able to give it his consideration first thing after breakfast. We all fixed now on the elevator?'

Ben looked at his watch. Pinnacle was headquartered on the American east coast, so presumably where McCarthy was it was about 4.15am. Ouch. Working for Mr Junior must be fun.

'Totally fixed any minute now.' In the meantime he noted his pad – email McCarthy green 2pm. He could ask the architect at 10am whether anything about the tower was green. He doubted it; while the tower was full of high tech, it all seemed to be boys' toys stuff rather than local materials and recycled rainwater. Quite what was environmentally friendly about a collection of outsize egos jetting from the far corners of the globe to Hampton next Thursday would no doubt occur to him by 2pm. He hoped.

As he had expected, the 10am site meeting was hard hats and excuses. Ben's plan had been to invest a maximum of five minutes oohing and aahing at the technical marvels. That was a good warm-up tactic with specialists, and allowed Ben to show off some of his file reading. But the tower had ideas of its own. For the first time Ben was seeing it up-close and personal, standing inside the shroud of scaffolding in daylight.

Gazing four floors vertically upwards he looked through the auditorium's reinforced glass floor, past more than a hundred transparent seats and the glass ceiling, straight up into shifting brush-strokes of cloud scurrying 20,000 feet overhead. Some opaque floor areas hid engineering spaces and toilets but when a flock of starlings swept past, he could not tell if they had passed above the auditorium or beneath it.

'It gets everyone the first time,' murmured Tom, the project manager, and Ben agreed.

Wrapped around the central column of the giant toadstool at ground zero was a glass doughnut – the lift. According to one opinion in the file, the fault was misbalanced pressure between the hydraulic cylinders on which the lift was due to rise. Correction: one of the faults.

As the cluster of hard hats approached, the lift lit up and an out-of-work actress enunciated: 'The doors of the lift are closing.' Parts of the doughnut wall slid apart. Ben did not go in.

By 10.20am all 15 specialists had arrived, or were represented. Ben laid it on the line:

'You and I know that with the Pinnacle Leadership Tower we are standing on the well-known "bleeding edge" of technology. It's painful. Every one of you is proud to be part of this project. All of your firms are planning to put pictures on your websites. In fact, two of you already have although you don't have permission.

'You know the tower was contracted to be fully functional three weeks ago. That means we're into penalty clauses.

That means lawyers are on the case. And that means you're losing money and we're losing time. We can all see a mile off what the lawyers are doing.'

Ben kept going. 'Now it's 10.20, Thursday. My proposal is we stop the clock on all the lawyers right now, get this lift working by 6pm Saturday, get the rest of the snagging done by 6pm Tuesday, and courier all the penalty clauses back to the department of hell they came from. Tom, you're the project manager, you're in charge. I'll meet with you on site every twelve hours from now on. 10am, 10pm, every day without fail.

'You all work on this 24/7. If you need to fly in experts, book their flights within the hour. Safety clearance needs the bureaucrats, I'll settle for Monday on that. But you and I –' he jabbed Tom in the chest '– are riding this glass doughnut to the top and back 6pm Saturday *at the latest*.

'That's Plan A. I aim to please, so here's Plan B. Let me read you a list of some of the companies whose top dogs are going to be here next Thursday.' Ben started on a roll-call of world-famous international and British businesses. 'That's for starters. Now that is, by my reckoning, some trillions of annual client dollars up for grabs in those organisations. And if on Sunday I have to email them all to cancel the opening because the lift is not working and Sunday is the latest I can leave it without looking like a complete dickhead, be assured that I shall in those emails mention personally each of you, your boss, his boss and your companies as responsible for the fiasco.

'So the good news is, you and your bosses and I are all going to be famous one way or the other by the end of next week. So let's be famous for succeeding.

'*There is no time* for you to confer with your bosses, and their bosses and your lawyers. I need you solving the problems, right now. So while we've been out here, my office – the dean's office – has been emailing your head offices with what I have just said. The email also says how pleased I am that you have all committed to Plan A.'

Ben headed back to the office not sure if it would do the trick. But it was a better shot than adding another 10-page letter to folders of correspondence already splitting at their seams.

Of course the lawyers hated it, and for the next couple of hours Ben's phone went crazy. Ben just swatted them back. Half of what he was doing was bullshitting them, but the other half was just wrapping up their own piles of bullshit and returning them to sender. Ben's gamble was that pissing off the lawyers would motivate the engineers. The engineers wanted the tower to work; they just needed not to look like the only dumb-asses who cared.

'Mr Stillman, this is Bill Andrews of Andrews, Caravajal, Sagan and Warner –'

'Mr Andrews, your client and I are really short of time. Maybe call back when you've shortened the name of your firm? Pension someone off? Thanks.'

Ben's day was now dissolving into a blur, but he was acutely conscious that the engineering problems of the tower were only one horn of his dilemma; the human side of the opening was equally lethal. He locked the office door for an hour to wade through the accumulating VIP list with Vanessa before she took her half-day off. She showed him how to switch the phones through to college reception.

Could the European vice-chairman of one of the major investment banks arrive by helicopter – no. One of the college's governors was being shadowed at work that day by his daughter, could she come – no. Could the Maharishi Swami Tandoori, one of the world's richest paupers who would be in religious silence that day, bring his aide to speak for him – um, yes.

1.32pm marked a gear-change in Ben's day. In the morning he had been seeing the wood for the trees, deciding, delegating, cajoling and instructing – showing leadership. No-one might follow his instructions and that was scary, but a different scary from having to cut trees down himself, which he now had to do.

In 28 precious minutes he had to produce from scratch an environmentally green confection to get Cardew McCarthy off his back. By then, Gyro would have sent him some briefing for the afternoon GSG meeting, he hoped. He would digest this before 3.30pm with the ham sandwich and minutes of the last two meetings that Vanessa had placed on the meeting table.

He needed to make a salad without leaves. The architects had confirmed that there was nothing particularly green about the tower; instead transparency had been the grand egotistical concept. In fact from an environmental point of view, it would be a particularly bad idea to ask questions about the synthetic glass-like material which had been used to make the auditorium's seats, shelves and tables.

Oh, well. Ben played for a few minutes with the calculator on a carbon offset website and then opened an email template on the computer. Its keys were light to the touch and the letters came up in a size comfortable for a 55-year-old to read; on a full-colour wide screen it was like being in the front row at the opera. Ben wrote:

Mr McCarthy:

The Pinnacle Leadership Tower is so many generations ahead of contemporary best practice that it cannot sensibly be measured in conventional environmental ways. The all-glass construction means that large parts of the tower are made of glass, which is a recyclable material.

The glass ceiling maximises the use of solar energy for lighting purposes in the auditorium, reducing fossil-fuel consumption. The glass walls mean that tomorrow's leaders who study in the auditorium will be continually reminded of the beautiful and precious environment around them, which it will be their responsibility to protect.

In the evening, the glass floor ensures that the electric light which is used passes through to ground level, enabling it in effect to be recycled, reducing the need for path lighting. Therefore, the tower demonstrates environmental leadership where it should be, at the heart of conception and design, and not tacked on as an after-thought.

In addition, we are committed to keeping the CO2 tonnage of the opening ceremony itself to a minimum. Our chef sources his produce locally. Of course this is not possible with the champagne but we are happy to consider the possibility of bringing this to the UK by barge and sail-boat.

We are totally focussed at this time on the various preparations for 21 June, but please let me know if further environmental analysis will be of assistance.

Ben Stillman
Chief of Staff, Hampton Management College

Ben hit 'send' with a comfortable five minutes to spare. Not bad, even if he thought so himself. 'Consider' was such a useful word.

He reviewed his notepad again, and checked the computer. Terrific – an email from Gyro headed 'GSG' had arrived 20 minutes ago. Ben skimmed it: there were a couple of paragraphs of background in horrendously incorrect locker-room language and then three points which he could make on Gyro's behalf at the meeting: exactly what he needed.

The Appropriate Language Training pilot could be rolled out to all staff. A multi-disciplinary working group could develop a gender module for the MBA, but only as an optional elective. And Ben could pledge Gyro's total commitment to appointing at least one, and ideally two, women to the four professorships remaining from the Pinnacle endowment, 'especially if they had nice tits'. Unquote. He flinched at the possibility that he might not have scanned the email in advance and stumbled into reading it to the meeting verbatim.

Ben clicked 'print' and picked up Gyro's email. It was a glorious day and he could do with a breather by the lake, armed with his sandwich and the GSG papers. Then he would visit as many of the faculty and administrative staff as he could. Right now he was starving.

The conversations with staff were friendlier and longer than he had hoped (several remembered teaching him). So with no-one in the outer office, when Ben returned almost exactly at 3.30pm, the Gender Strategy Group was already standing around the meeting table: a short, stocky farmer's wife in a black T-shirt and trousers, about 50 Ben guessed; an emaciated museum curator in headmistress glasses and coffee-stained summer dress, also probably about 50; and behind them Connie Yung, the newly appointed student governor in designer jeans and a sleeveless white cotton blouse.

Looking down the line, Ben thought Tesco, M&S and (maybe?) boohoo. The last time they had met, he and Connie had locked horns about Bakhtin so it would be good to kick off on a different note this afternoon. Ben reached out a hand and offered some words of welcome. 'It's good to see you, Connie. Your colleagues must be the Gender Strategy Group. I'm Ben Stillman, the dean's chief of staff for the next couple of weeks. You may know I did my MBA here.' The glance he got in return was friendly, but unaccompanied by a handshake.

He realised that the farmer's wife had held out her hand but then withdrawn it. 'You may address me as "chair". I was in here cleaning this office at eight o'clock this morning. You didn't notice.'

Ben instinctively made sure that the dean's email was buried deep inside his meeting folder; this one looked the type to be able to read other people's notes upside down. 'Oh, I'm so sorry. My mistake. It's a bit crazy around here, and my first day in the office.'

She pushed past him to occupy the dean's chair at the head of the table. 'I'm the head cleaner and the staff co-chair of the Gender Strategy Group. The dean, we understand, though we were not properly informed, is away.'

'In Hong Kong. A very urgent meeting at short notice connected with next week's opening. He is very sorry –'

'Clearly, then, I shall take the chair. You may tender the dean's apologies for his absence at the appropriate place on the agenda.'

The others arranged themselves around the meeting table – Ben with the wall of photographs behind him, the other two facing him with the wall of books behind them. Ben noticed that Connie's arms were slender and smooth-skinned, like vanilla ice cream that had melted in coffee.

Making the most of her regency, the chair took 10 minutes to proceed with apologies, minutes of the previous meeting and matters arising. Having mistakenly assumed that he would be running the meeting, Ben had counted on having the whole thing wrapped up in half an hour as Gyro had suggested.

That might be harder from where he was sitting now.

'Any corrections to page 2 of the previous minutes?'

Suddenly Ben sat up.

'Mr Stillman?'

'Nothing,' he mumbled. Don't mumble, he thought. Don't draw attention to yourself. 'Nothing,' he said again.

'Good. Any corrections to page 3?'

The museum curator shifted in her seat. She was a professor by the name of Tilney. 'If I might, chair, "obsequious" is mis-spelled in paragraph 6, and again two paragraphs further on. We are a degree-awarding establishment, so some visible competence in the use of language might make a pleasant change.'

Ben got up as if to pick up something from the window sill. He could see the screen of the dean's computer facing the farmer's wife, as he had left it before going to lunch. Thank God, it was dark – he had been mistaken. Everything was fine.

'Nicely put, Professor. Any matters arising?'

But everything might not be fine. Screens go dark if you leave them unattended. They hibernate. They save the planet. But they spring back into life if you hit a key, and the last thing that had been on that screen was Gyro's locker-room language. Ben had not anticipated being bumped out of his own seat.

'Are you rejoining us, Mr Stillman?'

'Of course. My apologies.' He moved towards his own place. It might still be all right; after this long a gap, if the cleaner hit a key, she would probably come up with a log-in screen. But he could not take the chance. If he could get her out of the chair, he could hit a key and deal with the problem in a second. 'Would you come over to the window? There's something Dean Gyro particularly wanted me to show you.' He moved to the window, pointing downwards.

'Is this a matter arising?'

'Absolutely. It could not be more arising. Or arisen. Honestly, it won't take a minute.' Connie and the professor started towards him. There was no movement from the cleaner.

'Here, out here, about halfway towards the lake. Or, do you think, more to the left?' Ben gesticulated inexplicably.

From the chair there was no hint of movement. 'What are you talking about? There's nothing in the minutes about the lake.'

'The statue of, ah, ah –' Ben tried to think of a famous woman. 'Florence Nightingale.' Just for a minute he needed the chair out of the chair … 'The nude Florence Nightingale.'

Up, she was up! The chair hoisted herself into a standing position. She was thundering, but she was not moving. 'Order, order. Back to our places. I'm calling the meeting to order.'

Connie was at the window, trying to be helpful. 'Where exactly are you talking about, Ben? I can't see anything.'

It was the wave of the chair's arm that did it, the touch of her sleeve against the joyously light keys. From the window Ben could see the screen light up. He threw himself across the desk at the computer and pulled out the power cord. Papers flew. Professor Tilney screamed.

'Are you all right?' asked Connie.

Shit. The screen stayed lit: it was a laptop with a battery. Ben hit the keyboard with his fist, pushing several keys simultaneously. Thank God! A log-in screen.

Ben excused himself to go the bathroom, washing the sweat off his face with copious running water and nurtured by its protected status as a men's room. Thank you God, thank you God, thank you God, he thought. It took a few minutes to pull himself together.

'Thank you for returning, Mr Stillman,' the chair said impassively. For precious moments Ben was grateful that his colleagues had used his absence to return the office to order, as if nothing had happened. But something had happened. Connie was blushing.

'We were concerned,' the chair continued. 'We were sympathetic. We know about the pressures of the job. We have raised concerns about what happened to your predecessor.' Then she softened, just for a moment. 'I know that you are only with us for a short time, Mr Stillman. But you might consider joining the administrative staff union? We have very modern benefits, and one never knows when the protection of a union may become useful.'

Ben nodded gratefully. He noticed that his own meeting papers had been replaced neatly in his folder, square to the table's edge.

The chair's next words came at him with a distant plangency, not the comforting of a sympathetic or even neutral teacher or trade union official, but the sentencing of a judge. 'But first, Professor Tilney has found a document which is pertinent to the proceedings and which she would like to read into the record.'

'The G-Spot Group,' began the woman in the coffee-stained summer dress, reading from the printed email that

Ben had not the least difficulty in recognising. That was how Gyro had begun, and from there his language had careened rapidly downhill.

'I didn't know Chinese people blushed.' Ben and Connie were alone in his office, Ben shell-shocked in the dean's chair, Connie looking at him from the window.

'I didn't know men wept,' Connie replied.

'It's in the Bible – Jesus wept.' Ben coughed. 'Look, I'm so sorry.'

'Stop that. Sorry for what? It wasn't your email. If we ignore the bits written in testosterone, what the dean offered was quite reasonable. In fact now we know why you dived across the table, it was even rather charming. Anyway, let's see what was on the computer.'

Ben wasn't sure why the whole episode had put him in Connie's good books, but right now he was happy to take friendship wherever he could get it. He tapped a key on the keyboard and entered his log-in. He expected the G-Spot email but it was one of the screens minimised behind it which had them both in hysterics: the curvaceously modelled men's underwear on the SmartPants website. Ben tried to explain but the words that came out of his mouth stubbornly refused to make sense.

'Don't cry again,' said Connie, clutching at Ben's shoulder as her hysterics failed to abate.

'I'll try. Look, I'll make some tea.'

In the relative sanity that followed, Connie explained the gentle inquiry into Vanish's departure which the governors had asked her to undertake; she had stayed on after the meeting to arrange to talk to Ben at a convenient time. Perhaps on Sunday, since she had tracked down Vanish and got an appointment with him on Saturday, and she had to be at the college on Sunday to start the last few days of her course.

Sunday suited Ben since (unless the GSG fiasco got him fired) the tower and its opening had to be his top priorities and Sunday was several days away. Surely his history with Bakhtin would come back into the picture with Connie at some point, but with luck that bridge could be crossed when he came to it. For now, being fired by Bakhtin seemed to have made her more sympathetic towards him.

Needless to say, reception had a pile of phone messages for him and it gave some relief to start working through them. He put to one side a message from Frank which wished him well, apologised that he was not around until Saturday evening, but offered him Saturday dinner in town – 'something to get you out of the prison compound'. It was well past 6pm before he got to the message at the bottom of the pile. The caller was Roger Sling, with a phone number in the First Improvident branch in Alderley. Sling apologised that he had left some messages for Vanessa before realising that Ben had now taken charge (Ben laughed to himself). Sling identified himself as the college's bank manager. He would value a meeting with Ben at his earliest convenience.

Ben had expected a long first day, and had got one.

FRIDAY 15 JUNE

FRIDAY 15 JUNE

When life, work, play and love all revolve around the same thing, you've got passion! The key to creating passion in your life is to find your unique talents and your special role and purpose in the world.
STEPHEN COVEY[3]

On Friday morning, Greg woke up feeling particularly sharp and proactive. *Being proactive is more than taking initiative. It is recognizing that we are responsible for our own choices.* As he swam his early-morning lengths, the pool surface was a ballroom dance floor with a hundred golden dancers waltzing with sunlight in response to his strokes. This morning he was thinking about the day's choices particularly carefully. It was his 25th birthday, although he knew he looked much younger. This was sometimes a problem in undercover work. He drank little, but being asked for ID when he met someone in a bar was annoying.

Gyro was staying in Hong Kong until Monday night to close a long sought-after deal, so today Greg had only two work engagements: taking the dean's new assistant to a midday

---

[3] *The 8th Habit: From Effectiveness to Greatness,* op. cit.

meeting at the district police headquarters, and driving Dianne to one of her Friday night London dinners.

If luck was on Greg's side she would decide early on which of her guests to sleep with, and with a lot of luck she would spend the whole weekend at her Kensington flat. In that case Greg would make it back to Hampton at a reasonable hour and be free until Sunday evening, but he did not count on it. VIP drivers did not make personal plans for their birthdays. In Greg's case Gyro would have agreed the time off effusively weeks in advance, but it would have meant nothing if something came up on the day.

In any case Greg's passion, his work and his play, was unmasking the truth. That was why he had volunteered for undercover training soon after joining the police. And for his birthday what Greg wanted – no, what Greg was proactively choosing – was the evidence that would tip Amelia Henderson's hand to commit departmental resources to averting whatever threat Frank Jones had in mind for the tower opening. The birthday present Greg wanted was audio monitoring in Frank's house; it was the obvious next step.

Of course, if Frank was not a renegade loner but linked to a cell, the threat assessment and response would shoot up the scale. However, even Greg's hyperactive observation had not detected any evidence of a cell. Frank's profile – his career as an academic, as well as whatever lay concealed beneath it – leaned towards the solitary. Greg had skimmed some of Frank's published papers in the college library. While he could make little sense of them, compared to the publication lists of other academics at the college, the papers were few and mostly single-authored.

After his swim and breakfast Greg drove the Lexus out to the boathouse, parking well back so as not to drive over any of the patches of discoloured grass that he had photographed from the air earlier in the week. The boathouse was one of two one-room buildings set in the woods close to the lake edge, a simple weatherboard hut with a sloping tile roof.

As usual Frank's boathouse was padlocked on the outside, but one of the things which had attracted Greg's attention on previous visits was that Frank had reinforced the door-frame and fitted a second lock into it. He had also closed up the windows from the inside with plywood. By the middle of a summer's day the interior would become unpleasantly warm. Greg listened for a minute or two, and then rapped on the door: nothing.

Greg's first goal was to look inside the hut. Then he would look at the grass patches, but that could be done anytime; pausing on a lakeside stroll was an innocent activity. An alarm was unlikely, as the structure had no mains electricity. To work inside the hut Frank had brought a portable inverter, producing 240v AC power from a petrol engine. Greg had seen and heard it, because the engine needed to be operated outside the hut.

For his own purposes Greg had brought a heavy-duty battery-powered cordless drill with a circular hole cutting bit. He also had a small digital camera, a torch, instant glue, masking tape and a well-padded anorak. He would cut the hole near the corner of the hut, opposite to the road and to the patch of ground on which Frank usually parked.

He chose a spot about two feet off the ground yet loosely covered by shrubbery. Too close to eye-level would cause the intrusion to be noticed sooner; too low would make it impossible for him to see what was inside. If he saw nothing, he would glue the circular plug of wood back. If he was unlucky, the hole might come out directly behind something large and close, which would mean cutting a second hole somewhere else. At some point Frank would discover all this, but with less than a week to the tower opening the balance of risk favoured action.

He knelt down, pulling the anorak over his head and the drill to keep the shrubbery off and to dampen the sound. Some chaffinches still chirped in complaint. The ground at his knees became covered in a mixture of earth and light wood shavings which he would need to smear around in an attempt to disguise. He put the drill down carefully and reached for the torch.

He took his time. The angle was awkward and the light beam narrow. Well, at least he had some vision; some angles were obscured but he had not come out directly behind a cupboard. He probed around with his pencil of light, trying to make out the outline of each object in his sight. After a few minutes he realised that although he was sweating and had dropped the anorak, he could do better by pulling it over his head to screen out the sun, killing the torch and letting his night vision kick in.

First things first: there was definitely no boat, nor anything like parts of a boat. There was a workbench against the opposite wall, but from his low perspective Greg could not see what was on it. One dark rectangular shape stood perhaps four feet high. That it was electrical could be seen by the wire clippings of different colours scattered on the floor. Were there chemicals? He made out nothing drum-like, nor smelled anything except earthy wood. In a far corner he could see part of a plastic sack, like a 25-litre bag of compost from a garden centre; but even if he had been able to read more than the odd snatch of writing on it, there was no guarantee that the writing described what the bag now contained.

Greg's knees and back were complaining about his awkward position, but his morale was high. What he had seen might not be a smoking gun, but it was not an innocent doll's house either. He took half a dozen flash photographs and decided not to glue the circular plug of wood back but tape it loosely in place, and kicked around the earth where he had been working. Then he turned to the circular patches of grass which he had noticed from the air.

Greg had the Lexus ready when the dean's assistant finished his twice-daily ten o'clock meeting with Tom, the tower-project manager. Ben climbed in the front seat and they set off on the 20-minute drive to the police headquarters with plenty of time to spare.

'We're there with the tower. Not exactly no worries, but we'll get there in the end. Tom thinks the lift will be working by tomorrow evening.' Buried in the pages of his notepad, Ben struck Greg as in a middling mood, a 50-50 mixture of tense and optimistic.

'That's good news, Mr Stillman.'

'It will be if it happens. And it's Ben, please. I want you to be part of this meeting with the police. We're discussing traffic arrangements for the opening, that kind of thing. You're the expert, really.'

The invitation took Greg by surprise. Doubtless it would come with a catch, perhaps a favour needed next week, but even so it was a chance not to be missed to share with his passenger his morning's findings, including the pictures on his camera. If Ben was Frank's plant, then showing the pictures was forcing the pace. But if he wasn't, then it was a chance to start raising Ben's suspicions, even if his attentiveness right now was driven by relationship-building rather than smoking-gun images.

'All the pictures really show is there's no boat in the boathouse.'

Greg persisted. 'But the grass circles, and the tracks from the boathouse to one of the circles?' Invisible from the ground unless you knew what you were looking for, Greg thought that the different colouration reflected re-growth of grass over scorched patches between one and two feet in diameter. In the undergrowth near one of the patches he had found a couple of inches of electrical wiring on which the insulation had melted.

Ben twiddled with the melted wire. 'It's something, but it's something to find out rather than something we have found out,' he mused. Greg took it that the use of 'we' was deliberate.

Ben continued, 'It's certainly not something for the police today. We'd look very silly if it's just Frank being shy about being an over-age boy scout, flying model planes and crashing them a bit too often. You know, maybe radio-controlled ones he makes himself with small petrol engines.'

Greg conceded the point, although he did not believe crashed model aircraft would make scorch marks two feet across.

Ben hastened on. 'What you've done is exactly right. You've been observant and you've brought what you've noticed to my attention. I agree that there's something to explain, but the chances are it has a very simple explanation. The first thing we do is see what Frank says he's up to in the boathouse.'

'But that could tip him off.'

'So we'll be smart about it. He's invited me to dinner tomorrow night. We know each other from before and, after all, he got me into this mess! We'll chat, have a few drinks, I'll get his story. And then we'll see what we think.'

Their meeting at Alderley district police headquarters lasted 40 minutes. Chief Inspector Haddrill was with a sergeant from infrastructure operations branch, formerly known as traffic. 'Traffic' had too much of a sense of movement about it to fit the road system in southeast England.

The meeting went efficiently. Greg explained one or two things, such as the parts of the grounds which the college usually used for overflow parking, but took care not to appear suspiciously expert in police matters or vocabulary.

Ben explained the guest list, the planned timings and general arrangements. Getting cars in and out smoothly would be the main headache, said Haddrill. As with any concentration of international business leaders there was some risk of a political protest, but Haddrill assessed it as low.

Virtual Savings and Trust did not trip any of the major alarms – arms, animal testing, abortion clinics, gambling, GM crops, pornography, whaling – and while it was always possible that one of the visiting Russians might be on another Russian's death list, the tower opening was not an obvious place to attempt a hit.

Another possibility on Haddrill's list was an attempted kidnap or hostage-taking. Again, with some simple precautionary measures, his overall assessment of the risk was low. For a couple of hours there would be a concentration of VIP targets in one place. But the other side of that coin was the private security the tycoons would have with them, in addition to the police presence. Ben confirmed that the Pinnacle family would certainly have some security people there.

So Haddrill's conclusion was that for both sets of reasons, traffic management and security, between 3pm and 9pm the college would become a one-way system. He opened out a map. Traffic would come in down Pynbal and go out over Crassock. At 3pm there would be a thorough sweep to identify all cars parked in the college and check them for any attached devices. From that time there would also be a checkpoint and camera on the approach to Pynbal. Expected cars would get windscreen stickers, unexpected cars would be turned back and everyone would be filmed.

A vehicle recovery truck would be parked beside the checkpoint; if someone broke down on the winding roads the jam could be cleared quickly, and within a minute it could be parked across the road to close it. The Crassock end would have 'No Entry' signs and a periodic motorcycle patrol. Finally, from 5pm Haddrill would take personal charge from the mobile headquarters which would be parked at the college. Strictly speaking this was not necessary, he explained, but modern policing was all about customer service and personal leadership.

Greg and Ben were impressed; Ben also got the hint. 'Dean Gyro will be very interested in this, and he is an international expert on leadership. If your duties allow, he would be delighted if you could join him and his guests for dinner at 8pm.'

Haddrill beamed and closed his colour-tabbed folder. Greg spotted his moment to throw something unexpected into the discussion and pounced. Afterwards, back in the car, Ben was not amused.

'I guess that was your sense of humour, was it, Greg? Springing the Prime Minister on us at the end of the meeting?'

Greg said nothing, keeping his eyes on the road.

Ben continued, 'I think if there was a possibility of the Prime Minister coming, I might just possibly have mentioned it to the police when I was going through the guest list. Or somewhere in between the discussion of demonstrations and kidnapping. For Christ's sake, Greg, there's no way the Prime Minister's coming, and that's not just me saying so, that's from the dean personally. I know you meant well, and

Dr Peach-Gyro means well, and I was sorry to have to come down on you so hard in front of the police.

'But you see what would have happened otherwise? Right now they'd be checking with Number Ten, and Number Ten would say we're raving lunatics. It would have embarrassed the college. If anything it would have made the Prime Minister less likely to come another time. Which, thanks to Dr Dianne, the dean is absolutely sure he will. But not this time.'

Birthday or not, for the rest of the day Greg's luck headed south. Even though he set off with Dianne Peach-Gyro at 4pm for a 7.30pm black-tie dinner, the traffic flowing into west London that Friday was excruciating. When Dianne was on the phone she was her cooing, solicitous self, especially when she murmured sweet words of absence to her husband. But that did not stop her biting through Greg's neck in one clean snap when he mentioned Ben's dismissiveness of the Prime Minister coming to Hampton for the opening. Ouch.

Afterwards, Greg realised he had only mentioned it to break the boredom after Dianne's phone calls had petered out somewhere near the Hammersmith flyover. It was lack of professionalism; for once his waiting skills had let him down.

Whatever the reason, Dianne made sure that he had a surfeit of remedial practice for the rest of the evening. The dinner was at Alex Bakhtin's mansion in Hyde Park, which raised Greg's hopes of being sent back to start his weekend straight away: clearly Dianne would spend the night, and quite possibly the weekend, with Alex. Instead she kept him waiting, not just while the other guests arrived and drinks were served (Ed Lens was dropped off by a government car but his driver didn't wait), but throughout the sit-down dinner.

Greg burned a couple of sticks of jasmine by the side of the gravel driveway as he watched the waiters through the net curtains in the dining room. Greg knew from Alex's driver that the curtains were designed to catch the flying glass of a bomb blast since some of his boss's money was Russian. He motivated himself by thinking of how things might be when he moved into the job that Amelia had in mind for him in the autumn.

When Dianne emerged, one of the last, she was on an arm which Greg had not expected – Mark Topley, the MP for Hampton and a minister in the Health Department.

'Run us to the Kensington flat, would you?' Dianne rested one jewelled hand on Greg's arm as he held the door for her. Her walnut hair gave off the mixed scents of Chanel and cigars. 'Greg's such a sweetie, the tops. And then I promised it would be no bother to come back in the morning and get Mark to his constituency surgery for 9am?'

'If it's no bother,' said the MP apologetically. 'I absolutely don't want to be any trouble.'

'My pleasure, sir.' As if I needed Saturday morning fucked as well, Greg thought. As if the minister didn't have a driver of his own. As if what Mark Topley MP absolutely didn't want was Dianne's apartment as the pick-up address in the government car-service log. Servants of the public can't be too careful.

For the briefest of moments Greg thought of the fun he could have if he could have whipped out a police warrant card there and then. But then the thought was gone. His unique talent was to uncover larger hidden truths than a condom and a few grams of something in a married minister's dinner jacket. He had a special role and purpose in the world. If Ben played ball and Frank lied to him about the boathouse over dinner tomorrow night, Greg might have his birthday present and be able to deliver it to Amelia before the weekend was out.

SATURDAY 16 JUNE (MORNING & AFTERNOON)

For the first half of Saturday morning, summer took a commercial break. As the sun rose the sky darkened and the temperature plunged. Winter previewed a series of new improved squalls with Siberian hailstones, rattling windows across London's suburbs like a riot and startling the squadrons of horses assembled to Troop the Colour before the Queen.

The Lexus which pulled to the kerb off Kensington Church Street at 7.30am shrugged the weather off, but Connie Yung was unable to do this. She rolled over in bed and pulled up the duvet. Why drive her beat-up Corolla to Guildford in this? Her appointment with Richard Vanish could wait another day. As Dorothy Lines had explained, what Connie had agreed to do wasn't a real inquiry; certainly not one upon which any pressing decisions hung. What did have a deadline this week was her final MSc project. Predictably Connie was behind with this, so having a clear day to make her conceptual analysis less tangled would be good news.

The hailstone riot beat Connie's attempts to sleep hands down, leaving her to ponder (not for the first time) why she had said yes – yes to becoming a college governor, yes to doing some ferreting around Vanish, or indeed yes two years ago to being sponsored by her employer to do a part-time degree in healthcare management? None of these things were necessary to doing her job well; indeed the opposite, given the hours they consumed.

As a personnel professional Connie knew part of the answer well enough. These were all markers of being a 'high potential', signs that she was 'going places'. But she did not want to go places; she had seen enough, and much of what she had seen – especially the politics and barely disguised egomania in the higher levels of private and public organisations – discomfited her.

Shifting out of the private sector into the NHS after Bakhtin had wrecked her food-packaging business still felt the right decision, even though it had been a painful wrench. Private-sector values were accumulating within the NHS like plaque, but having really smart colleagues who did care about patients made all the difference. The idea of 'going places', whether getting promoted or simply acquiring power, just made her feel car sick. Yet label herself 'low potential'? No thanks!

A mystery of the 20th century – Connie put it down to the divine sense of humour – was why the shiny new 'human resource' profession had attracted so many individuals with scant feeling for, or ability to deal with, the complexity of being human. Connie wasn't one of these, so she knew there was another dimension to her career puzzle; something difficult to pin down. Maybe because her big four-oh birthday was so close, some truths were too close to dodge – Help! Even closer was the lightning. Connie jumped out of her skin, so startled she didn't even hear the thunder.

When she had recovered sufficiently she took refuge in a faded silk summer dressing gown (summer!), put the kettle on and called Vanish. Afterwards she could ponder yet another of her yesses, said against all her intentions.

Vanish said, 'Next Saturday would be fine … but if you want to do something about it, it will be too late.' There was no shred of pleading in his voice, only certainty. So Connie went to see him.

The winter commercials finished in time for the Queen's 11am parade, and the only things which pummelled Connie as she steered her Corolla down the A3 towards the miasma of Guildford Saturday shopping were questions. 'If' she wanted to do something? To do something about 'it'?

Her friend Seth Carter came through on the hands-free. 'Just checking that you haven't chickened out on tomorrow afternoon?'

Connie and some other MSc students had planned a Sunday afternoon celebration picnic by the college lake – a multiple celebration of the end of the course, for which they had to be back in college, plus Seth's new job and (subject to chickening out) a warm-up for Connie's big birthday in July. Seth was making the opposite move to Connie's, from the NHS into the private sector, and had offered to buy the champagne.

'I see no chickens, but what about the weather?'

Typically, Seth had it nailed. 'Forecast checked half an hour ago. No problems at all. Leave your woollies at home – wear something off-the-shoulder and a little bit see-through. Sexy sunset guaranteed.'

'For whom?'

The noise of the car swallowed the first part of Seth's answer. 'Sounds like you're doing seventy in the old banger. Or taking the call inside a washing machine.'

'Yeah, right. Going to Guildford – something the governors asked me to do.'

'Oh, congratulations on becoming a governor! I heard the news.'

'Something tells me I'll know better tomorrow if congratulations is the right word.'

Vanish had picked an upmarket tea lounge off the high street, in a hotel with halogen lighting and 14th-century stonework. Connie assumed he had chosen it because it was quiet and he didn't want her to know where he was staying; judging by the price of a sandwich lunch with hand-picked organic salad from the garden, he wasn't staying here. She would have to foot the bill and reclaim it from the college. With luck both she and the college would get something for their investment.

Richard Vanish was in his thirties, with receding curly hair and freckles – much younger than she had expected. Twenty minutes into the conversation it was the years of personnel experience of which Dorothy Lines had spoken which saved Connie from snatching out of Vanish's hands the spectacles with which he kept fiddling. Connie realised that she would have to play the conversation long, so she spliced gentle questions about Vanish's background together with talking up the caring side of her HR responsibilities, and her innocence in becoming a governor.

As a personnel professional, Connie's questions were only apparently gentle. The more she dug, the less impressive she found Vanish's career. From university he had passed on taking an MBA and gone straight into academic administration somewhere even sleepier than pre-Gyro Hampton.

In the end the only intentionality she could ascribe to his career was divine retribution; God might reasonably be enraged at any higher education system for graduating such an ineffectual human being. Vanish had gained a pass degree in mediaeval history (perhaps that was why he had chosen the hotel) without picking up any knowledge of or passion for anything, including himself.

The pallor and banality of the conversation became interesting – 'Richard, another pot of tea? Let's be daring, I quite fancy those mini-bloomers with pork crackling' – when Connie began to puzzle how this misfit had ever become the dean's right-hand man. Vanish had started in the role two years earlier – in other words, after Gyro had arrived. However in the first year he had been off for six months thanks to a virus playing hell with his digestive system. Much of the time he had been bed-ridden, receiving nutrients intravenously.

Connie guessed that Gyro's plan had been to take a short-term hit for a long-term gain: accept an inadequate internal candidate into the role, pick a particularly inadequate one so he blows out very quickly and thereby overcome opposition to hiring a hot-shot on a lot more money from outside – someone like Ben. However, illness had been the joker in the pack. Employment and potentially disability legislation would have made firing Vanish a minefield.

'You're helping me build a very clear picture, Richard. Of the new dean. Of your job. Of tensions.' Vanish had backed up some of the concerns which Frank had articulated at the shopping centre. Unquestionably Gyro had brought in big donations beyond the college's dreams, which had paid for modernising the bedrooms, building the tower and endowing new academic appointments like the Bakhtin professorship. But as the college gained more bells and whistles, its running costs had shot upwards.

'Clearly one of the tensions is that Hampton needs to be famous enough to jack up its fees, especially for MBAs, pretty quickly if it isn't going to run out of money. That needs to happen within the next year or 18 months. It's a race against time. Am I correct?' Vanish nodded. 'But the governors are aware of that. Naturally the tension affected you, but it was not your responsibility.' Vanish nodded again.

Connie came to the crux of the matter. 'So there's something I'm missing completely on timing. You ask to leave your job suddenly, over the end of the May holiday weekend. When I called you this morning, you said next Saturday will be too late. What am I missing?'

The taking of a decision marched across Vanish's face. 'A loan for two million pounds which the governors know nothing about. It's due at the end of June. One-point-two million pounds was borrowed but it's a PIK loan, if you know what that means.'

Connie shook her head. Vanish was clearly scared, but at the same time calm and lucid.

'Payment in kind,' he explained. 'You don't make any interest payments, so you pay a ton of interest, because it all rolls up and adds on like billy-oh.'

'The corporate version of the kind of loan you or I might get from a loan shark.'

'If we knew the kind of loan sharks who knee-cap you if you haven't got the money on the day.'

Connie ran her hand through her hair. 'But we haven't borrowed the money from crooks, have we?'

'No. From First Improvident.'

'But that's one of Britain's biggest banks! In which case nothing makes sense. You say the governors don't know, but money doesn't move from banks to colleges without armfuls of paperwork: a resolution from the governors, auditors making sure the loan is on the balance sheet.'

'Normally, yes. But in this case one of the directors of First Improvident is the dean.'

'That's worse – he'd have to declare his position to the bank. The bank's a public company, it would have to report the loan in its accounts. The rules on this stuff are a mile high.'

'Which in this case haven't been followed.'

No … or could it be? Connie nodded slowly. 'I'm beginning to get you. Somebody in the bank had to help Gyro, or at least be paid to turn a blind eye. And if two million doesn't get paid within two weeks, the college is looking not just at bankruptcy but a fraud investigation.'

'Gyro didn't realise how much I'd found out – I guess I looked too dumb to worry about. But I realised I had to get out – fast. Before the police were over everything.'

'But there's nothing on paper?'

'Nothing in the college's papers. Gyro has some private papers.'

'And you didn't talk to the bank.'

'I didn't dare. But our manager, Roger Sling, has been getting really antsy. He sees our accounts so he knows the only way we could come up with two million pounds by the end of June is if the dean magics up some money in Hong Kong.'

'Frank was asking why he'd gone so many times in the last few months. This would explain it.'

'Or he's lining up a job for himself and will leave the college holding a baby it didn't know it had.'

Connie asked for the bill. Perhaps she had better claim the expense back right away if she didn't want to end up paying for lunch after all. Actually, what was she saying? Things might be much worse than that. If what Vanish said was correct, all the governors would be in the press and fired for incompetence, if not prosecuted for fraud. There might be no college to award her degree in September. How could any of this be? How much had Dorothy Lines really known when they had their little talk? And why had she ever allowed herself to become a governor in the first place?

For heaven's sake get a grip, Connie told herself. Richard Vanish – you've never met him before. He hasn't produced a shred of evidence. If he had been so concerned at the time, why had he no photocopies of these alleged private papers?

Because they were fantasies, imaginings intended to cushion his private humiliation at failure and being unemployed. The reason Vanish couldn't do a day more after the May weekend holiday was because the tower opening was coming down on him like a train and all his shortcomings were about to be exposed. He said his illness was physical, but she only had his word for that.

'Richard, I appreciate how difficult this has been for you. Really. If I were you, I would have been sorely tempted not to return the college's call.' Vanish nodded.

'I promise you I'll be making inquiries. Urgently. I'm sorry if that sounds weak.'

'It doesn't sound weak at all,' Vanish demurred. 'I haven't given you any evidence, have I?'

'Not unless you were willing to say what you've said to the police.' Connie's stomach clenched, not knowing what answer she hoped he would give.

The rabbit in the headlights with whom she had started lunch returned. 'No. Absolutely not,' he replied. Connie's stomach told her that was the answer for which she had been desperate.

'Of course.' Connie's HR training re-asserted itself: take charge, close the discussion professionally. 'We've covered a lot, but just take a minute to think if there's anything we've missed?'

Vanish paused. 'I don't think so. I mean, there was one thing, a file Greg Martin gave me on Frank Jones, about a month ago. But it was silly.'

'Greg Martin?'

'The dean's driver. Yes, I know. All I could think was that the dean wanted Dr Jones pushed out because he was asking too many good questions. I thought Greg might be doing what the dean wanted. Anyway, the file was all rubbish. But take a look yourself if you want. It's buried underneath some papers in the bottom drawer of my desk at Hampton.'

The weather brightened steadily through the afternoon but Connie's thoughts were churning too much for her to make the call during her drive home. Instead she drove to her local high street for a cappuccino and to browse a newspaper, but the choice by mid-afternoon was limited to topless or smug.

Smug proved to be a mistake. *The Times* carried the Queen's birthday honours, and a photograph caught her eye: Alexander Hector Lyapunov Bakhtin, by Her Majesty's decree created Lord Bakhtin of Wembley, for services to industry. Connie was speechless. When she had recovered her voice she was home, where the college switchboard put her through to Ben.

'I need to let off steam,' she warned.

'I'm standing behind the yellow line,' Ben assured her. Still, the shock wave which followed took him by surprise, like a high-speed train blasting through a country station.

'Just what is the problem with men? Tell me that. I mean, bastards or wimps, why is that the only choice we've got? Did somebody break into the factory where you get made and vandalise the settings? I can't believe it – Lord fucking Bakhtin. The dickhead!'

Ben ducked. 'Come on, you're spoiled for choice – bastards, wimps *or* dickheads. Is that stuff about Bakhtin in the news today?'

'The Queen's birthday, isn't it? Her official one. Lord Bakhtin *of Wembley*. So he's a footballer, is he?'

'No, though he owns a club. Or did he sell it? Anyway, Wembley was where he lived when he first came to England. I researched it for a speech once. Well, don't be surprised: once he became a big cheese he started doing all those sorts of things – hanging round politicians, sitting on boards, giving money away. Including to Hampton, of course. There's another thing I'll have to do on Monday – send him Gyro's congratulations.'

'Don't make me sick. Speeches and that – is that what your job was when you worked for him? Or did you get involved in running his individual businesses?'

'Oh, definitely speeches. Like Monday night. And a bit of group strategy, meaning whether to buy or sell particular businesses. Once Bakhtin owned a business he was pretty hands-off.'

'As long as the profits came in.'

'You've got it. Remember the yapping dogs?'

'I'm glad you didn't stuff my business. Relieved, really.'

Ben switched the subject. 'Look, tell me about Vanish – how was your meeting?'

So Connie poured that out. Ben whistled when he heard about the loan and then mused, 'So, even if he was ill for six months, even if he's right about the loan, that's still eighteen months when he didn't do anything about it? That's pretty feeble, although now I've seen what a mess he was making of the tower …'

'Exactly. That's what I meant by wimps and bastards. Why did Vanish have to be such a wimp?'

'Did he ever ask Gyro directly?'

Connie thought back to the conversation and sandwiches. 'No, he didn't. He was too frightened. I thought about it a lot on the drive home. His manner changed so much when he was talking about the loan, as if he knew his stuff for once. But you're confirming that Vanish was pretty useless, so the reason he knew his stuff probably was that he had invented it. He suckered me into not postponing the meeting so he got someone to buy him lunch and listen to his crazy ideas for 90 minutes. Sure, we still need to ask some questions – I've got no choice now I'm a governor – but that's how it looks to me.'

'And I'm in the perfect spot to ask questions. We can do our homework before Gyro gets back – who knows, he might bring two million with him. The bank manager wants a meeting anyway, and Frank's taking me to dinner tonight. Frank's got to be a good guy to talk to. His questions about the dean seem pretty on the ball, and we know he's as straight as anything.'

'I like the sound of that.' Sometimes a problem shared did feel like a problem halved. For Connie, this was one of those times. 'Could we talk some more tomorrow afternoon?'

'At the college?'

'A few of the health MSc's will be around towards the end of the afternoon. We have our last classes from Monday to Wednesday. If the weather's nice, we're planning a picnic by the lake.'

'That's perfect. It's a date.'

SATURDAY 16 JUNE (DAY & EVENING)
SATURDAY 16 JUNE (DAY & EVENING)

The 10am meeting didn't need umbrellas; the flying saucer overhead easily sheltered them from the icy cricket balls being hurled downwards from the heavens. However, the percussion of ice against glass was deafening. Ben's heart stopped when a sheet of hail tumbled off the outer auditorium wall. The fragments looked like glass.

'Don't worry.' Being a good project manager, Tom had cultivated the gift of rapidly reading his client's nerves and then calming them. 'It makes a hell of a racket but she'll sleep through this like a baby. The glass isn't quite bullet-proof but it's damn close.'

Tom had a stranger with him, but his expression told the story.

'Good news?' Ben guessed.

'Ninety percent. We've sorted the pressure equalisation between the riser cylinders. In fact we could take a ride up now, but we'll wait till six o'clock. I'm having a back-up of the equalisation fix installed in case the first system fails.'

Ben gave a thumbs up. This really was good news. 'The ten percent?'

'The announcements. Trickier than we thought. That's why Rakesh is here from Bangalore.'

'Welcome to the English summer.'

The newcomer grinned. 'Actually I'm from Yorkshire, just doing a two-year rotation in Bangalore. Pleased to meet you, Mr Stillman.' They shook hands and exchanged cards. Rakesh Pradhan was assistant chief engineer of Proximity Communications.

'What's the situation right now?'

Rakesh exhibited a purposeful command of the situation. 'We've had a change in the last six hours. Before, we had reversal – the announcement said opening when the doors were closing and vice versa, now it's random, or apparently random. So sometimes it says opening when the doors are opening, and sometimes not. What we have done over the last forty-eight hours is eliminate totally the hardware faults. That's positive because it means that pure brainpower can crack the situation. As of midnight last night we have the whole set-up connected to Bangalore, where we have a dozen specialists on the case.

'I know these guys, Mr Stillman, some of them are so bright it scares me shitless, if you will excuse me for using that word. They are on this 24/7 because this is like a riddle or crossword puzzle to them. The wives and kids of these guys are not going to see them until they've cracked it. So fundamentally, this is now a dead problem. It just may not be quite dead by six o'clock this evening, and for this Proximity Communications and I deeply apologise.'

'Rakesh, I appreciate that. Keep me updated. And if the worst comes to the worst, can we just switch the announcements off for the opening day?'

Tom nodded. 'Exactly.' The relief on his face that Ben had arrived in the nick of time was unmistakable. For nearly three weeks there had been no-one in the college who could grasp what was needed to get the tower opened at all, let alone on time. Admittedly, no-one had been an improvement on the person before …

The good news meant that Ben did not need to be lashed to Gyro's desk all day. He popped back into the office briefly, to send Gyro a progress report. Since it was a Saturday morning he was surprised to find the infamous cleaner hoovering Gyro's carpet – all he got in return for effusive greetings was the smile of a *tricoteuse*. There were no incriminating emails on the desk, just architect's drawings of the lift.

Of the phone messages – including two more from Roger Sling – there was only one that he needed to return right away. As expected, Casey Pinnacle was proving to be one of the most irritating of the VIPAs, as Ben had started to call them – Very Important Pains in the Arse. Impossible to pin down as to whether he was definitely coming to Hampton on Thursday, or whether he might be in Baluchistan or perhaps just showing up for the dinner, Casey kept peppering the college with irrelevant questions, as if he had confused it with Wikipedia.

Ben left a message saying he would respond on Sunday. He had decided to have most of Saturday off. Subject to the lift performing at six o'clock as Tom had promised, Ben would really have something to celebrate over dinner with Frank.

The storm passed and gradually the sky lifted. For lunch he had chatted up the kitchen staff and got a freshly made margherita pizza brought to his bedroom. After lunch he sat on his bed with his shirt unbuttoned, the weekend *FT* unread and work papers scattered around. For the thwack of tennis from the Queen's Club men's championships he turned the TV up. A medium- to well-done Spaniard was getting hammered in straight sets by a tanned South African, their skin tones and tennis whites equally incongruous under a sky like a damp, grey Kleenex.

Ben flicked through his notepad, listing on a fresh page for Sunday things as yet undone. Painting the tower with green words seemed to have shut Cardew McCarthy up. He grimaced hard at the next scrawl: the 'GSG'. What a cock-up – for once those were exactly the right words. But a cock-up in a teacup. He made a note not to forget on Tuesday morning to tell Gyro about it. Face to face would be better than email or over the telephone, and the closer they were to a successful tower opening the more likely Gyro would just say, 'Screw the lot of them'.

Some names from the latest spreadsheet of Thursday's acceptances caught his attention, among them Alex Bakhtin and Connie Yung. Alex's presence on the list made obvious sense. He had given the college millions; why not come to see his late wife's glass throne installed in its matching *palazzetto*? So Ben would encounter him on Thursday. After a moment, he decided that that would be a good thing. No-one could land on their feet faster than Ben had landed at Hampton; he could rub that gently in Alex's face. Connie was invited as one of the governors.

A quick browse through Gyro's accumulating in-tray revealed a one-page memorandum from the associate dean for quality. Some MBA students were unhappy about the low grades Frank had given ethical appraisals which he had asked them to make of their own companies. She was reviewing the assignments in question and would submit a report on Monday. A telephone rang, although Ben could not recall giving his room number to anyone. Perhaps Frank, cancelling dinner? Ben turned the television down.

'Hello, dear, now don't fuss. You know I can't bear a fuss.'

'Mum!' said Ben. 'How great to hear from you. But how did you find this number? Is something wrong?'

'There's something wrong when I have to get a stranger to tell me that you've changed jobs. I called your old office. Alex's secretary – '

'Tahmina?'

'You should know, dear, you sat next to her. Yes. She said to try Hampton Management College. That was the last place she knew you had been.' Ben's mum paused. 'For a moment I thought you'd done a runner. Imagine that.'

'Well, to tell the truth, the move was a bit of a surprise for me, too. It all happened pretty quickly. I'm just at Hampton for a couple of weeks helping out, and then I'll come and visit. I want a job without so much travelling, you know? I want to put down some roots.' This was news to Ben, but the words came out of his mouth with conviction. 'How's Dad?'

'He's fine. He has his check-ups once a month and they're fine. Well, it will be good if we get to see more of you, you know that. Will you come next week? The Archibalds' daughter is back from New York. I'll see if she can come round to dinner.'

Ben winced. 'Let's just have dinner ourselves, shall we? I haven't taken you and Dad out for ages.'

'You'd tell me if you were gay, wouldn't you? They had this quiz in the magazine to see if you're a gay-friendly mum and I scored eighty-three. I'd never forgive myself if you were gay and I didn't know.'

'Mum, I'm not sixteen. I think I'd know if I was shagging boys instead of girls.'

'Yes.' The syllable sighed its happy acceptance of omniscience, a mother's fate. 'And you have made sure to get clean underwear? Because you've not been back to your flat since last weekend, I'll be bound.'

'Trust me, Mum. I've been to the ends of the earth to get clean underwear.'

'That's nice. Well, let us know when you know. To make up your room for you, I mean.'

'I'll come lunchtime Sunday week. The twenty-fourth. I'll be finished here. Book for three people at Da Luigi. And don't forget, you can always call me on my mobile.'

'You know I won't have any truck with those ridiculous phone charges! Lots of love then.'

The phone call with Connie lifted Ben's spirits; he had suspected that Richard Vanish had a screw loose, and the picnic sounded a perfect way to unwind. By half past five, the damp grey ceiling over southeast England had dried and started to come apart. Stabs of sunlight were pushing through, yellow tinged with rose, as if they had bled slightly. Given good progress with the lift and to give himself the night off, Ben brought the next site meeting forward to 6pm.

All the scaffolding had now been removed, revealing the tower fully for the first time. It shimmered – patterns and colours of light changing with the clouds and refracting unexpectedly in the curved glass. In some places the tower became opaque, impossible to look through, while in others it vanished tantalisingly into the silver birches and the hills behind. The tower looked breathtaking but also achingly vulnerable, like an infant spaceship that had lost its tribe somewhere in the starry reaches and was now sucking warm milk up a fat straw.

Tom was grinning as he handed Ben a hard hat and high-visibility vest. On a Saturday evening, after two and a half days of round-the-clock operations and with victory in sight, the rump of the site crew was small indeed – just two people, watching as the curved wall of the doughnut opened and Tom conducted Ben inside.

'The doors of the lift are closing,' said the actress as the doors opened. 'The doors of the lift are closing,' she repeated but in a different intonation as they closed. Tom shrugged, and they both laughed.

Ben gripped the handrail. He was glad that the lift's floor was not transparent. In no time they shot above the college buildings and glimpsed the lake and the dean's house beyond, before entering the auditorium's underbelly. Gingerly, Ben stepped out. The actress did not approve. 'We apologise. Lift door functioning is temporarily inoperative. Assistance is being called.' Between his size nine feet were the helmets and uplifted faces of the watching crew. Ben flinched slightly because he had no idea whether his socks might be showing through worn soles.

Transparent amphitheatrical seating encircled them. Ben looked through the seats to six starlings flashing past with hints of green and purple in their plumage. The temperature was pleasant; Tom explained that they had been taking the air-conditioning up and down through its paces. From a control panel Tom ran through the lighting combinations – uplighters, downlighters, mood lighters and spots, all of them fixed to one of the 12 titanium girders which radiated out from the central column like a rib-cage.

The girders were in both the floor and the ceiling and became thinner as they extended, before meeting each other at shoulder height at the auditorium's widest circumference. Ben had to admit it was impressive, and for the Pinnacles value for money was beside the point. Whatever its merits as a lecture theatre, money could certainly be made on it as a nightclub – something that Casey had probably already spotted for his after-battle party.

'It is something.' The quality of the acoustic was remarkable. 'It is that,' Tom agreed.

'What's left to fix?'

'A lot of small stuff.' Tom pointed at one of the coral-like acoustic tiles in the roof. 'Three of those are loose. It's not a glue job, they need to be recast.' He led Ben up a sloping aisle to a glass door that he pushed open. They stepped out onto the terrace, like Saturn's narrow ring.

'The rubber seals on the terrace doors are as the architect specified, but in bad weather they leak. We're getting new ones made. They won't come from Germany for another two weeks but they're not critical for Thursday. And of course there's the lady of the lift, but Rakesh and his crew are all over her. If they have to they'll reboot the whole announcement operating system and download a completely virgin system from India.

How happy was Ben? Delirious. 'Or we'll simply pull the plug on her for the duration of Thursday. With a roomful of smart people, what do you reckon? Some of them might just be able to work out for themselves whether the doors are opening or closing. Well done, Tom. Brilliant. Get some sleep. And count yourself in for dinner on Thursday night, if you want. Be my guest.'

Frank was in high spirits when he picked Ben up at the college to head to the new, four-and-a-half star Kings Arms. Expansive and chatty, he apologised for the state of his four-wheel drive. He had had a couple of days' break in the country – 'the real country. Some friends of mine are making a mint doing executive breaks on a farm where they let you milk cows and feed pigs. Try it before you look at me like that.' An automated car wash had taken care of the smell but left some residual streaks of mud.

'Since when the shaved head?' Ben asked. 'Since my MBA, that's for sure.'

'New Year's. Friends have been saying it for some time. They were right, don't you think?'

'Definitely. Not that you looked bad before.' Unlike most of Ben's teachers, Frank had always had moments of style, such as carrying off on occasion a leather jacket – something beyond most 40-year-olds. For dinner he had changed into a long-sleeved silk shirt and fashion jeans stitched with silver thread. Ben guessed that Frank probably ran or did cardio in the gym. He himself had run out of the excuses of being in his twenties and having an impossible jet-set job. Once Ben finished at Hampton would be a good time to start some serious cycling again.

Two of the Kings Arms' stars were also new since Ben's time as a student. Now it was virtually a leisure complex: a sports bar that doubled after 11pm as a night club, a gastropub and a small hotel – the Kings Arms had been a focal point of social life in Alderley since the English wars of religion.

The latest of these was the War of the Apostrophe. Following a repainting and rebranding two years ago aposotrophes were no longer to be seen, along with workboot's and football strip's. By 8pm, sports bar and gastropub were both packed. The rigid smiles of the waiting staff alerted them that the kitchen was probably running badly behind, so they skipped first courses in favour of a couple of pints in the garden. Frank still enjoyed the occasional roll-up.

Ben asked about Vanish.

'Richard was not cut out for that job, not at all,' Frank confirmed. 'A really decent bloke but he and Gyro lived on different planets. Richard thought nine till six was a long day, Gyro probably thought it was a long lunch.'

Ben steered the conversation towards the college's financial situation, about which they agreed equally quickly. Gyro's strategy was more of a gamble than he liked to let on. His trips to the Far East needed to produce some return soon. But anything like fraud was ridiculous (what would Gyro get out of it, for one thing?). Gyro was on a very loose rein from the governing body because they were in awe of him. Among the college staff, few stood up to the bullying which was Gyro's frequent resort when he didn't get his way.

'We're a management college, we shouldn't be a financial house of cards. I just want the governors to stop being frightened of asking questions like what are you up to in the Far East, and by the way you need our agreement. Don't you think, though, the new governor looks like good news?'

'Connie Yung?'

'Yes. I taught her a few classes – not as many as I taught you. But I went back to look at her scores. Pretty impressive, across the board.' But the point was, Frank continued, Gyro was a strong guy, not a bad guy. Hampton wasn't Enron.

'God knows which budget he raided to get me on the plane to Hong Kong, but I got the impression flying out with him that this will be the time he comes back with the loot.

He kept his cards close to his chest but there are donors out there who would make rich Brits look like chicken feed,' Ben observed.

'Well, that will help. But in a way that's not the point. Loot or no loot, the governors should say, what's our Far East strategy? Why Hong Kong, not Singapore or Djakarta? Should we be fundraising or recruiting? Competing or building alliances?'

When dinner came – duck and chorizo pie with poached pear for Ben and a risotto with artichokes and porcini mushrooms for Frank – it did the job splendidly. Ben went on to wine, Frank on to tap water with ice and a slice.

They were in no rush. Ben gave Frank a version of his first few days, although the meeting with the Gender Strategy Group did not make the director's cut. Stories about Gyro wandered into a broader discussion of America's fondness for occupying other people's countries. 'Come on,' Ben remonstrated. 'Had Gyro personally called the shots on Iraq?'

'No,' replied Frank, but to judge by some of the photographs on the dean's wall he was quite connected to some of the types who had. In his second year at Hampton, Gyro had accepted money from an arms manufacturer to fund a specialist programme in international logistics. If Hampton had been part of an ordinary university campus, there would have been protests. The turn of the conversation reminded Ben that Frank had volunteered to teach ethics at the college – something else that was new since Ben's time.

'Well, no other faculty were interested, I can tell you,' Frank snorted.

'It gets you into a few scrapes with some of the MBA students.'

Frank looked up and then smiled wryly. 'Another complaint?'

'Some students think their marks are too low. I haven't seen any details.'

'The ones who think they are paying Hampton to make them successful Gordon Geckos ... yes, we have our moments. I push them harder than the dean would like, but I think it's necessary. I want us to take our teaching responsibilities for ethics seriously. But I guess the acid test of any teaching is whether what people learn turns out to be of any use.' He gestured. 'Out there, outside Pleasant Valley. In Alex Bakhtin's world, for example. You went straight there, didn't you, after you graduated?'

'Pretty much. The MBA helped, but I had a break. Someone who knew me knew Alex wanted a few people.'

'So the certificate on the wall didn't get you the job, but it helped. Then what?'

'What Hampton taught me was how to take an all-round view of a business and a market. A shareholder's perspective. I only realised afterwards how few people, even in a really successful 26,000-person global business, look at a business that way. I mean really few. And what you taught on finance helped so much. I'm staggered by how many people just blank finance out.'

'They joke about rocket scientists in investment banks, but it's true – after physics, finance is like pissing up the wall.'

'When I started with Bakhtin first I had to do a couple of staff roles, but then I was given a real business. A manufacturing business in the north of England, in plastics. Nothing out of the ordinary. Alex gave me 12 months to double the profits.'

'And what you learned here helped?' Frank looked genuinely curious.

Ben poured himself more wine. 'Yes and no. What helped was figuring out pretty fast that there wasn't a textbook way to do what Bakhtin wanted. Our margins had already started to flatline and competition was increasing – new technologies, different choices for our clients.

'Without the MBA I would have spent more than a year thrashing around trying one thing after another to boost profits, finding out too late that none of them could hit the spot. It was a mature market. I might have succeeded at first, but the profits would have been competed away. Some time after that Bakhtin would have fired me.'

'So Alex was greedy. What happened then?'

'After the first month I went back to him and said there wasn't a way to get the profits he wanted. The MBA meant that I could show him why. I felt really scared doing it, but he was pleased I'd read the situation quickly and had had the balls to come back to him.'

'So you didn't double the profits.'

After the better part of a bottle of cabernet sauvignon, dodging the question should have been easy to do. But it wasn't. Frank had been pacing his drinking (had that been a plan, Ben wondered?). Now, Frank held Ben in his gaze. His bald head was like the dome of a radar tracking system. Frank believed in truth, and his former student gave it to him.

'I quadrupled them. Or maybe quintupled them, I lose track. That's what landed me the job as his right-hand guy. I remember he said to me after month one, "So you've figured out the answer isn't in the textbook, now go find it somewhere else. You've got 11 months." '

'How did you do it?'

'Luck. A health scare. Our market was food packaging. Our main competitor used stuff which we didn't, and which it would have taken them more than six months to replace. When there was a health scare about it, the supermarkets blew them out of the market within a week. Eventually they got studies done which showed their ingredient was safe, but by then their firm had gone under.'

'A health scare.' Frank was frowning. 'That was very lucky. For you.'

'You win some, you lose some, right? Believe me, I've had my share of the dice landing the other way.' Ben milked his former teacher's loyalty for all it was worth. 'Let's get some brandies. I'm not saying another word to the college's ethics expert without them. And there are some things I want to ask you. Like, why you ended up at Hampton. It was a dump, right? You were head and shoulders ahead of most of the faculty. So why are you here?'

'It was luck, but you're saying you let Bakhtin believe it was cunning. Have I got that right?' Frank was still frowning.

'Is this dinner or a *viva*?' Ben protested. 'Fair play, right?'

'You're right, fair play is important.' Frank made a gesture to move the conversation on. 'OK, I'm at Hampton because it seemed like a good idea at the time – the relevant time being a long time ago. The college didn't have much of a research reputation, but the teaching load was light. And I've always had a weakness for being a smart-arse on my own.'

'You switched over from physics?'

'Yes. My PhD was in molecular physics, but if you can do the maths, finance pays better. Funnily enough I've been looking at some physics recently; the maths is even worse now. Anyway, tell me another way to live by a lake this close to London?'

'You're right about that,' agreed Ben. 'So you sail? You've got one of the boathouses, haven't you?'

'As a kid I sailed all the time.'

'Do you have a boat?'

Frank laughed. 'Here? Maybe half a boat. I'm building a replica of the first rowing boat to cross an ocean – Samuelsen and Harbo rowed the Atlantic from America to France in 1896.'

Ben shifted. On the one hand he was trying to hide a disquiet – a small one, like a mouse nibbling at some unimportant crumbs of cheese. The photos inside the hut showed no rowing boat, half-finished or otherwise. On the other hand, part of him felt more comfortable now that both of them had something a bit uncomfortable to chew on. Not that it was a competition, but one-all was still a decent score. 'You're kidding. How long will that take?'

'I should have finished a year ago. It's just a hobby, really.'

'You'll need some machinery, I guess, to shape the planks of wood and that? Electrical gear and stuff.'

'No, not at all. The whole point is to do as much of it by the original technology as possible. Hand tools.' Frank held out his right hand. 'I'm a bit stronger than I look. Why do you ask?'

'Doesn't every former student want to discover their star teacher's human side? You must show me the boat some time.'

'Star teacher? Well, well,' Frank chuckled. 'We must do this more often.'

Ben pushed again. 'So when can I see the boat?'

'Whenever. Any time after next week – exam-marking week.' Frank rolled his eyeballs. 'Care to give a hand?'

Ben asked for the bill and for the manager. If possible he wanted to look at the bedrooms. He would bet money on at least one VIPA discovering on Thursday night that they wanted a bed but the Ritz was too far to walk. It would help to have something more presentable than a student bedroom up his sleeve. Frank excused himself for a smoke.

Since VIP overflow from the college was business the manager wanted to have, he came off his break. Ben was given a quick tour of a 'deluxe executive double' (not much different from a college bedroom, but with snobby toiletries) and 'the kings suite'. The suite had potential, and was available on Thursday night. Although the bedroom was barely larger than its queen-sized bed there was a spacious en suite bathroom and a living room, ersatz in its decoration but with two arm chairs, a period mantelpiece and a desk.

The manager went back downstairs to check in some guests, leaving Ben with the key. The suite's rooms were clean. He checked the lights and the taps; they were all fine. The room was non-smoking but that was par for the course. As he turned to go, he noticed the clock on the mantelpiece. A cuckoo clock in the shape of an Alpine hut surrounded by a tableau of rustic figures – an authentic fake, powered by battery.

Why did he do it? Perhaps the mouse of doubt in his life wanted company. Ben wound the time on from 10.20pm towards the hour. The mechanism swung into noisy gear. A window flew open and let fly a drowning cuckoo sound. He had heard that sound before – in the background of the telephone call in which Alex had fired him. At the time Ben had thought Alex was flying over India. Why would Alex have been in this bedroom of the Kings Arms? And why, if he had been round the corner from the college, hadn't he given his own speech on Monday night?

SUNDAY 17 JUNE
SUNDAY 17 JUNE

Sunday was Ben's fourth day in the dean's office. He arrived early. While so far turning the tower opening around from being a fiasco had gone better than Ben had dared hope, he needed no telling about the dangers of complacency.

Roger Sling's agitation had reached far enough to leave his home number in the message, so Ben called him. They batted apologies back and forth and agreed to meet at the college first thing on Monday. The main focus of the site meeting was on the announcements. By 10am the team in Bangalore had had a full 24 hours working on the problem remotely. Rakesh's optimism was unshakeable that Proximity Communications would have the issue properly licked. By contrast Ben and Tom continued to draw comfort from their private fall-back – simply switching the announcements off.

The announcements issue wasn't the only thing needing proper licking – there were the VIPAs. Among these, Casey was the prince. Like playing tennis with a nutcase, all Ben could do was to keep returning the serves and banging the idiotic ideas back to his opponent's baseline. It was exhausting.

'Good to speak to you too, Mr Pinnacle. I got your message. Funnily enough, I do have in mind that Thursday is the one-hundredth birthday of VST. A display by the Red Arrows aerobatic team would indeed be a lovely surprise for your father, to mark the occasion. The Red Arrows have no problem doing very fine displays. And I'm sure they would have no problem doing orange-and-gold coloured smoke in your corporate colours.

'Here's what would be a problem, to the point where anyone could forget about me doing it: any suggestion that I ring our Ministry of Defence on a Sunday to ask for a Red Arrows flypast at Hampton this Thursday, when they have taken the trouble to produce a very fine website explaining that all requests for each summer need to have been made by the preceding September.'

Ben paused. 'Yes, indeed. You are American, and we are British. As we speak our armed forces stand toe-to-toe with yours, blood brothers and sisters in the unceasing war on terror. Moved as our Ministry of Defence will undoubtedly be by this fact, as well as by the urgency with which the one-hundredth birthday of Virtual Savings and Trust has arisen, I fear it will not suffice. On their website – did I mention they have a website? – the Red Arrows thoughtfully explain that they do not do weddings, funerals or birthdays.'

Another pause. 'Quite. Exactly. Now, to be the epitome of helpfulness is my only goal. At any other moment of the year, I would offer to spend the rest of my Sunday compiling a spreadsheet of all the countries in the world whose air forces have aerobatic teams, and how much it would cost to source alternate supplies. But it being as we speak almost exactly one-hundred hours to the opening of your father's tower, and with the odd thing remaining on my 'to do' list, with huge gnashing of teeth I must refrain from making this offer.'

'By all means. Try entering "small country with aerobatic team" on eBay. Why not? It's my pleasure, sir. Dean Gyro's delight that you will be joining us on the day is surpassed only by my own.' Ben replaced the receiver.

The mouse of Frank's lie was still in Ben's mind, but overshadowed now by a giant rat. To the mystery of Alex making one of his top achievers redundant, without warning, apparently to cut costs, had been added the mystery of where he had been, and why, when he had done the deed. Round the corner?

Of course Alex was a lord now. Ben was on the point of sending Alex a congratulatory email blind-copied to Gyro when he took a leaf out of his mother's book and called Bakhtin's office on his old number. In his time only occasionally had Tahmina needed to come in on Sundays to catch up, but now struggling with two jobs she might well be there. If she was, Sunday would be a good day to ask her where Alex had actually been on Monday night. What he heard made hara kiri unnecessary; he was humiliated and disembowelled by the words.

'Lord Bakhtin's office, Charlie Driesman.' Charlie – his friend. His rival too in the Bakhtin empire, hardworking as anything but not quite so smart – or had Ben called that wrong? Charlie – sitting in his old seat on a Sunday.

His job had not been made redundant after all; just given to someone else.

'Charlie?'

'Is that Ben? Good on you, mate, what are you up to?'

'Congratulations. I guess you got my job.'

'Thanks. I was gutted to get it this way. What Alex was thinking I have no idea. But I knew you'd land on your feet.'

'I did, thanks. I'm doing a project for Hampton – pulling chestnuts out of the fire for this big opening we've got on Thursday.'

'I know. It's in Alex's diary.'

'Of course it is. Anyway, it's high exposure. I'm going to meet more bosses of large companies in a day than I would've in a lifetime, so hopefully I'll land something interesting.'

'You lucky bugger. Anyway, what can I do for you?'

'Easy enough, just pass on congratulations to the boss, from Dean Gyro and myself. And tell him I'll particularly look forward to seeing him on Thursday.'

'I tell you what, he'll probably hire you back. Now he'll have to do speeches in the House of Lords, and he loved your speeches. I can't write speeches for toffee.'

' "Sorry" isn't a long speech. He could try saying it to me on Thursday. But he won't, of course.'

Charlie grunted. 'True.'

There was a silver lining in Charlie being a mate – it was no sweat for him to right-click on Bakhtin's diary to see not only what it said for Monday night, but what it had said previously. The entries had been made by Tahmina. Originally, it had shown the glass-chair presentation at Hampton College.

That had been changed in favour of en route to India, which in turn had been replaced by 'KA private'.

'So who's KA then?' Charlie's curiosity was aroused. 'I assume it's a she.'

'That's my assumption as well,' said Ben disingenuously. His next call would be to Greg. They could trade information. Ben could confirm that for whatever reason (private sexual practices? But with a portable petrol generator?) Frank wasn't telling the truth about the contents of the boathouse. Greg could confirm where he had driven the dean's wife on Monday night, returning her to the college before the end of Ben's speech. The only good thing about being shafted by Bakhtin was that by the time he told Connie about it, the two of them would be on the same side.

Seth Carter could have been excited or forewarned by the fact that full written details of his new remuneration and benefits arrived from his employer by email on a Sunday; he chose to be excited. At quarter to five he drove his VW hatchback (goodbye to that, soon enough) into the college car park, where Connie and two others were waiting for him.

Seth had raided the Alderley shopping centre for two drinks coolers and ice, one of them for food. Between them they also had a rug, a solar-cell garden light and an old, pre-Walkman, ghettoblaster. They drove a few minutes along the Crassock road and parked past the staff houses by a couple of soaring plane trees, their bark scraped by winter storms and a few JRs and APs who had loved TCs and LGs.

Sitting in a grass meadow by the water's edge the group was easy to see from the far side of the lake. By twenty past the party had started, with all but three of the 25 course members there, the course administrator, a couple of faculty and Ben. Feeling flush with his guaranteed first-year bonus Seth had gone a bit mad on Waitrose champagne. Exercising her clout as a governor, Connie had persuaded the college to lend them glassware, so the party was bubbling. Chilled jazz played quietly. Fish in the lake popped up from time to time to approve.

'Very nice party,' Ben complimented Seth, who had his arm around Connie's shoulders.

'She's worth it, believe me. Connie's a special lady.'

'Congratulations on your job. I gather it's one with sane people like me in the private sector?'

Seth carried on through Connie's derisive snort. 'Oh, thanks. The NHS has been really great to me, and I may well come back, maybe as a chief executive.' Connie redoubled her snort. 'In the meantime I feel like I've escaped under the barbed wire. Connie went the other way, you know; she started in the private sector and then decided she couldn't stand the crap. Anyway, she reckons I'll last about five years. Why not, make some money, and then see what's around. Who knows? Maybe I'll set up my own business!'

'Exactly. Make some money, buy out the college and have this as your back garden.' Ben gestured around him. Yesterday's weather had vanished without trace. The sunset looked promising. 'Anyway, what's the business you're joining?'

Connie roared with laughter. 'Oh boy, this a good one. Do your stuff, Seth. Show us your A-grade private-sector bullshit. We know you can.' She bit into a king prawn that had fallen into a linen cupboard of filo pastry. Just as men were either wimps or bastards, it struck her that the same was true of king prawns. Too often they turned out either to be wimp prawns that were barely worth eating, or unnaturally macho prawns which had been using various gym supplements on the side. But these ones hit the spot, cold and delicious with the champagne, of which Ben was well into his second glass.

Two enjoyable nights out in a row, Ben thought. He didn't like to think when was the last time that had been true. 'What's the business?' he repeated. 'I might know it.'

'I don't think so,' said Seth. 'It's a bit specialised. Proximity –'

'Lift announcements!' Ben interrupted.

'You might think of lift announcements as a simple business.'

'I do,' said Connie.

'I wouldn't blame you. But it isn't – it isn't simple, and it isn't just lift announcements. There's all kinds of stressful communications situations in confined spaces when the wrong message, the wrong tone of voice, the wrong speed of speaking, could make the difference between life and death.'

Connie could not suppress her giggles any more. They flooded out like passengers down the exit slides of a 747 in which a man in a hood had smoke coming from his shoes.

But Seth's 747 was at full throttle down the runway, reaching for lift-off into his new intercontinental role. The NHS was just Britain, but now he was joining the global village (business class).

'Think about the voice alarms in the Eurofighter, or on the space shuttle. They're all Voice 2.0. The system detects how you are responding to the announcement and adapts to your stress level. All kinds of predictive algorithms kick in to adjust what the announcement is saying and how to say it.' Seth put his glass down in order to gesture with both hands. 'Proximity's mission is the creation of calm focus. For example, we might switch to an older man speaking more authoritatively, or a woman speaking more gently, or an African voice. It's interactive. It depends on you.'

Ben said, 'Come on! Give a serious example.'

'Believe what you like but in five years, every new car sold in the United States or Europe will have one of our smart boxes inside it. It will sense if the car has been in a collision, and if so what type of collision, and if you are conscious. It will speak to you to provide you with information which will keep you alive and calm until help arrives. Shock, and mistakes made during shock, is one of the biggest killers in accident situations, and we can halve it.'

'Blimey. But what will your role with them be? Not the crash dummy in the car programme, I hope.'

'No. For some of our most exciting applications, we think the British NHS could be in the vanguard worldwide.'

Connie cut in at the mention of her employer. 'Like what?'

'Number one on the list – self-surgery. Within two years this will be ready to hit the big time and the British NHS is perfect for it.'

Did Proximity have a special training course to ensure its people always said 'the British NHS', Ben wondered? It did make the company sound effortlessly global. 'Does self-surgery mean what I think it means?'

'Yes, but you're not on your own. You're in a specially designed chair environment. We set up two cameras, one as back up, hook both of them through to the computer, and the computer talks you through the whole thing. Calmly. Appropriately. And Voice 2.0 will produce that calm focus.'

'Well, I can see that. It wouldn't do to stress out in the middle of transplanting your own brain, would it?' Connie pushed Seth away playfully, holding her head in her hands exaggeratedly. 'God save us from the private sector.'

'Of course it won't be suitable for all procedures, or all people. That's where your GP will continue to play a critical part. But for other procedures, it's got huge advantages. No waiting lists. A surgeon – yourself – who speaks your language and has got all the time in the world because he isn't operating on anyone else. And right now it takes years – sometimes 10 years – for improvements in surgical procedures to filter down to the man in the gown with a knife in his hand. That means patients die.

'With self-surgery, your computer guidance will always be up-to-date through the internet. In terms of front-line care, it will be like a 10-year leap forward – at practically no cost. I shouldn't really say this, but in fact we've already done a demonstration at Number Ten.'

Connie came back with a vengeance. 'You gave the occupant a brain transplant, I hope. For God's sake give it a rest, Seth. They don't start paying you any bonuses for another month. Put my CD on.'

They put Connie's CD on later, because first there was early birthday cake – a cheesecake with one candle. The crowd had thinned down to a gang of friends. It was still light, but evening light. Seth packed up glasses, coolers and rubbish (some bits he picked up several times as the champagne took its toll). Connie handed Ben a magnum of Rioja. He used the corkscrew like a pro, but the bottle had a screwtop. After pouring everyone a glass he propped the bottle in the lunar glow of the garden light, using the sun's light a second time. Underneath the grass, the earth was moist from the wet pounding of the day before.

Eight of them danced, and then six. Some of them lay down to paint night-pictures with the glowing end of a Rizla and some crumbly Moroccan. The tracks Connie had burned on the CD ranged from Fatboy Slim, Everything But The Girl, Bob Marley and the inimitable Tina Turner to new stuff from the Cure. Had she screwed up, she wondered? Such a range of music must make her seem old to someone 10 years younger. Anyway, Ben was still dancing.

When English men got drunk and danced, it reminded Connie of a street party. Arms and legs, hands and hips were all over the place, forming conga lines and opening their front doors to anyone. But the unpractised wildness of the gesturings also said that come sun up, those bodies would be frozen again, each a suburb of silence where a sprained neck might commute to work for years next to somebody else's shoulder without ever asking to borrow an aspirin. If it was a clue to his life, Ben's body in motion struck her as positive: underneath it all it was the body of a man in whom life had not destroyed the capacity to be happy.

Connie knew when the last track had started. She moved next to him as it did, pretending to look in the other direction at the headlights of a car reflected in the lake from the other side. The track was a cool-down number with the spiced lyrics and harmonies of the Indigo Girls, but for a moment Connie could not remember which song she had chosen. It turned out to be 'The Power of Two', in which someone claims to be stronger than the monsters beneath your bed, and smarter than the tricks played on your heart.

She turned to him. 'I did think about finishing with one of my own, but one of my friends called it "jump-and-shout music". I think she may have been right.'

'One of your own what?' Ben was happy, his shirt undone.

'Tracks. For a while I was a singer-manager in a student band in Manchester. Being the manager meant being sober enough at the end of the night to stop us getting ripped off by the venue.'

'Wow.' (Wow as in, gosh, you were young once? Or just, wow?)

'Come for a walk. We've been studying here on and off for

two years, and this week is our last. There's supposed to be a viewing spot up on the hill, but I've never been.'

They walked for 10 minutes up the hill, cooled by the beginning of a night breeze. She liked the way Ben did not walk too fast without making a show of it. He seemed – what? Honest, for a start. Likeable. Sexy. (Did the young always seem sexy to the middle-aged? No, she thought, remembering at work how irritating she found most of the junior male doctors.)

Ben stirred. 'You remember saying all men were bastards or wimps?'

'I was right.'

'So what am I?'

Connie reflected. 'All right, all men are bastards, wimps or wanna-bes. You're a wanna-be, like the other MBAs.'

'And according to you, is that good or bad?'

Suddenly they both laughed, realising at the same moment what she was going to say. 'It depends what you wanna be!'

'Not Bakhtin, at any rate.'

'You probably wanted to be him when you came to study here.'

'Maybe.'

'We're here,' Connie announced. They had turned a corner and the hill had flattened out, creating a space where a couple of cars could retreat from the road. Beneath them the lake looked as if it had been scraped out of the valley with an ice-cream scoop.

Watching the lights excused both of them from speaking for a while. The teaching and administration building was dark.

Fluorescent lights gave a partial animation to the swimming pool, the car parks and parts of the residential building, but the scene was dominated by the flying saucer, glowing like a giant version of the garden light they had used earlier. Long black shadows from trees and other buildings radiated away from the tower like lines holding up a circus tent. At its top and around its rim blinked red hazard lights.

'It *is* a great view,' Ben ventured.

Connie wondered if he would make a move. Apparently not. The last few weeks of being 39 did not seem the age for hanging about. Because she had stayed off the red wine she could taste liquorice on his tongue. A public roll in the hay did not appeal, so she put her arm through his and led him back down the road towards the college.

MONDAY 18 JUNE

Talcum powder. The scent of tropical rain. Connie's body at 37°C. But before that – now he remembered – dancing. So coffee was in order, quickly.

It had been after two when Connie had set the bedside alarm. They had settled on eight o'clock as a compromise between Hampton and a lie-in, so Ben had kept his mobile switched off. It was seven now and he was awake. He might as well get going. Outside, the sun had already done a substantial chunk of its morning shift and was expecting tea and biscuits.

At Bakhtin Ben had not thought of himself as unhappy, but this morning he was happy in a way that was tantalising and different. He was a happy man in a welcoming bed in a righteous world. Bakhtin had wronged him but on Thursday Ben would get justice face-to-face.

Uncomfortable as it had felt to give Greg confirmation of Frank's duplicity about the boathouse, Ben had gained in exchange rock-solid proof of his own suspicions. Greg had delivered Dianne Peach-Gyro to the Kings Arms for 90 minutes last Monday evening. Who had turned up to collect his boss? Bakhtin's driver. Game, set and match, my lord?

One detail to improve things still further would be to confirm Connie's name. He was 97 percent certain that 'Connie' was what he had called her two dozen times during the night. But then damn it, why had 'Candy' popped uncontrollably into his head? Sometimes it was so embarrassing to be a man, like when you get a leak in your pants.

Oh, for goodness' sake, think straight! He didn't know any 'Candy'. But then, how well really did he know 'Connie'? It mattered because he very much hoped he would see her again – soon. As a governor she would be at the tower opening and gala dinner, so he had high hopes of Thursday night.

The rise and fall of breathing next to him suggested that he had a few minutes in hand. After easing himself out of bed Ben did a hamstring stretch and invented some other exercises which involved moving his sleeping partner's belongings around. Success! 'Connie Yung' was embossed on the badge students were supposed to wear in class. Exactly. 'Connie' was what he had meant. Still, a reminder scribbled on the inside of his left arm would do no harm. Then he threw on yesterday's clothes, gave Connie a kiss and let himself out.

Ben's shaving gear was in his own room. His good mood lasted the minute and a half it took him to walk there. Round a corner, down some stairs, round another corner was the dean's secretary, Vanessa, camped outside his door. He doubted that she had ever before been in the state of agitation he witnessed now.

'Where have you been?' she hissed. 'The dean's been trying to reach you since six. It's disgusting. He got me to drive in and find you. Where's your mobile?'

Ben patted his pocket. It was there. He checked his zip. What was disgusting?

'Then turn the bloody thing on and call him,' Vanessa continued. 'And run! Over to the tower.'

Liquid nitrogen was dripping onto Ben's guts. 'It can't have fallen down! The noise would have been deafening.' How could Gyro have heard something in Hong Kong when Ben had slept like a lamb?

'I need to get Harry to school – thank God I didn't bring him in the car. What on earth would I have said to him?'

Ben ran, fumbling with his mobile's power button as he went. Normally it yielded instantly, but this time he gave up on it, deciding that he might as well get a first-hand view of the tower disaster before dealing with a garbled account of it. He turned the corner of the building.

The flying saucer was intact but a group of students in various states of dress had gathered around the tower's base, obscuring his view. Obscuring his view of what? The lift, he realised immediately. The fucking lift. Deep down he had known it – last week's good news had been too good to be true.

But no, the lift was working. It rose above the spectating heads most of the way up to the auditorium and descended again. Then it rose again. He could see something wrapped around the lift. Oh, for goodness' sake – just some protest or other! Surely security, or even a student in the crowd, had had the wit to call the police.

As Ben pushed his way through the group, some of whom were starting to laugh, his angle of view changed. The lift had been programmed to keep moving up and down: there was no-one inside it. To the lift someone – well, certainly a group, this was too complex for one person – had wired up some wooden boards. Painted on them were on one side the knuckles and fingertips, and on the other side the thumb and wrist, of a curled male fist. The fist rose and fell with the lift, stroking the shaft.

Obviously the tower had temporarily fallen victim to some pranksters: though to what end, or how it should all have come to provoke Gyro's instantaneous ire on the other side of the world, Ben did not see.

Once he had called the dean, he did. Gyro flung his words like mortar bombs, and they clung to their victim like napalm. Someone must have rigged up the artwork at dawn, not long afterwards posting a two-minute video on the web. Within half-an-hour corporate web-watchers, scanning constantly for any conjunction of the word 'Pinnacle' with trigger words or phrases (protests, law suits, threats, injuries, kidnaps, deaths, loss of profits or other obscenities) had flashed an alert to Cardew McCarthy. The on-screen legend said:

HAMPTON – PINNACLE – WANKERS!
CAPITALISTS FUCK OFF!

Gyro's final words had been clear enough. 'Fucking get the lawyers! I'm texting you the name. Get the police! Get that video taken down *now*! Whatever it takes. Get it down before Junior wakes up.'

When he reached the office the cleaner grinned at him. He nearly hit her between the eyes but didn't have the time. First steps first: the maintenance team disabled the lift at ground level, stopping the offensive motion. Ben had no hopes of early results from forensic evidence – fingerprints, DNA, or paint sourcing; in any case the thing was clearly a prank. Still, the police had been called. Tom was on his way to look at how the lift controls had been breached. Greg had taken to dispersing the crowd and keeping the crime scene intact as if he had trained for it.

Ben grimaced when he read the details of the lawyer whom Gyro wanted on the case. Still, it was an international firm, so they would be able to move swiftly in different national jurisdictions to get at the video's host server.

'Mr Andrews, please – it's urgent, I need you to page him if necessary. This is Ben Stillman in Dean William Gyro's office at Hampton Management College. Thank you.'

Two minutes of silence nearly made him redial, but then he heard a throat clear. 'Bill Andrews.'

'Mr Andrews? This is Ben Stillman in Dean Gyro's office.'

'I recall that, Mr Stillman. And my firm is still Andrews, Caravajal, Sagan and Warner. I'm afraid none of my partners have taken up your generous suggestion of retiring so that we shorten our name. But it's not all loss; I was given some suggestions for changing your own name, to as little as four letters.'

Top lawyers: you get to pay them a fortune and you have to crawl to them as well. '*Touché*, sir. Very good of you to take this urgent call. Are you somewhere where you can look at this web address?'

By the time he had finished with the lawyers, his mobile was going crazy but Greg had brought Chief Inspector Haddrill in. Ben realised that not only had he had no breakfast, shower or a shave, but his shirt bore a trail of lipstick. The trail started at his collar but rapidly headed south. There was nothing for it but to get out his notepad. The three of them reviewed the video.

In the circumstances Ben was grateful for the chief inspector's years of practice at keeping his thoughts to himself. After a moment Haddrill said, 'We need to consider the possibility of inside information.'

Greg nodded.

Ben said, 'Why do you say that?'

'Because the lift was not working until Saturday. Apart from the contractors, only the relatively small number of people who were around the college on Saturday or Sunday would have had this information. Presumably it would be straightforward to make a list?'

Ben nodded.

'While the offending contraption may well have been built weeks ago, someone then moved quite fast.' Haddrill pointed to the screen. 'These pictures were on the web within thirty-six hours of the lift becoming operational. The ISP, all of that, we'll look at too – if they have been careless we might get a fast result that way. But let's assume not. At the moment we should assume a possible combination of internal and external resources.' Haddrill turned to Greg. 'I am assuming that we are not dealing with any kind of visit by the Prime Minister on Thursday.'

Ben was adamant. 'It's not in the plan for Thursday, and never has been.'

'That's also my information,' agreed Haddrill. 'So, looking inside, what have we got? Disgruntled members of staff? Or students – anyone just failed a course, or missed out on a job at the Pinnacle company? That's Virtual Savings and Trust, isn't it?'

Greg looked at Ben. I know what you're thinking, thought Ben – Frank and his shed. Conceivably Frank might have built the fist in his shed, though what they had glimpsed of its contents had not looked like a fist at all. Ben was torn. Frank was a mentor and becoming a friend. Yes, Frank had lied about the shed's contents on Saturday, but there could be a hundred explanations for that short of terrorist melodrama.

Greg was still looking at Ben, and Haddrill had noticed. Not mentioning Frank at all was not an option. Greg would go out of his way to mention it later. Ben's silence would only accomplish the undermining of his own position.

'Maybe two possibilities,' said Ben. 'One – Dr Frank Jones, a lecturer who has been here some years. Greg can tell you more about him. It's possible he's been building something in the boathouse which he rents from the college at the far end of the lake. Let me make my own position quite clear. I think it's a total red herring. Frank was one of my MBA tutors and he wouldn't hurt a flea. Also this whole thing –' Ben made a gesture with his hands '– is just too naff for him. But let's deal with it. Greg, when we're through here, take one of the Chief Inspector's men over to the boathouse and open it up. It is college property. Whatever we find, I'm sure Frank will explain.'

Action and confirmation – Greg was delighted. He could not wait.

Ben was not finished. Distressing though it was to recount the GSG meeting last Thursday he did so, consoling himself that it would certainly earn the cleaner a police interrogation. There was the answer, as plain as daylight: a graphic attack on the phallocracy plotted by the cleaner with the evil grin. The clincher: the cleaner had been in his office unexpectedly on Saturday, when the architect's plans had been on show.

Haddrill's response was disappointing. 'I see why you think this is relevant, Mr Stillman. I'm glad you mentioned it and I will keep it in mind. But let's not move precipitately.'

For goodness' sake why not, thought Ben? Extraordinary rendition to Guantanamo Bay would be a good first step.

Haddrill read his mind. 'In your own and the college's interests. Let's say we come out of this office and throw the book at, what is it, the Gender Strategy Group. No doubt they have lodged a complaint about the dean's email. Threatening someone who has lodged a sex discrimination complaint is victimisation, leading straight to a tribunal hearing in which this memo and the video would be evidence. But we will make inquiries.'

When they left, Vanessa was there with a mug of black coffee and a croissant which he grabbed with both hands. She had got Harry to school and herself back under control.

'Thank God you're here, Vanessa. What kind of crazy people are we dealing with? Anyway, the police have it under control.'

'Is the tower all right for Thursday?'

'Mercifully, it seems to be. It was a prank. Tom will do a full check.'

'Well, that's the main thing. And the tower was not going to have been ready before you arrived.'

'Thank you. I'm sorry you had to come out looking for me,' he added.

Vanessa smiled. 'You probably want to shave and get a clean shirt.'

Ben nodded.

Vanessa glanced down at her pad. 'Roger Sling said you and he had a meeting first thing.'

'Oh shit! I can't believe I forgot.'

'He said you made the appointment on Sunday morning, so you might have been overworking? Anyway I've dealt with it. He needed to see the dean as well so I've put him in the one slot we had left – 2pm on Thursday. That's with you and the dean.'

'You're magic.'

'And don't forget the dean's back tomorrow, so you need to move desks today. Maintenance put in a computer point on Friday, but on Mondays they are only around until three. We need the waiting chairs and coffee table taken away, and a desk brought in.'

'Good point.'

'Unless you'd prefer to be in Vanish's office.'

'No thanks. If they need to cart me off to the loony bin, they can take me directly, not via a broom cupboard.'

The call-back he wanted from Andrews came through at lunchtime.

'The video's down. Of course there will be clips circulating whoever knows where, but the main site is down.'

On the screen Ben clicked back to where the video had been, to be greeted by the comforting message that the content was temporarily unavailable.

'Where was the server?'

'In Germany. Nothing exotic. Of course, they can't help with any useful information about who uploaded the video there. On this occasion that might even be true. But one of our Frankfurt attorneys will visit them again tomorrow and call them daily until Friday. We want to dissuade them from getting any clever ideas.'

'I owe you,' said Ben.

'You do. You particularly owe us for the flurry of work you created last week with your Gettysburg address to the tower contractors. You have no clue of the grave legal risks you created.'

'I guess not. And you want to be paid for it.'

'We will be paid for it, Mr Stillman. I think I am just confirming that it will not prove difficult for us to be paid for it?'

'If you keep the video down, I reckon the chances of that are good.' No doubt when the invoice came to be presented it would not lack for zeros, but by then Ben would have moved on.

Good news deserved to be shared so Ben told Gyro right away. He promised a final round-up shortly before four o'clock, when Gyro would be at the airport waiting to take off back to Heathrow.

By mid-afternoon there was mixed news from the tower. 'You'd best listen for yourself. To be honest, it's hard to describe.' Tom, Rakesh and Ben were standing by the tower, with the lift back to normal – other than a problem with the announcements which Rakesh was trying to explain.

As they approached the lift a faint, continuous murmuring sprang into full clarity as the lift doors slid back with a swish. The announcer was the same actress but her speech repertoire had changed. She was also unable to stop. 'The announcement is beginning. The announcement is continuing. The announcement is ending. There is no announcement. There is no announcement. When there is an announcement, we will make an announcement …'

'What the fuck?'

'Pretty much our sentiments, Mr Stillman. Unfortunately, in the course of the pranksters messing about, they've done something weird to the circuit boards. To be honest, the guys in Bangalore have never seen anything like it.'

'Well, shut the woman up completely.'

'That's more complicated than we thought.'

'What?'

'We've tested and re-tested it. Since this morning's attack, the only way to shut off the announcements completely is to cut off power to the whole of the lift.'

'You're joking.'

'Regretfully, sir, I am not.' Rakesh's gloom attracted Tom's nodding agreement.

'Well, come up with something! We're paying for solutions, not problems.' The conversation had taken Ben beyond edgy; suddenly he recalled Gyro's question about being defeated by lift announcements.

Haddrill matter-of-factly summarised the situation. There had been some fingerprints on the wooden fist. Whether they matched the national database they would know by the end of tomorrow. Realistically, that was unlikely; a more likely question would be whether the college wanted to fingerprint staff and students. Ben said with relief that that question could await Gyro's return the next morning.

The boathouse had drawn a blank (it was empty), Haddrill continued. Other lines of inquiry would be pursued but, in the meantime, the chief inspector ran through some enhancements to the security plan for Thursday which struck Ben as entirely sensible – practical without overreaction.

Greg's version of the story, when he caught up with Ben, went in a different direction. 'Frank's hut. It's empty.'

'I heard. That's good!' Ben replied. 'The more good news the better.'

'No, it's bad – very bad. It's not that there was nothing suspicious in it, there was nothing *at all in it*.'

'Greg, I find that comforting. If Frank is planning to surprise us all on Thursday, he will find it hard to do with *nothing at all*.'

'You're not thinking straight.'

'I might grant you that. It's been a day from hell.'

'Don't you see? What you talked to Frank about it on Saturday, it tipped him off. He hid everything on Sunday. That means he's got another hide-out.'

'For both of our sakes, Greg, give it a rest. We've raised your suspicions and the police have listened to them. End of story.'

'I'm asking for sniffer dogs. If there were explosives in the shed, we can find out tomorrow.'

'N – O – no. Forget it. Don't think and drive, just drive. Dianne must need taking somewhere. Take the rest of the day off! It's an order!'

The two men eyed each other unsympathetically. Ben watched incredulously as Greg reached into his jacket for a box of incense sticks, lit one and planted it in the ground. The scent of jasmine eddied this way and that between them, as if unable to make up its mind whom to trust.

Greg exhaled. 'I'm sorry, Mr Stillman. I should be more understanding. It's been quite a day.'

'Thank you, Greg. You do a thorough job, and I appreciate it.'

'Thank you, sir. It's only right for you to sleep on things. I can wait. I'll wait till the morning before I contact the police.' He held his hand up to stop Ben from speaking. 'You're in a state, Mr Stillman, I can see that. I don't need to do anything before the morning – there will still be time for them to test the boathouse. I'll secure it overnight so no-one can get in. But try to stop me in the morning, sir, and it will be a different story.'

'Why's that? Because the dean will be back?'

'Frank put you in your job, Mr Stillman. You knew him from before. You've popped up out of the blue, able to start right away, just before the opening – how coincidental is that? If Frank hasn't been meddling with explosives in his hut, he hasn't got anything to worry about. Neither have you. None of us have. We'll know tomorrow. But if you stop me tomorrow – well, you see how it would look.'

The day had been getting on top of Ben, and now he surrendered. He hadn't had a cigarette in years but wanted one badly. He went out without telling Vanessa where he was going, because he did not know. Suddenly he remembered there was a cigarette machine in the college bar, where he bought a pint of lager to get the necessary change. He downed it and bought another.

How likely were the police to bring in sniffer dogs on the say so of a boy-band member of the Hitler Youth? And even if they did, so the fuck what? They would find *no explosives* and

Ben would be out of Hampton in another four days – and not back any time soon, if he had any say in the matter.

On the bar was a flyer for Luscious, some local singer, advertising a gig. Ben adopted it as a beer-mat. Waterdrops dribbling from his glass made her psychedelically-coloured hair run wild, spilling like snakes from a basket. The effect matched Ben's mood. Luscious? Oh yes, according to the file, Gyro had engaged Luscious to sing at the tower opening and then during drinks before the dinner. Gyro – flying back from Hong Kong – airborne half an hour ago … Shit, shit, shit.

Now he was done for. Ben had missed the final update call which he had promised to make, leaving the dean 14 airborne hours to stew on Ben's failure as he flew back. And he had completely forgotten that the maintenance shift finished at three. So now he would have to strike camp and move from Gyro's office into the broom cupboard: the one he had sworn not to check into on his way to the insane asylum.

His phone rang again. The voice of a friend, soft, concerned. The voice of a woman. 'We just got out of class. I heard it was a crazy day and wondered how you were.'

Ben rolled up his left shirt-sleeve to refresh his memory. On a day when so much had gone wrong, he really, really, really did not need to screw this up as well. 'Connie!'

'Join me for dinner? I hear there's turkey rissoles on the college menu tonight.'

He would have loved to, he replied. Turkey rissoles would be the sanest, friendliest things he had encountered all day. But he couldn't. He had to move office, and he had to stay up half the night writing the 20-page report for Gyro on readiness for Thursday which he had planned to do during the day. And then, he omitted to add, he planned to get semi-smashed; he'd leave just enough grey cells standing to get himself up in the morning. But tomorrow night, or maybe Wednesday, would be great. Talk tomorrow, they agreed.

TUESDAY 19 JUNE (MORNING)

(ƆNINᴚOW) ƎNUႱ 6l YAႻSƎUT

Seagulls can be caught by wrapping food round a stone and throwing it in the air. The gull swallows the bait while still on the wing, gulps down the stone with it, and the weight causes it to crash. Obviously this is a technique for use over land rather than at sea.

JOHN WISEMAN [4]

In an exchange of emails Greg had confirmed to Ben that setting off from Hampton at five would have them at Heathrow in time for six. He omitted to say that by then he would be already be halfway there, alone. Greg smiled at Ben's agitated phone call at ten minutes past five but what made Greg smack his lips was the text he sent back to Ben: 'New instructions – dean's office at 7.30am'. New instructions! – that felt good. And it was true, even if the instructions that Greg was passing on came from a source Ben was not expecting.

Result! Amelia Henderson had promised action to bug Frank's house. That was gratifying progress but would take 24 hours. That could be too late; the big day would be here in 48 hours and it was getting bigger. Greg knew his duty: be proactive and take no chances. So this morning he would

[4] *SAS Survival Guide,* HarperCollins (Collins Gem), Glasgow (1993)

bring down two seagulls. It was time to stop wondering what Frank was hiding. He was a clear and present threat to Thursday and needed his neck wringing now. Ben was not such an obvious threat, but why take chances? Plucked out of nowhere by Frank, suddenly at the hub of everything, Ben was doing exactly what a Frank plant would do – keeping his nose clean. So let him flutter his wings for a while longer, before being grounded with severe indigestion.

On the journey back Greg needed less than half an hour to do what he needed, which faced him with a dilemma of pleasures. Should he lurk around the dean's office to monitor Ben's reactions to the wounds which he would shortly receive, in case Ben gave something away? Or in case the wounds needed extra salt? Alternatively, should he wait at the boathouse for the police to show up? A reasonable bet was that the explosives experts would take a while to come.

Concerned by the switch with the car, Ben intended to be first to the dean's office, two bound copies of his readiness report in his briefcase. He was not. The dean's chair was already occupied by a woman. The last time that had happened had not been a good omen.

The chair swung from side to side, propelled by slim, tanned calves bred on the latest running machines and salon treatments. Steepled fingers graced with two platinum rings and a yellow stone waited in impatience. A low cleavage revealed rolling sand dunes awaiting a storm. High heels in mango yellow matched a very short skirt in the same colour. Dianne Peach-Gyro had called the meeting, which began when Gyro arrived five minutes late.

'Why do I waste my time? Why do I waste my time? What a shambles, the pair of you. Neither of you returned my calls yesterday.' The trail of nail varnish in the air indicated Gyro and Ben in turn, but Dianne was not waiting for answers.

'While you have been making panda bear eyes at Communist fat cats who intend to have the college for dinner, this idiot wasted my time by provoking a delegation of the sisterhood to call on me threatening a strike. By going on bended knee I have held that off until next week. I thought we might want to do that so that the Prime Minister can come here this Thursday to announce the most important breakthrough in Hampton's miserable history.'

'Darling, congratulations!' exclaimed Gyro.

'Thank you. I wanted to tell you yesterday but that plan needed one of you to be sufficiently bothered to return my call. The announcement will be for eight million pounds of investment in this college, as the first step in a one-hundred and twenty million national investment programme in British business schools to bring management skills in the NHS up to world-class standards.

'The fact that on Thursday a range of business leaders of the highest international distinction will be here to mark the opening of the tower will provide, in the Prime Minister's view, an excellent symbol of what achieving "world-class" in Britain means. I agree.'

Gyro rushed forward and pecked his wife on the cheek.

'Darling, I'm speechless.'

'That makes a pleasant change. Of course there are details to be sorted. I assume that is what we are paying Ben for, if he can spare any time between incidents of gender warfare.'

'Of course he can, darling. But how did you pull it off?'

'On your travels you won't have had time to notice, darling, but our little island changed its prime minister a year ago. Right away I saw that the new one needed to put a stamp of his own on how to modernise the NHS. The choice and markets agenda was old hat; the gap for something new was wide open.'

Dianne shrugged. 'The jig-saw pieces were staring us in the face. Hampton trains NHS managers. Better managers means a better service for patients and investing in the skills of our workforce. Spice it up to be world-class – I'm afraid I traded shamelessly on your reputation, will you forgive me? – stir for twelve months and now Ed Lens is gagging to hear from Ben as we speak. Indeed he and I were waiting for a good part of yesterday. Never mind: the concept and the headline figures are agreed, as is the pertinence of launching this Thursday. All that's left is dotting i's and crossing a few t's.'

Gyro looked at Ben sharply. 'Ben will be on to it right away. He might be able to manage a little punctuation.' Ben could see Gyro pondering how to retrieve the initiative. 'Talk to Ed, Ben, and prepare an options paper for Dianne and me to consider this evening.'

'My thoughts exactly, darling.'

Ben struggled to have something to offer, remembering the fundamental problem about the Prime Minister coming on

Thursday which Gyro had left ringing in his ears. He coughed. 'We have to keep in mind the pre-eminence on Thursday of the Pinnacle family.'

Gyro had his arm round his wife, as if they were posing for a photograph. They might as well have spoken in unison, although it was Dianne who said the words. She agreed with Ben, but quite dismissively. 'Of course, that goes without saying. That's why you're here – to come up with win-win solutions. A win for Junior and a win for the Prime Minister.'

'Exactly,' Gyro confirmed. 'I hope, Ben, you are not going to disappoint us any further.'

'I very much hope not,' Ben replied. He produced a copy of his report. 'I've been sitting on the contractors' necks. We've got really good progress on the tower, including the lift –'

'Don't push me, Ben,' Gyro scowled, tossing Ben's report onto his desk. 'Who caused Thursday's fiasco? You. Which caused yesterday's global abomination – a child could work out that much. Yet you kept me in the dark! What were you thinking?'

'I'm really sorry. It was a mistake.'

'I'm hoping you weren't a mistake. Get on to Ed Lens right away. And one other thing: get hold of Dr Jones. I want to see him in here at nine sharp.'

'My mistakes were not Frank's fault.'

Gyro rolled his eyeballs. 'Since he recommended you, let's say the jury's out on that one. No, another complaint from the MBA students is a step too far, and getting up to no good in the boathouse is the final straw. Greg has briefed me fully and I've spoken to Haddrill already. I said I want the specialists in.

I want the boathouse and its surrounds swept for explosives by lunchtime.' Gyro turned back to his wife. 'The Prime Minister! I knew it all along. No-one else could pull it off for Thursday, but I knew you would.'

'That's kind of you, darling. All I did was notice the opportunity. The person who pushed all the buttons was Mark Topley. He's been just the sweetest. Having him as our MP and Minister for Health was such a stroke of luck. But you must be desperate for some breakfast. I asked Annette to make your mother's home-made waffles.'

At lunchtime Connie pulled up outside Frank's house, a five-minute drive or a decent walk from the main college buildings. There were six modest semi-detacheds in three pairs, each with small front and back gardens.

Sometimes the larger part of being responsible was not forgetting. Connie had not forgotten her conversation with Vanish on Saturday, especially the threat to the school – and to herself as a governor – if there turned out to be a large, imminently payable, under-the-counter loan. She had persuaded herself that the allegation was probably a self-serving fantasy. Nevertheless, some things could be checked. The obvious first check was with Roger Sling, the college's bank manager. Ben had been due to meet Sling on Monday but that meeting would now be on Thursday. So be it.

Connie had worked out that there was another check that she could make today, now that Gyro was back from Hong

Kong – had he returned with any money? Not only Vanish, but Frank as well, had talked about the number of Gyro's recent visits to the Far East, with nothing to show for them so far. So on Monday night she had emailed Gyro chattily welcoming him back to the UK, saying she was enjoying her first few days as a governor (it could not hurt to remind him) and hoping that he was landing with fabulous sacks of money to the college's benefit.

She hadn't expected to hear anything back straight away – she was too unimportant – but he had got back quickly with a cordial voice message. She had picked it up at mid-morning break. At that point she emailed Frank, asking if they could meet at lunchtime, or any other time that day – she would skip class if need be. Ten minutes ago he had emailed back, 'Definitely – lunch?'

Connie had not been inside any of the staff houses before. A semi-circle of glass in the front door at head-height threw the only available light into the narrow hallway. It was stacked with papers and books. At the end was a kitchen and a small toilet under the stairs. A single living/dining space was divisible into two by remarkably out-of-fashion sliding panels. Two bedrooms and a bathroom upstairs, she imagined. Well, if you lived in England, you did not need to imagine, you knew.

'Come in!' Frank looked pleased to see her. Pleased? More like relieved. 'I was making myself a cheese sandwich.'

'I've eaten. But a cup of tea – green or herbal if you have it?'

'Two green teas coming up. Take a seat in the living room, I'll be with you in a minute.'

The furnishing of the living/dining space was eclectic, but less so than Connie would have feared for a 45-year-old bachelor. Bookcases of course, a small bust of Gandhi, a 15-year-old turntable and a stack of records (records!), two armchairs and a handsome circular dining table with four chairs. On the main wall hung an original canvas, a large semi-aquatic expanse of grey and white serving as the backdrop to something limb-like with a trickle of red. Connie felt a twinge. Was it saying something about hidden depths? Frank's presumably.

An imitation-silver candelabra of three intertwined fish on the dining table picked up the semi-aquatic motif.

'I'm glad you've come round,' Frank said as he emerged with the cups of tea. 'I've just been fired.'

'What?'

'Well, agreed to go. By noon on Thursday. I said yes on condition that the pay-off was in my bank account by noon tomorrow.' He recounted an icy meeting two hours earlier. Gyro said that he could not overlook another complaint from a group of MBA students about his ethics teaching. 'I said their marks were low because their ethics were low, or had I missed the point of it all? But the truth is I've been a thorn in Gyro's side for too long. I think this wanker protest nonsense was the last straw.'

'Was that you?'

'No, nor did Gyro have anything he could pin on me. But saying I thought it was quite witty didn't help.'

'I'm so sorry.'

'Don't be – though there is one thing you could do for me.'

'What's that?'

'Come here to dinner on Wednesday night. I'd like to have a last supper but just with a couple of friends. I had you and Ben in mind. While most of the faculty here aren't against me, they're too much in favour of a quiet life to be for me. Will you?'

'Of course. I mean, we'll need to ask Ben, but I know how much he respects you.'

'Calling me his star teacher on Saturday was going a bit far. Anyway, now the star's out, which makes your role as a governor all the more important. You can ask questions. If you want.'

'I want. That's why I came round.' She talked about her meeting with Vanish on Saturday. Ben had mentioned some of it to Frank that evening at the Kings Arms, but now Connie pulled no punches. She described the suggestion of the off-the-book loan, as well as the fact that Vanish had no hard evidence. Frank whistled in astonishment. 'If there is a loan,' Connie continued, 'Vanish thought Gyro was counting on raising money in Hong Kong to pay it off – that's why he's made so many trips recently. Since Gyro's back today, I emailed to ask him politely to ask if he was bringing back bags of loot.'

Frank nodded. 'To be fair to the bastard, he has done exactly that a number of times, like getting the money for the tower.'

'Here's his reply this morning.' Connie put her phone on speaker and they listened to Gyro's message:

'Good to get your email, Connie. It's great to be back with everyone so excited about Thursday. How did my trip go? Exhausting. Positive. But you're Chinese yourself, aren't you, so you know how it goes. No money for the college right now, but a big pay-off soon.'

'Jam tomorrow, in other words,' Connie concluded. 'Which is why I wanted to talk to you. What should I do next? As a governor?'

Frank was concentrating. 'Play the message again, will you?' She did. 'He may have chosen his words carefully. If it's an off-the-books loan, and he has come-back money or a pledge to pay it off, that money will have to be off-the-books, too. Like directly from some Chinese big-wig to the bank, bypassing the college. It wouldn't be money for the college right now, would it?'

'I hadn't thought of that,' Connie acknowledged.

'Ben told me that Gyro's diary – his official college diary – for this trip is just like the other Hong Kong trips: completely blank. That could also make sense if Gyro's raising money off the books.' Frank looked up; he had reached a conclusion. 'I bet the answer will be how Sling is on Thursday. It will be as plain as day if there's a dirty loan still hanging over his head.'

In the background Connie was aware of a car pulling up outside. 'You're right. But obvious in his body language, not necessarily in any documents. So I'll invite myself to the meeting. Just turn up unannounced. Ben knows when it is. Gyro will wonder what I'm up to, but I am a governor. Frank, I knew you'd see a way –'

Two sets of footsteps down the front path were followed by a hammer-blow to the front door. Greg was outside with a police officer in tow. 'The dean called in the police this morning to do an explosives check on the boathouse,' said Greg.

Frank stood guard on the path and pursed his lips. 'What a surprise, Greg. I'm sure it has everything to do with you. I always thought you were a secret Santa, disguised as a jumped-up shit. So how did the boathouse do?'

'It passed. But we also want to test the house.' The police officer seemed content to let Greg do the talking.

'This is outrageous,' Connie protested. 'Where's your warrant?'

'The house is college property. Under the terms of Dr Jones' lease – '

Frank pulled Connie back and then waved his arms, holding his hands out. 'Forget it, forget it. You can come in on two conditions. One is that you test my hands right now. The other is that you are out of here in ten minutes. You make me sick.'

Greg eyed the offer he had in front of him and took it. While the officer used tweezers to take discs of cotton out of a packet and wipe them on Frank's outstretched palms, Greg slipped inside, picking the places to be swabbed. Each time the officer popped the swabs into a machine in the car's boot, which a minute later spewed out some lines of letters and numbers on a roll of paper, like a till-roll in a cash register. Frank and Connie stood still and watched the bizarre performance.

'Your ten minutes are up,' Frank declared.

Greg came out of the house wearing an expression as inscrutable as Frank's. He said something to the officer and turned around. Strips of print-out fluttered on the officer's clipboard. The house had no basement but Greg had selected cupboards, the attic, the bathroom, the front hallway and some curtains for swabbing.

'You're clean as a whistle, sir,' the officer said to Frank. 'You had your curtains dry-cleaned a few months ago, but there are no explosive markers. Not now; certainly not last week; and probably not in the last three months. We're sorry we've had to bother you, but police work is mostly about eliminating people from our inquiries. Each step brings us nearer to our man.'

'Watching your face almost makes the day worthwhile,' Frank called out as the unmarked car pulled off with Greg in the passenger seat.

Connie realised that she was shaking. 'They thought you were a bomber?'

Frank took her by the arm. 'Search me,' he said. 'Mind you, they just did.'

Connie reached for her phone. 'Ben needs to know what's happened. He can speak to the dean.'

Frank shook his head. 'It won't do any good – as far as the dean's concerned, I'm gone; the more gone, the better. Ask Ben to dinner Wednesday night. Early, say 6.30pm? I'll be up most of the night packing and Thursday's a big day.'

'I'll check again, but the Prime Minister will be in Africa on Thursday.' Amelia Henderson spoke as if Africa were up the road from her native Inverness but encryption made her words jagged.

The day's results spoke for themselves, Greg thought. Frank would be off-site by noon on Thursday. If Frank had had plans for Thursday he would now have to change them. With luck he would have to communicate, and the bugs to hear that were now in place. But Amelia didn't like Greg's tactics. 'You were impatient, rushing over to his house. Two hours later with a warrant, we could have taken the house apart.'

'I told the officer to tell Frank he was all clear. I mean he *was* all clear, but I had guessed that was going to be the result from the way he let us go in. So I thought it through, like you keep telling me. Even if a house search found something, we wouldn't know who he's working with. A second team could have a second bomb.'

'You're over-reaching. We haven't got one team yet. One person isn't a team.'

'Whereas now Frank thinks he's in the clear he'll drop his guard – which is good, because – I'll admit it – he's been more careful than I had expected. I was sure we would find traces at the boathouse.'

'No trace cuts two ways. Yes, he's no amateur lone bomber. It might mean training and sophistication or it might mean he's a harmless academic with a hobby he doesn't like people to know about.'

'So we protect against the threat. Because he's going to be out of the picture on Thursday, if he is a threat he'll need to talk to his handler urgently. With the bugs in and his guard lowered, we'll find out who he talks to.'

Amelia was silent for a moment. 'OK. It's not a perfect plan, but it's not bad. Well done. What matters is if Number Ten suddenly plans to go to Hampton we will be ahead of the game. We've got your eyes on the ground already, which is a huge plus and makes us look smart.

'Of course, we can kill a planned visit if we need to, but there's no need. General terrorist chatter is flat – nothing's going on as far as our usual suspects are concerned. Thanks to you we've spotted one ornery academic who may have something to hide but he's out of the picture cleanly. Our scoreboard's looking good. Be patient and it will stay that way.'

Greg grinned.

TUESDAY 19 JUNE (AFTERNOON)

(TUESDAY 19 JUNE (AFTERNOON))

The black-and-white photographs lining the stairs had Ben craning his head while trying not to fall over. At first glance, there was a sameness about the portraits of Britain's past Prime Ministers, as if they had been taken by the same photographer around the time of the abdication crisis. Ben was also trying to follow Ed Lens' receding back. Attempting the two tasks together meant that he walked into the person who was going down.

In the polls the Prime Minister and First Lord of the Treasury had been going down for some time, but a cheery 'Good afternoon' rang out as if Ben was a long-lost voter from his constituency. He had been coached to give an upbeat greeting and grin at a certain point on the stairway whether or not anyone was there. The delayed effect of the grin on his cheek muscles produced the amount of smile which the image wizards desired when the Prime Minister walked out of the front door and into Downing Street six seconds later.

Ben had seized the opportunity of Dianne's announcement to get out of the college and out of the path of any lava flow from Gyro about the feminists. In any case, he badly needed to get face-to-face with Lens to check out whether Dianne's wild rantings had any substance – and if they did, to steer them towards the safe harbour of a Prime Ministerial visit *after* Thursday. On the drive into London he had concluded that that was the win-win-win solution: the college got its moment of fame; the Pinnacles didn't get upstaged; and best of all he, Ben, would be out of the picture.

When Ed had met Ben after the speech eight days ago, he had asked if Bakhtin had been to Number Ten. Oddly, here they now were. Did Ben's rapid switch of role from Bakhtin to Hampton strike Ed as odd? Not at all.

'Smart move,' said Ed from the corner of his attic office, 'given Bakhtin's key role in this programme. Dianne's idea, no doubt.'

Ben fished for safe ground. 'She's certainly a smart woman.'

Most of Ed's office was taken up by combination-locked filing cabinets in battleship grey. Presumably the locks were equally effective at stopping thieves getting in and skeletons getting out. The floor sported several defensive fortifications constructed out of broadsheet, tabloid and NHS newspapers and some weekly magazines.

Half-concealed behind one cabinet was a poster of the five cavorting nudes of Matisse's *La Danse*, with a coffee-stain in one corner, but otherwise the walls were empty. The agile energy of the figures was reminiscent of Ed's own wiry physique. Or perhaps it represented an active and public-spirited citizenry, keeping themselves fit to avoid placing gratuitous demands on the National Health Service.

The sash window looked out into the Downing Street garden, scattered with its plastic tricycle, toys and a sandbox. The window was open but since they were under the eaves, the room was hot. Ed was not much older than Ben but red braces suited him. The sweat marks on his shirt testified to his constant gesticulation, always pointing, correcting or adjusting.

Bakhtin's key role in the programme was one of the first things that Ed explained. The headline figure for investment in British business schools was £120m. This was to buy a major upgrade in the skills of NHS managers, to enable them to cope with the new choice-driven, customer-focussed health world. It would mean more and better courses like Connie's, taken up much more widely by senior clinicians as well as managers within the NHS.

Overcoming the split between doctors and managers was a top priority. The money would pay for such things as attracting higher calibre, world-class faculty to teach the courses (what Hampton had been doing under Gyro was showing the way). There would also be investment in more specialised course content, such as state-of-the-art interactive business games drawing on advances in decision theory as well as relevant lessons from health economies overseas.

Naturally, Ed explained, the figure of £120 million included quite a lot of packaging. In the pathfinder phase there would only be £32 million, in tranches of £8 millon each for four business schools; anything after that would depend on the programme's early results, not to mention general elections, public spending crises or outbreaks of war. For that £32 million, European business schools would compete to be one of the lucky four – or three, since Hampton had taken the lead place.

They would be less lucky than at first appeared, because each participating school would have to raise half of its £8 millon from its own sources: the government would simply match-fund. Lord Bakhtin had kicked the programme off by agreeing to top up his gift to Hampton from £3 million to £4 millon; he had also agreed to chair a panel of business leaders to front the programme. In other words, he would be the programme's chief fund-raiser and arm-twister. For that he had got a seat in the House of Lords.

Ben marvelled at the ratio of bang to buck. In extra cash, Hampton would get £1 million more from Alex and £4 million from the taxpayer. £4 million was all the government would be spending anytime soon, but they would be getting their £120 million headline. The political arithmetic was wonderful.

And, Ben mused, despite having been Alex's chief of staff for a year he had not pieced any of this together. Granted, the diary had recorded various meetings at Hampton about the gift. Ben had only gone along to one or two: it had been an intimate personal matter rather than a business one, concerning Alex's late wife and tricky negotiations about large amounts of personal money. Presumably some of these 'meetings' had then become intimate in a different way, with Dianne beginning to spin her spider's web.

Ed was on edge. Ben was not surprised. Looked at from a business perspective, the sketchiness of the thinking behind how spending £120 million would actually improve things for patients was flimsy to the point of non-existence. But the danger preying on Ed's mind was something else entirely.

'We need to sex the thing up. We've chucked billions at the NHS already, but there still isn't a clear narrative in the public's mind about the benefits. The dimension we're missing here is *transformational*.' He grabbed a pen off his desk and scribbled the word in small capitals in a miniature notebook which lived in a jacket pocket. Ben saw that the other words written there were *MRSA* and *nano-oncology*.

'How does spending this money transform the whole situation? How does it enable Cinderella to go to the ball? That's what we need to crack. Otherwise no deal, no launch at Hampton.'

Seeing half a loaf, Ben grabbed it. The overwhelming priority was to unhook this Prime Ministerial circus from the tower opening in two days' time. 'I agree. And given just a few extra days beyond Thursday, we could come up with something absolutely transformational.' Surely? About as surely as he could compose a violin concerto. But even a few days' grace would get him clear of the scene, and Gyro and Dianne could have the pleasure of sorting out the promise.

'Besides, the Prime Minister's diary must have been committed for this Thursday months ago.'

'It was.' Ed flicked between windows on one of his two computer screens. 'Since last November, this Thursday and Friday have been down for a surprise visit to a British disaster relief operation in sub-Saharan Africa.'

'And is there a disaster?'

'Oh, always. This week, flooding on a major river which may overwhelm the dams. We need enough flooding for the Land Rovers we have donated to look dramatic and useful, but not enough to flush them into the Indian Ocean. We were going to have had helicopters, but they have had to go to Afghanistan,' he added wistfully. 'The final call on whether the Prime Minister's going won't be made until tomorrow afternoon.'

'So we need to be ready to go on Thursday?'

'Definitely. Security, everything. You've got some top business names and plenty of Yanks showing up at a British business school. That's exactly the message about "world-class" that the Prime Minister wants to get across. And you've got Bakhtin giving money, so we can plonk our £4 million down right away. But by 6pm tonight you and I need a story-line about why better management is transformationally sexy. That's what everyone is looking to us to deliver.'

Driving back to the college Ben had the sun roof down and, when he could, the accelerator. There was an adrenaline rush about coming with pressing business from a meeting in Downing Street, even if you had not the faintest idea of what you were doing. 'Sex up' the government's announcement – by 6pm?

Ben overtook a truck sitting on its assigned speed limit. He recognised the company name on it from his time in Bakhtin Enterprises. The blast of passing the 30-tonne container blew his hair one way and then the other. He realised that he was feeling the same way he had felt when Alex had challenged him to double the profits of Warrington Plastics. Back then he had learned that when the answer was not in the textbook, sometimes it was somewhere else.

Learning that lesson had made him, for a while, one of Alex's golden boys. Now he felt uncomfortable about what he had done, and if Connie found out it would be a disaster. So far, Alex firing him had helped him and Connie make common cause. But the clamminess of Ben's hands told him he needed another of those career-making smart answers now. Where to find it? This extra challenge had forced its way in when the tower opening already boasted a superfluity. At the moment Ben was far from a hero in his boss's eyes; he daren't drop another spinning plate.

He broke the news that a visit by the Prime Minister was a possibility to Haddrill via hands-free, adding that the possibility of it being Thursday was one which he was doing his best to avert. The chief inspector's no-nonsense efficiency continued to impress; he would get a team right away onto creating Security Plan B.

To review that plan Haddrill wanted a meeting at the college on Wednesday morning. They were already perilously short of time; to wait until late afternoon, when they might or might not have got definite news from Downing Street, would create far too many headaches. 'Let's just have difficult challenges, not impossible ones,' Haddrill concluded.

In the meantime Haddrill wanted as soon as possible – like now – the names, addresses and nationalities of everyone who would be on-site on Thursday: staff, students, visitors, caterers, the lot. He had already reviewed one VIP visitor list, but now their offices should be told to bring photo IDs. Ben made more calls to get things moving right away. While he could not yet hint that the Prime Minister would be coming – indeed rescuing flood-ravaged African families would surely be more televisual – in these security-minded times no-one would second-guess the police's judgement that extra checks were prudent.

Rakesh of Proximity Communications spotted him as he pulled into the car park. He came over, excited to the point of gibbering. More exactly – Rakesh and 10 Indians (or Yorkshiremen) whom Ben had never seen before. 'It's fixed,' he exclaimed. 'After Monday's problems we completely ditched the previous installation, because it could have been hacked into in some way.' Ben nodded. 'So we've installed instead a completely state-of-the-art system, of course at no cost to the college. The components arrived this morning from Los Angeles.'

At last. To have been defeated by a lift announcement would have been humiliating indeed. 'Where did all your friends come from?'

'You may not have seen yesterday's *FT*?'

Ben gestured at the tower. 'The attack, remember?'

Rakesh gave a million-dollar smile. In fact, for him personally that estimate was pretty accurate. 'Proximity Communications was bought over the weekend. All our stock options crystallised.'

'Congratulations!' This was one key reason why Ben had done an MBA – to understand sentences like that and to learn what to say in response, ready for the day when he could do some crystallising himself. Crystallising meant jam tomorrow had become jam today – crates of it.

'The new owner called me. Personally, on Sunday. He told me, because of everyone who will be here on Thursday, and because of Mr Wilson Pinnacle Junior, whatever I needed to totally fix things I could have.' As they walked, Rakesh gestured. 'So these guys flew in from all over. Remote working is all very well, but hands-on is still the best.'

They arrived at the tower, showing their IDs to one of the security guards whom Ben had hired after Monday's attack. The woman who had auditioned to be an autistic cat had gone, presumably to a West End production; now the lift greeted them like a *maître d'* in a top-of-the-market Californian resort overlooking Big Sur. 'The elevator doors are opening.' 'The elevator doors are closing.' Thank God – once only, and in that order.

Rakesh asked if 'elevator' was a problem. Ben shook his head; Thursday would be as much a scrum of Americans as of anybody else. The glass doughnut rose up into the body of the auditorium. The effect of the glass shell and seating was still visually stunning, but now the trimmings of a fitted-out space were appearing as well – water-coolers, red carpets, indoor plants. Ben waved at Tom who was having a meeting with the electrical contractor.

'Elevator' was not a problem, but riding up to the auditorium hammered home that other things were big problems – like the brutally unfixable fact that the auditorium would already be full to capacity without the Prime Minister and his entourage. Making room for them would mean displacing some of Pinnacle's guests, virtually all of whom were flying in from far-flung business empires. And Pinnacle was paying for the whole thing.

They descended. Rakesh pointed to two postage-stamp sized sensors which had been installed in the doughnut's ceiling. 'Our very latest technology: Voice 2.0.'

'Don't tell me.' Ben held his hand up. 'They're working out if we're stressed.'

'How did you know?' Rakesh was amazed.

'Let's say I did some homework at the weekend. But you've disabled them, right? I've had it up to here with clever stuff.'

'Exactly. We've dumbed them down to use just the 1.0 functions within the 2.0 capability.' He patted the doughnut wall paternally. 'But when you're ready for it, you'll have the smartest lift in Europe.'

'I'm sure its parents are very proud.'

It was after 3pm. Ben could put off no longer making his way to his new home, Vanish's broom cupboard somewhere on the ground floor. He walked past it twice before remembering where it was. Inside, the air-conditioning scraped and grated but did not cool, the window barely opened and in one corner were deposits suspiciously like mouse droppings. Dumped unceremoniously on his desk was the 20-page readiness report on the opening which he had given Gyro that morning.

On the front page was scrawled 'Noted. WCG. 6/19', with no thanks or congratulations.

After a while Ben conceded that there were advantages to the room. It insulated him from what surely had to be the three-ring circus of Gyro, Dianne and Greg. He walked over to the administration department to check progress on the information which he had promised Haddrill. The extra work involved and its urgency meant that he left with his back metaphorically bleeding, if not from daggers then at least from staple guns. Did Ben care? Did he hell.

From his office he fired off a draft to Ed of part of the note which they owed their respective bosses by 6pm. Ben had focused on the part of the note which mattered to him most: the timing of the Prime Minister's visit. He had grasped that failing to come up with a sexy story-line was not in fact a disaster; undoubtedly it would earn him an ear-bashing from Dianne, but no sexy story-line would guarantee no visit on Thursday.

With the compact size of the auditorium vivid in his mind, Ben was convinced that the tower simply could not accommodate the Prime Minister, a couple of assistants, a security entourage and a TV crew without displacing Pinnacle guests on a scale about which even a Prime Minister might think twice.

What helped Ed get it was suggesting that the obvious newspaper headline was 'gate-crasher'. The displaced guests would have high-up media connections and no loyalty to a British politician. In the version of the note which Ben wrote for Dianne and Gyro, no hamming up was needed. From the college's point of view embarrassing one of the world's top business leaders in front of the global business élite, just after lifting more than \$30 million out of his pocket, spoke for itself.

Cardew McCarthy arrived early. Except for his moustache, the vice-president for corporate social responsibility at Virtual Savings and Trust looked exactly as Ben had imagined. His back was used to check the straightness of the platinum-iridium standard metre at Sèvres. His shorn and knobbled scalp could have helped beginners learn Braille. And – why did Americans wear such things? – he had pressed into service a gold blazer, an orange shirt and orange trousers. You could sharpen steak knives on the creases and test sunglasses on his rendition of VST's corporate colours. McCarthy was 27 minutes early for his meeting with the dean, so reception had sent him along to Ben.

Ben took him for an inspection of the grounds. With the lift working well, going up into the auditorium was a pleasure. The lines on McCarthy's face softened as the bold concept of the tower absorbed him bodily. Ben hit him with as much police and security babble as he could muster: plenty of rank, uniform and method seemed the best way to reassure an ex-military type.

'Of course, your bobbies won't be carrying guns.' The trickle of humanity in McCarthy's voice was easy to miss, like the Colorado river threading its way along the floor of the Grand Canyon.

Ben said, 'After 7/7, you'd be surprised.' He enjoyed saying '7/7' to Americans; it confused them no end.

When they arrived at Gyro's office, Vanessa gave Ben one of her widest cheer-up smiles: God bless her! At least someone had faith in him. 'Do go through,' she said. 'The dean won't be a moment.'

They went in. McCarthy gazed out of the window while Ben looked at the desk. It seemed an age since he had tried to make it his own. His eye strayed to the coat-stand by the door carrying Gyro's doctoral robes. Doctors! He'd hit the jackpot! Doubling the number of doctors in the NHS! It was 4.55pm. Abandoning the college's guest he hurtled back to his broom cupboard, phoning Ed as he went. Ed was delighted.

Connie was incredulous. 'Doubling the number of doctors in the NHS?' The last few days had become one thing after another – in fact, just like her day job. Hampton was supposed to be somewhere she could get away from the murderous circus and think. Now Ben was coming out with this infantile nonsense; had he lost his mind?

It was 7pm. Connie and Ben were in the dinner queue at the college canteen. 'Chicken please,' said Ben. 'I know. But Ed loved the idea.'

'Gravy?'

'Thanks, but not on the chips. OK, not to worry.'

Connie put her tray on the counter and poured herself a glass of water. 'But they won't be medical doctors. They'll be doctors of management.'

'Vegetables?'

'A bit of everything, thanks. Not just management, I've suggested expanding the programme beyond business schools. So there will be doctors of nursing, psychiatry, anaesthesiology …'

'… and finance and law! And you will never double the number. Have you the faintest idea how many doctors there are in the NHS? The vegetarian lasagne, please.'

'Not enough, the public thinks. According to Ed, that's what matters. A bottle of the Rioja please, and two glasses. The one you've got on special.'

'Parmesan on the pasta?'

'Thanks.'

'Gravy?'

'No. Well, whatever Ed says, in my opinion it's mad.'

'That's what I think as well. But it works for Ed, so that's what's gone into our note. It's with the Prime Minister and Mark Topley overnight, and I've emailed it to Gyro and Dianne. I'm on call to discuss it with them later tonight, otherwise we could have gone to the Kings Arms.'

They grabbed a table.

'The Sea Horse is interesting, if you haven't been there. But look, did you get my message about tomorrow night?'

Ben nodded. 'Frank's. Sure. Early, you said – 6.30pm?'

'He's packing overnight and Thursday's a big day.'

'Too big! The thing about this Ed guy. He may be crazy, but I needed him to help me nail down the coffin lid on the idea of –' he mouthed the final words '– the Prime Minister coming.'

'Ed sees that's crazy?'

'Absolutely, I got him there in the end. Upset VIPs pushed out of the tower leaking stuff to the media, headlines like "gatecrasher".'

'Let's be grateful for small mercies. I tell you, I don't understand why at the top of organisations, there are so many crazies.'

'And arseholes. No, neither do I. Look, Connie, about Thursday night – you're coming to the tower opening?'

'After all this, wild horses wouldn't keep me away. Don't forget I'm coming in for the meeting with the bank manager as well. We've got to get to the bottom of Vanish's loan story.'

'You're right. You know afterwards there's a gala dinner. Not this stuff –' Ben gestured towards their plates '– fucking expensive caterers. Would you be my guest? Stay the night? When I started this job, I had no idea how much I would be celebrating getting out of here.'

'It's a dress-up?'

'Black tie or national dress.'

'Cool.'

'That's a yes?'

'It is.' Connie frowned. 'You asked me to look at this.'

'Oh yes. The file Greg gave Vanish on Frank. It was in his desk, where he said.'

Connie had folded the grey cardboard folder in half to fit it into her bag. She unfolded it, and riffled through the few sheets of notes it contained. 'Vanish was right, it's rubbish.

There's nothing there, other than enough to want me to march Greg towards the nearest psychiatric hospital.' She picked out one note. 'He claims that for two months he regularly went through Frank's rubbish. Every Thursday he would put the sack in the back of the Lexus and take it home.'

'He found nothing, I guess.'

'Once.' Connie read from one of the notes. 'Three pieces of electrical wiring in different colours, between two- and three-metres long. Each piece had melted at one end.' She closed the folder. They were sitting side by side; she turned to face Ben directly. 'All it tells me is that you don't have to be mad to work here but it helps. Who the hell does Greg think he is, anyway? What they did to Frank yesterday was unbelievable, but Greg is just an amoeba: it was Gyro who made all that happen. Frank kept asking questions which Gyro didn't want asked, and now he's got rid of him.'

'It looks like that,' Ben agreed. 'We'll find out a lot tomorrow.'

'This place must be getting to me, but I'm beginning to wonder if Vanish was right? The bank manager, Roger Sling – from what you said he was quite agitated to get a meeting quickly.'

'He was.'

'And Gyro's come back from Hong Kong empty-handed? Again?'

'It seems so. Mind you, I'm in the dog-house at the moment, so he might not tell me. He could be holding back to make a big splash tomorrow.'

Connie thought for a minute and shook her head. 'No. He might not tell you, and he might plan to wow us all tomorrow with how many millions and from whom. But he would have put an email round the governors telling us to expect an announcement tomorrow. For one thing, he knows how to keep us on-board. For another, he couldn't keep it all to himself; talk about a big mouth and an ego to match.'

'I agree,' said Ben. 'But don't forget the other side. He's brought more money – real money, not just talk – into this place than all his predecessors put together. And tomorrow, more top CEOs are going to remember Hampton than ever before – more by a long way. That's a return on my investment in a Hampton MBA. As a governor, you've got to be in favour of that.'

Connie gave Ben a quick kiss. 'I'm in favour of you finding out what you want to be. Then I can decide what I think about you.'

WEDNESDAY 20 JUNE

Sixth Rule of Good Luck: Sometimes, even under the seemingly right conditions, Good Luck doesn't arrive. Look for the seemingly unnecessary but indispensable conditions in the small details.

ALEX ROVIRA and FERNANDO TRIAS DE BES[5]

Greg uncoiled out of the turn at the end of his 35th length. He was enclosed from neck-to-toe in his speedsuit, an eliminator of friction in aquamarine, turquoise, orange and purple, and he swam like the teeming life of the Barrier Reef. But even tomorrow, the height of summer and the longest day, compared to Australia the British sea and sky would be pallid, as if wartime rationing had never ended. Quite possibly a department of the British government issued sunshine coupons, and the sun only came out when people had collected enough.

In terms of big battles, he had won. Thanks exclusively to his persistent observation and decisive action, Frank would be gone by noon tomorrow, and with him the biggest threat to the college – or, if the Prime Minister came, to the security of the state. And the upstart Ben, though not down and out, had

[5] *Good Luck: Create the Conditions for Success in Life & Business*, Jossey-Bass, San Francisco (2004)

been put in something closer to his proper place. A moment of achievement to savour. By the time he reached length 39, Greg had summarised his position like this: an outsider, an unseeded nobody still in his early twenties, had just come through a bloody first set and won 7-5. However, that was only the first set.

To calm down after his triumph, last night Greg had re-read one of his favourite writers, Eckhart Tolle. Tolle held up this example: A man won an expensive car in a lottery; in response to his friends telling him how lucky he was, he replied, 'Maybe'. A few weeks later in his car he was involved in a terrible crash, and ended up in hospital; in response to his friends telling him how unlucky he was, he replied, 'Maybe'. While he was in hospital the slope on which his house stood collapsed into the sea. Again the man's response to the good or bad fortune in his circumstances was, 'Maybe'.

In this way, Greg taught himself as he reached length 43 that the more advanced response to his successful removal of Frank was, 'Maybe'. Maybe there remained somewhere in the college small details that his acute observation had missed. For example, if Ben was Frank's plant and back-up, then the obvious place for Frank to hide the contents of the boathouse while still keeping them close to hand was in Ben's room. How could Greg have missed that? But what other details might still be escaping him?

The college's swimming pool had been enhanced as a millennium project, the only modernisation of significance during the pre-Gyro era. Now the changing rooms were entered through an atrium and the pool had been reconceived as an overflowing bath or infinity pool. The millennial significance of these developments weighed with Hampton's then-dean sufficiently for his pleas to alumni to produce £186,000 – at the time a sum unheard-of in the college's fund-raising.

As he towelled himself dry, Greg felt a chill down his spine. For months Gyro had mocked the possibility of the Prime Minister coming tomorrow, but all that time Dianne had been confident that it would happen. Any minute now she might be proved right. If she was right, and had known months ago that she would be right, then (indisputably) she had the foreknowledge to present a very serious threat to the life of the nation.

The person on the inside of the college, Greg reminded himself, need not be the hit-man or a suicide bomber. The insider needed only to leave unlocked a door which should be locked, pass on a police patrol schedule which should not have been passed on, or infiltrate a name onto the guest list.

As he walked out of the building towards the main car park, he crossed a grassy knoll. He made a promise. If the Prime Minister was coming, Greg's country would not find him wanting. He added Dianne to the list of possible suspects. If the Prime Minister was coming, the opening arrangements would have to be changed. The first tell-tale clue to her intentions, a small detail for which he would watch, would be how closely she positioned herself to the Prime Minister in the revised plan.

Dianne's hair appointment was at 10am in Kew. Giancarlo's drug habit had gotten so bad that once she had emerged with arrestable dandruff, but she always returned for special occasions. Only one word could describe the expression Greg read on her face: triumph. As soon as the Lexus pulled out of the college car park, she dialled a direct line at the House of Commons. 'We're on. The Prime Minister. Tomorrow.'

Greg recognised the voice of Mark Topley on the speakerphone. 'What a star – you've done it! What happened? You know how keen the Prime Minister is on do-gooding in Africa.'

'That's off, entirely off. The Chinese have launched some laser from space diverting half of the Zambezi and saving millions of lives. From the British point of view it's a total disaster. The last thing anyone wants now is pictures suggesting that a few Land Rovers is all we could come up with.'

'So now Thursday and Friday are blank in the Number Ten diary.' Topley groaned. 'It will be awful. He'll have a round of catch-up meetings with every department. Best get my retaliation in first and call in sick.'

'Well, you are the Minister of Health. Now listen, I've come up with a solution to the logistics which I think you'll like. I was up half the night doing it. Gyro will be in the tower with Junior and his guests. The Prime Minister won't go into the tower. We're saying it's because of his busy schedule, although in fact it's because the tower will be full. Instead, a few minutes after seven he will arrive by helicopter at the lakeside where you, I and a BBC camera crew will greet him. Oh, and Alex – Alex Bakhtin.

'The PM will make the announcement to camera with the tower in the background, and then fly straight out again.

There will be excellent pictures of you, and because the visit publicises the opening Pinnacle Junior will be flattered. But he's not upstaged and his guests are not pushed out.'

'What can I say? You're a genius.'

'To be honest, it was an elementary solution which should not have needed my attention to achieve. However, I'm not carping because Number Ten are orgasmic about our young man's proposal for sexing up the announcement.'

'That's brilliant as well. I'm sure he caught it from you. Kiss, kiss.'

'Don't forget you'll need an afternoon shave. I'm not going to all this trouble to have you turn up with five o'clock shadow.'

Greg thumped the steering wheel in admiration as Dianne ended the call. 'You said all along it would happen, Mrs D, and you were right.'

'Thank you, Greg. It's nice to feel appreciated by somebody.' Dianne had dressed casually for the hairdresser: teal jacket, white silk T-shirt and jeans with miniature diamonds in the stitching. Her right hand landed on Greg's thigh. 'And someone appreciates you, too. Don't think all your swimming goes unnoticed.'

'Thanks, Mrs D.' Greg kept his eyes on the road while he thought – this woman! Had he ever met anyone like her? Dianne never lost focus. Dianne always got what Dianne wanted – one hundred percent. His challenge was to work out what she wanted now. Was it him, or was she flattering to distract? To distract him in particular from the possibility that she might be a threat to the Prime Minister?

'Now we've got confirmation, it's all hands on deck as

regards security.' Dianne's hand returned to her own deck. 'Get Vanessa to book a car to collect me at 12.30, would you? Chief Inspector Haddrill wants you back at the college for a site security meeting at 11.00. He thinks you're a key player.'

Greg stiffened with pleasure but still he needed to check his idea. After all, it was only a theory.

'So will you be on telly, Mrs D? Standing next to the Prime Minister?'

'I should think so, Greg. I'll be his host, welcoming him to Hampton. Because the dean will be in the tower, I'll be representing all of us.'

How's that for a credible threat, thought Greg as he pulled up in front of Giancarlo's – the British Prime Minister blown up on national television. The bomb would be in her handbag. Except that he, Greg, would be there to save the day.

Greg raced back to the college at well over any relevant speed limits. He needed to do this more often (which meant when he wasn't carrying any passengers). Otherwise he would lose the high-speed skills he had gained at the police college. Graduating fifth meant he had been selected for two weeks of capture-evasion training in Utah. Live on the edge – or atrophy. Back at college he had one thing to do before joining Haddrill's meeting: check Ben's room for contraband.

On the day before the opening Ben was up to his eyeballs in work. The receptionist knew Greg well and lent him a duplicate keycard without thinking twice about it; Greg said he had a package to deliver that Ben wanted in his room. Greg dismissed the need to worry about disturbing tell-tales such as hairs placed across drawers or wardrobe doors since Ben could not know whether they had been moved by the cleaner.

The room was bare, with Ben's few clothes, a hired dinner suit and some shirts, and socks tossed in the corner to be washed. There weren't even any depressions in the carpet suggestive of the heavy equipment Greg had seen in the boathouse having been stored temporarily.

The 11am meeting took place in the staff room, which was being co-opted as security central. Once a spacious room, Gyro had taken a large bite out of it for servers and switches to run the college's expanded computer network. In a process of humiliation, handsome armchairs had moved out and the space that was left had become a miscellaneous clutter. In the corner sat bottles of tap-water purified by abracadabra, pump-flasks of conference tea and coffee and offerings of milk from plastic cows.

Ben's notepad was buckling under the scrawled weight of a week's intensive activity. Next to Ben was Haddrill, who had brought with him two uniformed officers, introduced as Inspector Walker and Sergeant Lomas. All three were in shirt sleeves, in Haddrill's case complete with three-star shoulder tabs. Haddrill's peaked cap lying on the table in front of him was one of two signals that with the Prime Minister's confirmed involvement, the game had gone up several notches. The other signal was Amelia Henderson. Haddrill introduced the two of them as strangers, which Greg had expected.

Haddrill chaired the meeting, but seemingly by Amelia's permission.

'Obviously we expect a happy, trouble-free occasion to celebrate the opening of a new building and a century of success for a highly respected business,' Haddrill began. 'I stress this point because there remains a considerable VIP aspect to tomorrow. While that underlines the need for rigorous security, I want all officers on checkpoints fully conscious that they are not herding cattle.' Ben nodded vigorously.

'Lomas will be in charge of armed protection. Obviously now we will have checkpoints on both roads into the college. There will be two armed officers at each, two at our mobile command post in the college, two at the lakeside landing point, and two on the tower terrace. I'm afraid the terrace will need to be out of bounds to all guests.' Ben nodded again and made a note. While they had hoped to let guests roam on the terrace, capacity had been calculated on the basis that everyone would be inside the auditorium for speeches.

'Ben. Greg. Tomorrow we would like the two of you plugged into our local communications network from noon onwards. We won't be bothering you with all our messages – ' Haddrill smiled politely, meaning that the police would retain separate secure communications '– but it will mean we can reach either of you immediately in the event of any unexpected situation with arriving guests.

'When the opening gets formally underway in the evening, Ben will need to be with the dean in the tower so Greg, we would like you to be at the lakeside. In fact, Greg, a priority after this meeting will be for you and me to decide the helicopter landing site. We have to bear in mind security, accessibility and the need for a camera angle to the tower in the background.'

'No worries.' Greg turned slightly to look at Amelia who gave the barest of nods. Haddrill's plan meant that he would be separated from Ben at the critical time. However, Greg would be close to the Prime Minister and Dianne. What harm could Ben achieve inside the auditorium with armed guards on the terrace and the Prime Minister several hundred metres away? Greg kept his eyes peeled for any sign of discomfiture from Ben at Haddrill's plan, but there was none.

Inspector Walker rustled his maps of the grounds. 'Our guess at the best landing is here –' he pointed to the grassy area at the foot of Crassock which was usually used for overflow parking '– while we create some alternative overflow parking behind the student accommodation block. But obviously you know the area and we don't.'

Haddrill resumed his flow. 'This afternoon Inspector Walker will need your help, Greg, to prioritise search areas. We don't have the men or the dogs to search all the woods in the valley, but with your knowledge of the grounds we can make smart choices.' He paused. 'Obviously this will mean some interruption of your normal duties.'

Ben leaned forward. 'I've already discussed that with the dean, Chief Inspector. Dean Gyro is adamant that in these rather rushed circumstances the college must offer you unstinting co-operation. Greg knows these grounds better than anyone else. For obvious reasons Dean Gyro and his wife will not be doing much travelling over the next 48 hours and where necessary we can book local taxis.'

Greg sat up, visibly taller. His crucial role was being recognised. Had Amelia talked to Haddrill behind the scenes?

As if he sensed the question Haddrill added, 'Implicit in all these arrangements, and indeed in the two of you sitting here in this conversation, is that a certain amount of work has been done on your backgrounds. Which, I am delighted to say, has proved entirely positive. We regard you as being on our team.'

Greg tried to look serious while grinning broadly. Lulling Ben into a false sense of security was an excellent strategy, the kind he would have suggested himself.

Sergeant Lomas unfolded a large-scale map of the college buildings and their surroundings, which had been divided into differently coloured sectors. 'Because of the number of contractors, cooks, waiters and so forth, as well as temporary guests, from 3pm tomorrow we envisage operating a colour-coded sector perimeter system.

'Anyone without the right coloured lapel pin for the sector they are in will be challenged. The two of you, Professor Gyro, Dr Peach-Gyro and a handful of other individuals will have pins giving you complete access. I need hardly stress that, no matter what happens tomorrow, on no account give or lend your pin to anyone else.'

If Greg could have brimmed any more with pride he would have wet himself. But every drop of pride brought with it a pill of responsibility. Under the table he wiped the palms of his hands on his trousers.

'Finally, Ms Henderson, your department. I regard it as a great honour to have your personal involvement.'

Amelia opened a slim document case and took out three sheets of paper. She smiled briefly at Ben and Greg. 'Perhaps I should explain that my department is rather back room – risk management. Chief Inspector Haddrill is, and will be throughout tomorrow, the commander in charge.' She focussed on Ben. 'From the information that your people provided yesterday we have noted certain points.

'You have one lecturer who comes from Iraq and was politically active there. He has joined a trade union here though he is not yet politically active. You also have a student on your advanced project management course who has a connection with the rather large Saudi bin Laden family. And you have a woman student from Palestine, a pharmacist studying financial management. Of course, pharmacy presumes some understanding of chemistry. We will be making inquiries and keeping the situation under active review.'

'The college needs to do nothing?' asked Ben.

'Nothing is precisely what we need the college to do. Or say. Other than advise Chief Inspector Haddrill of any guest changes, staff or contractor sickness – anything like that – without delay.'

Haddrill summed up. 'To conclude, in talking to your colleagues, the cover story for tomorrow's heightened security arrangements is a surprise visit by the French Minister for Industry. After all, this is an international business school.' Haddrill smiled. 'It is also our standard procedure to avoid attracting unwanted attention. The experts –' he gestured towards Amelia '– are confident that no-one in their right mind, or out of it, could be bothered to attack a French

Minister for Industry. It's a pleasure to be working with you, gentlemen. I think we've covered all the details. Tomorrow will be a long day.'

Half an hour later Greg was standing next to Haddrill in the grass meadows on the north side of the lake, not far from where Connie had held her birthday picnic. A few cirrus clouds raced high above. They had already visited a couple of other sites but, in Haddrill's view, this was by some margin the best location. There was enough flat space for the helicopter, with a clear line of sight for the television camera to the top of the tower.

Haddrill had put on sunglasses. He pointed inquiringly at the three pairs of semi-detached houses where the treeline met the road a few minutes' walk above them.

'Houses for some academic staff,' Greg explained. 'You know about Frank, but he will be gone by noon tomorrow.'

Henderson gestured. 'We'll search the others this afternoon. Tomorrow afternoon we'll search the woods over there.' He pointed across the lake towards the southwest, near the boathouses. 'Tomorrow's forecast is like today's – fine, nearly cloudless. The angle of the early evening sun and the problem of reflection in the lake means if I were going to plant a sniper, it would be there. You did a good job with Frank. I look forward to working with you tomorrow.'

Greg was exultant – this was the real thing. This was the happiest day of his life, the happier for its implication of greater things to come. When Haddrill had gone, Greg stayed behind to soak up the view. He lit incense and let the car radio browse. After some Vivaldi it moved onto one of Handel's anthems. He turned up the volume on the six car speakers, left the door open and sat on the grass. The aroma of Emperor orchids, his favourite incense, was the aroma of heaven. Like kings down the centuries, Greg surveyed the place where his hand would tomorrow slay the enemy.

Unlike anything he had heard before, *Zadok the Priest* began with an interminable waiting, which for Greg was erotic. At first like a stream rushing this way and that over pebbles, and then broadening, becoming a river, and then a lake like the one in front of him; but always waiting, waiting for something which would complete it.

Tomorrow the Prime Minister would come by helicopter. He thought back to his own helicopter trip over the lake with Casey Pinnacle seven days ago. Now the lake's end – the end of waiting – hurtled towards him, and as he went over, the end turned into cliffs. For a while he hung effortlessly, floating like a rainbow above a shocking abyss from which the choir's voices thundered. The words rose up to him like a fine mist, and he wrapped himself in them as had every English king claiming his divine right at every coronation since 1727, 'Zadok the priest and Nathan the prophet anointed Solomon king. And all the people rejoiced …'

The music entered him. It seduced him. For nearly three centuries, it seemed to say, I have wasted away until this day in your life when I found and crowned you. *I have only existed to express the meaning of this day.*

BOOK TWO

THE OPENING

THE OPENING

(ƆNINЯOW) ʏ⅃nſ 6 ʏʌᗡNOW

BEN

She's from Inverness. She's holding her hands open; the hands say "trust me". 'It's about learning everything we can learn from the worst breach in national security since the Cold War. It's as simple as that. If you're frightened, don't be.'

I'm not frightened but Connie is, a bit. We've been to the best lawyer I came across when I worked in Alex's office and he says the agreements are watertight.

Amelia Henderson says this in her office. It's an easy five-minute walk from the underground station at Temple. Connie and I came out of the tube to be swept along in the 8.45am crowd of lawyers and legal assistants. But they headed north for the Royal Courts of Justice or the legal hive nearby, while we walked hand-in-hand beside the River Thames to this town house. A summer shower threatened.

Beyond Amelia's desk I look across the river towards the Oxo Tower, the South Bank and the London Eye. Amelia invites us to settle into comfortable armchairs. A widescreen television is bracketed on the wall between two bookshelf-size speakers; opposite is a plain, government-issue wall clock.

Amelia's desk is clear except for a remote control and an A4 notebook. The pages look to be a 50-50 mixture of virgin and heavily written-in.

A lady called Fatima brings in plunger coffee, a pot of tea and some milk. Felt lining around the door's edges means closing the door is not a casual job.

'Sound-proofing,' Amelia explains. 'We'll be sharing classified material with you which we don't want just anyone to hear. May I?'

'I'll have tea, please,' says Connie.

Amelia pours. 'Ben?'

She and I both choose coffee.

'The fact you're going to be shown classified material is another reason, on top of the assurances you have received, why you've got nothing to fear. We're here to learn together. I'm sure you've got some things you'd like to understand better about what happened.'

Connie and I both nod. You could say that again, I'm thinking.

Amelia laughs and opens her notebook. 'So, any questions before we begin?'

It all happened less than two weeks ago but it seems so much longer. Will our memories be up to it? I'm still holding Connie's hand. Her nervousness hasn't abated much. Why not emphasise the safety barriers once again? 'Our lawyer has taken us through this, but –' I say as I glance around '– I imagine you're recording this –'

Amelia nods slightly, and immediately I realise that lack of memory is not going to be the problem, but the flood of too much. Until now I hadn't remembered the tiny nod she gave when we first met, in the security-planning meeting at Hampton. Now I realise she was nodding to Greg. It's all there and, frankly, unforgettable. I continue, '– perhaps for the record?'

I expect Amelia to grasp the point and she does. 'Good idea. So, you have full immunity from prosecution. The Crown will not penalise you in any way for anything you say during these sessions, or make public any part of it without your agreement.' Her stance softens. 'So if it was you who ripped the ear off Tommy's teddy-bear, or you've got some money under a mattress which the taxman doesn't know about, now's the time to tell mama. Anything more serious than that and I will definitely have lost my job, but you will be fine.'

We both pass up the opportunity.

'We need both of you to speak completely freely, or the truth will escape us all – forever. We want you to spark off each other's memories. If you were being investigated, you would be interviewed separately.

'You're free to leave whenever you want. However, you may not make notes, record or disclose what I tell you, or any classified material that I show you. We're under the Official Secrets Act.'

Connie rallies and we drop hands. 'How long do you want us for?'

'I'm pretty sure just the day,' Amelia replies. 'But probably a long day. We really appreciate your help.

'I want to start with the dinner at Frank's place on the night before the opening. That's the last time – almost – anyone talked to Frank. His last supper.' Amelia presses buttons on the remote control, as if keying in a number. A still of Frank's semi fills the screen with his Toyota 4-wheel drive parked in front. I guess from the digits in the corner of the frame that the picture was taken on 22 June, the day after the opening.

'I'll start with some nuts-and-bolts questions, if that's OK. Thinking about quite specific things like cars and tables quite often jogs other, more important memories back into the mind. So Frank's car – it was there when you arrived?'

Connie sits up. 'I arrived about twenty minutes before Ben. Yes, the car was there.'

'So far as you could see, packed, half-full or empty?'

'Empty. I remember thinking he was behind with his packing.'

With luck we will find answering Amelia's questions less stressful than worrying about answering them.

Connie carries on, 'When I was inside the house I could see things – papers mainly – were in a mess. Frank hadn't started properly packing at all. He said he was going to stay up all night to do it. He said he didn't want to serve supper surrounded by bare walls and packing crates.'

I add, 'Of course, we couldn't see any packing crates. I guess we assumed they were stacked in a bedroom. In fact, it was thanks to the packing that I mentioned the Prime Minister.' Connie shoots me a sideways glance but I think the only thing which makes sense is to take Amelia at her word – play things straight.

'How did the Prime Minister come up?' Amelia asks.

I explain. 'Frank kept saying he would be packing all night

because he had to be out of the college by noon. Gyro had insisted on that when he fired him on Tuesday.'

Connie interjects, 'But he only agreed to go if Gyro got the pay-off money into his bank account by Wednesday, and Frank told us they did. He said he wouldn't put it past the college and the bank to be in cahoots to snatch it back, so he withdrew it as a banker's draft and sent it to his brother to look after.'

I expect Amelia to ask how much the pay-off is – £50,000 Frank told us – but she doesn't. She must know that already from his bank records. Anyway, I resume: 'So I said noon now really is noon, because guess who's coming to the party? The Prime Minister.'

Amelia leans forward. 'Frank was surprised? Or he knew already, would you say?'

I say, 'He seemed as surprised as anything. I'd swear it was genuine.'

Connie agrees. 'In fact he couldn't believe it. He kept asking why. When you said you had dreamt up this scheme to double the number of doctors in the NHS, the three of us just laughed and laughed. In fact, do you remember, Frank fell off the settee.'

Connie and I giggle. Good, she's relaxing.

Amelia changes the line of questioning. 'What was Frank wearing?'

Connie nods. 'A Ramones T-shirt – an old one. Scruffy jeans. Bare feet, I think. I noticed because it looked like the same T-shirt he was wearing the day before.'

Amelia gives Connie a friendly we-women-notice-these-things smile before clicking the remote a couple of times. These are stills from different angles of Frank's living/dining area, much as it had been on the night. However, instead of the large painting there is now dust and an unfaded rectangle of wall, the size of a coffee table. 'Any particular memories here?'

We point together, 'The turntable.' I continue, 'A Rega. Frank lectured us quite a bit about it while we pretended to be ignorant digital bunnies. The finest in the world, he said, made in Westcliff-on-Sea in 1979. When Phil Spector worked with the Ramones.'

Connie's pointing. 'We talked about that photo on the mantelpiece. He sang at university, and then for a year semi-professionally.'

It's a black-and-white studio shot of three men in their early twenties, all in slim-line dinner jackets and holding eight-inch cigarette holders. Frank is sitting on a chair the wrong way round and looking straight into the camera. The other two are to either side behind him, one looking forward and up, the other in profile, looking at 90 degrees to the camera. Frank explained it had been a kind of impoverished Three Tenors.

'Was he maudlin? Had he been drinking before you arrived?'

Connie shakes her head. 'Not maudlin, just reminiscing. To judge by the bottle, he'd had one glass of champagne before we arrived. He certainly hadn't had a bottle and a glass.'

'And he drank how much before you left?'

'How much did we get through?' Connie asks.

'Two bottles,' I remember. 'The champagne was whatever

was on special offer when he bought it, but with dinner there was the Smith Haut Lafitte. That was an amazing white; he'd kept it for a special occasion. We were having duck but amazing wines stand up to whatever you throw at them. He could have spent a hundred pounds on it easily. We knocked back the two bottles pretty evenly between the three of us.'

Connie snorts. 'I don't think so! Put me down for one glass of each – I drove home, remember. Between the two of you, yes, that was pretty even.'

'So had Frank cooked the duck, or was it a store-bought job?'

'Very special! Home-cooked Peking duck in my honour.'

'Very nice. Meaning because you're Chinese?'

'Yes, but mainly because I'd become a college governor. Frank was big on me picking up the mantle of awkward question-asker.'

'What about drugs, either that evening or to your general knowledge? Because of what happened to his body, we're blind on that side of things.' Amelia purses her lips at the indelicacy of 'his body'.

I take that one. 'No, nothing. I mean, he was getting through roll-ups in his usual way, maybe a bit faster. But only tobacco. No funny trips to the bathroom or mirrors on the coffee table.'

'So,' says Amelia. 'This is the last object I need to ask about.' The slide shows the painting that had been on Frank's wall, but it doesn't capture the texture of the original. In the foreground are two bare feet seen from above, as if hanging off the side of a boat. The texturing of skin, veins, nails and dirt in creams and browns is infinitely fine.

Beneath is the sea painted in shades of grey, layer upon layer, tangible and shadowed. Deep down in one part of the sea there is a white luminescence, varying from pallid to intense. While the water's ripples make the shape of the luminescence hard to describe, it's too long and thin to be a reflection of the moon – it's closer to a slit. A tiny trickle of blood dribbles from one foot into the luminescence.

Connie shakes her head. 'I know this is important so I've thought about it a lot. The painting is how he gets me to come back to his house on Thursday afternoon. But I'm the one who says very early in the dinner, out of the blue really, that I really like the painting. I don't know why I do, it's not by anybody I've heard of, but something about it just feels like Frank. I felt a twinge the first time I saw it. But there's no way he knew in advance that I would say that.'

'The painting felt like Frank then, or feels like him now?' Amelia wonders.

'Both. He said the artist called the painting *Jaws II*, but he hated that. Frank's far more – I don't know? enigmatic? – and gentle than the idea of a shark. Before, I think it was as simple as the idea of hidden depths that made me connect the painting with him. Now, I'm thinking *Jaws II* was a better title than Frank gave credit for. Not a shark's jaws, more like the jaws of truth, waiting to explode out of the picture and grab you.'

I start to see something I hadn't seen before. 'Connie, you said you really liked the painting early in the dinner, but it's much later that Frank offers it to you. That only comes when you've explained you're going to gate-crash Gyro's meeting with the bank manager, but will then need to change into your dinner outfit.'

Connie says to me, 'I was assuming I'd borrow your room.' She is not sure whether an explanation is required so she turns to Amelia. 'My MSc class finished on Wednesday and I didn't have my own room any more.'

I've got a point and I'm running with it. 'That's when Frank jumps in and says come and change at his house. It's at the end of dinner; we're going soon. He's keen, grabbing the spare house keys out of the bowl and giving them to you. You're hesitating so he says he'll leave the painting for you all wrapped up, ready to take away. So you say thank you very much, you'll come round in the car about three, let yourself in, pick up the painting and change.' I look up excitedly. 'He could have given Connie the painting right then, at dinner – instead, he made up this stuff about wrapping it. I mean, it's not as if the painting needs wrapping because it's valuable?' I look at Amelia for confirmation.

'It's worth about four hundred pounds. Not a lot, really.' Amelia sucks on her pen. 'So by the end of dinner he wants you, Connie, to come by on the next afternoon. Ben's point is that Frank didn't have that plan at the beginning of dinner, or he would have said something as soon as you talked about the picture.'

Connie asks Amelia, 'Will I be able to have the picture?'

'Of course, I'll get it delivered next week. We've scanned it every which way: it's got no hidden treasure, I'm afraid. You're both doing ever so well, if I may say so, but shall we take a short break?'

CONNIE

Ben is getting on much better with all this, I can see. For him, it's like saddling up for a hunt. The fact that Frank is the object of the hunt doesn't seem to bother him much. But there's another reason, I've been noticing. Between Ben and Amelia there's a kind of masters-of-the-universe bonding. She's very senior, a lot more senior than she gives off, and Ben likes that. Being in charge, in control, foreseeing things, making difficult calls, taking decisions – he thinks that's what he's born to do. I don't. Anyway, that's what I'm thinking as Amelia kicks off round two.

Amelia's changed her interview plan (or she says she has). 'Let's run with the idea we had when we left off, that something happens during dinner which makes Frank want something he hadn't thought of at the start – which is getting you, Connie, to come to his house on Thursday afternoon. So think about the subjects that came up during dinner. What mattered to him? More exactly, what does he find out that he didn't already know – besides the fact that the Prime Minister is coming?'

I know where this is going, but we can't get there right away. It will be painful enough when we do. Ben doesn't see any of this. No wonder he's not stressed.

There's an obvious safe place to start, so I take it. 'Frank talked quite a bit about his brother and his brother's family, didn't he Ben? That was new to me. He felt very deeply about them.

'For a few minutes we talk about family. To judge by the photographs in the living room as well as what he said, Frank didn't have any family of his own – no partner, no children, no step-children. However, he has a brother who has a six-year-old with Down's syndrome.'

Amelia moves us on. 'That was sad news to the two of you, but it wasn't news to Frank. It builds up our picture of him but I don't see Frank's mind changing because of it.'

We lapse into silence for a minute. It won't be long before Ben, the keen 30-year-old, comes up with something.

He does. I can count on him. 'His academic paper, Connie. You asked him which one he was proudest of. He kept putting you off but you kept pushing.'

It's true. So what if I can't understand academic stuff, this is his life's work! Of course I pushed. Eventually he disappeared and came back with a 30-page, double-spaced typescript and told us about it. 'It was a study he did in his twenties, quite soon after he switched from physics. He used a very radical methodology to estimate what pay was really necessary to motivate CEOs. After all, they have so many other motivations – power, celebrity, flattery and so on,' I recount.

'And the opportunity to deal with challenges, which are really important,' Ben cuts in. 'It's not all selfish.'

'Agreed.' I continue, 'Anyway, Frank got very excited about the conclusion of his paper. Remember he was early in his career then, and he thought this was going to make his name in management research. His analysis suggested that most large company CEOs don't need to be paid anything at all; in fact many of them have so much money, *they* would pay the company to be given the role. However, they have to be seen to be super-heroes worth gigabucks. So Frank concluded that CEO pay should be set by secret auction: the company pays them a fortune but they bid against each other for how much they will give back to the company secretly.'

'What happened?' asks Amelia.

Ben takes up the story. 'No journal would accept his paper. He tried for years. They said his methodology was too fanciful, but what he concluded was they were scared of the answer. He thought business schools had sold out the quest for truth in favour of the quest for business approval.'

'And money,' I add.

Amelia leans back in her chair and stares at the ceiling. 'The problem –'

Ben stands up. His arms are moving vigorously. 'I know what you're going to say. The problem is, once again, we're talking about something which clearly mattered to Frank a lot, and which is news to us. But nothing about it changes during dinner.'

'You have it in a nutshell,' says Amelia.

Ben says, 'So maybe something happened when I push him on what he's been doing in the boathouse.' At last! 'It bugged me why he was lying about it, but my questions didn't get me anywhere. Still, maybe something clicked inside his head, because I remember now he got a bit rattled and came back at me on something completely different – a blatant switch of subject.'

Amelia says, 'That's interesting. What was the subject?'

Ben says, 'I'm not sure – the main thing is it had nothing to do with the boathouse.'

I say, 'Bakhtin.'

'Oh yes,' says Ben, 'he asked me if I had heard what Bakhtin had done to Connie's business.'

I explain to Amelia, 'I was human resources director in a medium-sized plastic packaging business before I decided to join the NHS. We got torpedoed and went under with all hands. Ben, you had better finish the story, I think.'

He does. 'I said I had heard something, but it's a large group and Bakhtin expects his businesses to operate very independently. I said I was in an analytical role at headquarters. What do headquarters people ever know about what's going on?'

BEN

Amelia is going to ask me about my lie, I'm sure of it. But instead she glances at the clock. 'My goodness, look at the time!' she exclaims. 'Let's turn to how dinner ends. Who decides it's time to go rather than have another drink?'

'I do. I apologise that it's only half past nine, but I have a hell of a day coming up.'

Connie says, 'And Frank needs to pack. So I'm going to drop Ben back at the college and then head home. That's the way the conversation is going.'

'And then?' Amelia asks.

Connie says, 'And then Frank wishes the two of us all the best in our future lives. He's kind of speaking to us as if we were a couple. At least that's how I remember it.' She looks at me.

I nod. Is she anxious once more? I think it's just a tear in her eye because we're remembering a goodbye moment. 'Frank fetches a poem and reads it to us. He says it's his favourite. It's how he says goodbye. He gives me a hug, and Connie a peck on the cheek and we go.'

'To your separate beds?'

I think, that's a bit personal, isn't it?

'Yes,' says Connie. 'Ben hadn't had much sleep that week and was yawning his head off. And I had to look through my wardrobe at home for something to wear to the gala dinner.'

'What's the poem? More importantly, what do you think Frank is saying in the poem?' Amelia looks expectant.

I say, 'I hadn't heard it before. I don't remember the words, but I thought it was a bit romantic. Like wishing us luck as a couple. It was a very simple poem, a bit like that song Doris Day sings, "Que Sera, Sera".'

Connie kicks me hard. 'You idiot, you're unbelievable!' She looks up at the ceiling. 'What is the point of men?'

She turns to Amelia. 'It's a poem by Erich Fried, originally in German, called *What It Is*. I think Frank's talking about the kind of love that has the courage to be honest. Frank dedicated his life to truth, to seeking out the truth.'

'I agree about Frank, but not about the poem,' I say.

'Let's listen to it, shall we?' Amelia says. She presses buttons on the remote. The screen goes blank. We hear background noises and then Frank is speaking.

Connie screams.

I jump out of my skin. 'You bugged Frank's house?' I exclaim, shocked.

Frank recites:

> *It is nonsense, says reason*
> *It is what it is, says love*
> *It is misfortune, says calculation*
> *It is nothing but pain, says fear*
> *It is hopeless, says insight*
> *It is what it is, says love*
>
> *It is laughable, says pride*
> *It is frivolous, says caution*
> *It is impossible, says experience*
> *It is what it is, says love*

When he's finished, Amelia plays with the remote and gives another of her nods. 'In Frank's case we were rather late into the bugging game. Unfortunately, he didn't call anyone or talk to himself, which is a shame, so the dinner party is our prize exhibit. Classified, as I told you.'

'Why ask us about the dinner when you have it all on tape?' Connie is nearly hysterical.

'Because we don't have it all on tape. I'm not talking about sound quality – technology can clean up the words. What the technology can't tell us is what the words mean.

What the poem meant, for example. As we've just seen, it meant different things to the two of you.'

'You're checking up on us, whether we're being honest.'

Amelia stands up. 'In part. After lunch we're going to talk about what happened on Thursday. For most of that we'll only have your word for it; we only have audio for one bit.'

'When I come back to Frank's house,' Connie says, quietening down.

'Exactly. So if the two of you had decided to play some peculiar game, we would have saved ourselves a lot of bother.'

'That's hilarious, *you* talking about us playing a peculiar game!'

I'm looking at Connie, wondering if we are going to walk out and not come back. Amelia looks at us and says, 'I've been completely honest with you. I think, curiously enough, that is what Frank would have wanted. Would you like to know what I think his goodbye poem is about?'

That's an unexpected offer. After a while, Connie nods.

'For me it's about what he's going to do the next day. It's nonsense, it's misfortune, it's pain, it's hopeless, it's laughable, it's frivolous and it's impossible – but it is what it is.'

The room goes very quiet. We all sit down. Amelia offers us the chance to remember how the dinner party actually ends – what Frank says after the poem. We say yes. She's on the remote for the last time before lunch.

Frank says, 'You take care. It's all going to work out fine.' He's talking to Connie as he gives me a hug. 'And you look after him.' Then he is giving Connie a kiss, and patting her pocket to make sure she's got the spare keys to his house.

'Stay overnight tomorrow if you want. I'll put out some clean sheets. As I recall, the beds in the student rooms are singles.'

Someone like me is a bit drunk and says, 'Have you been in one? In your time here?'

'No comment,' Frank replies, laughing. 'No comment and not interesting.'

Someone like Connie says, 'We'll be the judge of that.'

Frank says, 'Come tomorrow and be the judge of everything.'

THURSDAY 21 JUNE (TO MID-AFTERNOON)

The tower opening day began as it would end, in magnificently clear light. Breakfast was offered in a college dining room filled with triangular blocks of the sun's nuclear energy and shade. A study group from one class was sitting by the windows; Ben and Vanessa were in the opposite corner for some privacy. A white van like every other in England pulled up outside.

Of all days, Ben began today as he meant to go on – in charge. He had asked Vanessa to join him for a working breakfast. Ben's choice was to keep things light and ready for action: working grapefruit segments, two working boiled eggs and some working toast. Escaping from Gyro's office and having breakfast cooked by somebody else were treats for Vanessa, and she was celebrating by having the full English, including kidneys. Both of them were studying the masterplan of the day – all coloured index tabs, annotations and timings down to the minute (I wish, thought Ben). But it was a terrific piece of work by Vanessa, and Ben told her so.

Ben and Vanessa were working through the list of outstanding problems. With his back to the other table, it was only by intermittent glances Ben realised two men and a woman he did not recognise were standing by the table of students.

Vanessa explained the latest problem, which had arisen overnight. 'The Maharishi Swami Tandoori wants us to fix a room.'

'Offer him a student room.' They had six to spare.

'He wants a suite.'

'Okay. The Kings Arms. I knew there was a reason I went there. Tell him they have an exquisite suite which is famous for its cuckoo clock.' One of the strangers was showing the students some sheets of official-looking paper.

'Good thinking, master. But not quite good enough. He wants us to provide a suite with two young women. Girls.'

Ben was confused. Young women? Girls? Was Hampton now some kind of brothel? A woman student stood up, left the group and went with the visitors. Ben saw the man in charge telling the group something like, this will just take a few minutes. The students were very polite, a credit to the college.

Vanessa explained the problem again.

'Oh shit,' says Ben. Improvise, improvise. 'Okay. Tell him we will arrange this. But hush-hush, with a very high-class agency. Top, top girls, like they use for Arab princes. Lay it on with a trowel. Do you think two girls will be enough?'

'You might have the experience to know, but I don't. I expect he would have asked for more if he needed more.' Vanessa was sucking the goodness out of a rasher of streaky bacon after dipping it in brown sauce.

'Tell him three girls. A blonde, a brunette and a redhead. They will come to his suite at the Kings Arms at 11pm. But in case of problems, I need his personal mobile number, on which I will leave the telephone number of the agency.'

'If you're expecting me to find this agency, forget it.'

'Vanessa, get with the programme. There is no fucking agency. It's just bullshit. But he won't find out until 11pm and that will get us through the tower opening. He's not going to write to Gyro about it to complain, is he? But make sure you make a big song-and-dance about getting his personal mobile number.'

After breakfast Ben headed off towards his office. He detoured to walk past the tower, which was ringed by security hired by the college. Tom and his engineers were making final checks. Tom's BMW and another white van were parked at the base of the tower.

The photograph on the flyers had not exaggerated: Luscious' waves of psychedelically-coloured hair resembled a Beatles album cover. She was in jeans and a busty long-sleeved polo neck while a security guard helped wheel her sound system into the lift. Tom waved and gave a thumbs up sign. Not looking where he was going, Ben walked into someone who had been on his mind a lot in the past week.

'Alex! I mean, Lord Bakhtin.'

'My goodness, Ben.' The visitor ran his eyes over Ben from the satin interior of a £5,000 hand-made suit. 'I had heard you were here. How is it all going?'

'Very well up to a point.'

'What point is that?'

'This point. The point of bumping into you.'

Alex's expression shifted slightly. 'But you are expecting me, I think. Certainly your security people had me on their list. They gave me a lovely pink lapel pin.'

Different coloured pins would admit to different areas; Ben had not yet picked up his. 'You fired me, you scheming coward. And you lied. You told me I was the best thing since sliced bread but you were lining up Charlie Driesman behind my back.'

Alex assessed the situation silently.

For Ben, nearly two weeks of bile was erupting. 'Come out with it, you bastard. What didn't I do that you wanted, you *selfless* git?'

'Be careful whom you accuse of lying, Ben. When I said you were the best, I wasn't lying. Some days Charlie hasn't got a clue and I could string him up; I never had a day like that with you.'

'Commitment, then? I didn't give you enough hours in the day? Eighteen hours a day, seven days a week, for how many years?'

'Oh, commitment. You were committed, Ben. Though these days everybody is committed – everybody who matters. It's a *sine qua non*, not a competitive advantage. We're at a business school, aren't we, so let's put some of their expensively taught concepts to use.'

'What then?'

'You really don't know, do you?'

'I fucking don't!' The singer and the tower security guards looked over. A woman came out from the college building behind Ben and began to approach.

'You're not ruthless enough, Ben. I can only have one apprentice. You'll probably be the best apprentice I ever have – the best at being the apprentice. But I have an apprentice now so that in ten years' time there will be two or three senior people around the group, people whom I have trained and trust through and through, one of whom will have the potential to seize the business out of my hands and run it brilliantly after me. You would never be ruthless enough for that. So, onwards and upwards.'

Ben was stunned. Alex appeared to feel mild curiosity at Ben's ignorance and a slight irritation at being detained.

Not ruthless? Well, Ben knew how to reply to that. 'Venice in the Evening' by the new Australian designer Haribel Mâché reached his olfactory nerves too late. 'So what were you doing screwing the dean's wife in the Kings Arms while I was giving your speech?'

'This is your business because – ?' queried Alex in puzzlement, before turning to plant a peck on the woman's cheek. 'Dianne, a little reality seems to have upset the nice young man whom I sicked onto you. I'm sorry. But he'll be gone soon, won't he?'

And the fight was over. While a shrug of Dianne's shoulders re-arranged her breasts, her scent enveloped and re-arranged both men as if they were pieces on a chessboard. Now they were her two fighting cocks, presumably fighting over her. She smiled at Ben, and then Alex, resting one forefinger on each.

'Ben is a very nice young man. Of course on a bad day that's three strikes down – nice, young and man – but today he is our absolute hero. I won't hear a word said against him. Now, Alex, come with me. London's top colour specialist has come down. No pouting – you're going to look your very best for the television cameras if it's the last thing I do.'

Towards the end of the morning Ben and Greg headed to the police mobile command post. It was in the main car park, a blue-and-white articulated truck with a large painted number, a satellite dish and several radio aerials on top. A constable helped them put on small ear-pieces.

'We'll be saying a lot which you won't hear,' Haddrill reminded them. 'But you'll hear anything we say on the open circuit and, of course, you'll hear when we call either of you.'

'To respond to us, just hold the button down like this while you speak,' explained the constable.

'Let's try it,' said Haddrill. After a couple of goes they had the idea.

'No need for that 'over and out' stuff,' the constable added helpfully.

Haddrill looked at his watch – nearly noon. They all looked around. Two officers in short sleeves with protective vests and automatic weapons were patrolling the tower terrace. There were two more on the other side of the car park, two in the dining room, and other pairs out of sight at the checkpoints on the two roads into the college. Ben and Greg now had lapel pins with yellow tops: access all areas.

Ben's mobile gave the chirrup he had programmed for Vanessa.

'Yup.'

'I'm texting you the Maharishi's personal cell number.'

'Wonderful.'

'The caterers have got a towing-car to the ice truck that broke down. So it will be late but it will be here by 3pm, which is okay.'

'Even more wonderful.' Although the college and the tower were air-conditioned, it was a hot, cloudless day.

'And a group of students is getting agitated that one of them has gone missing. A Palestinian. Missing, possibly abducted. They're concerned because her father wasn't keen on her coming to England to study.'

'Well, tell them they're in luck, the place is absolutely swarming with police. Tell them to report it right away. But just in case there is something funny going on, report it yourself as well.'

He responded to a text from Connie checking that the meeting with Roger Sling was still on for 2pm. The moment when he and Greg walked out of the command post was when Ben started to feel that he had the hang of this security thing, although he could tell the ear-piece would fall out all afternoon and annoy him. Greg looked as if he had been born with his.

'Ms Yung. Always a pleasure, and sometimes a surprise.' Gyro surveyed the group assembled in his office for the 2pm meeting. Apart from Connie and Ben there was Roger Sling, who looked to Ben like a damp jellyfish with a nervous condition.

Connie was in one of her power outfits – elegantly cut jacket and trousers in blue pin-stripe, open-necked blouse with a lot of straight edges. 'Your deputy told me she was going to let you know: as part of my induction I asked to sit in on a range of meetings. This one with our bank manager looked particularly appropriate. Who knows, I may be able to help with the Chinese angle.'

'The Chinese angle?' Gyro's eyebrows buckled momentarily into a circumflex. 'Well, well. You're right. There is a Chinese angle. Connie – may I? – you certainly know how to make your mark. If all our governors were up to your speed I'd hardly be needed. Never mind. Roger, your meeting I think? What's on your mind?'

That was unkind, thought Ben, watching the bank manager squirm. Words slipped out of Sling, twitching like fish on a slab. 'Been a while since … your travels … update … end of the month … the …' (violent coughing) '… loan.'

Damn it, thought Ben, there *is* a loan.

'Which loan is that, Roger?' said Connie brightly. She made a show of taking a copy of the college's report and accounts out of her bag.

'Yes, help us, Roger. Which loan do you have in mind?' Gyro purred. He wore the smile of a chef with a jellyfish in his sauté pan.

Sling took a couple of sheets from his briefcase. Ben passed them to Gyro. The letterhead was of a bank in the Netherlands Antilles, not First Improvident. Gyro gave the papers barely a second's glance before standing to give them a view of his back. When his gaze returned, calmer than ever, he looked at Connie and Ben, barely acknowledging Sling. 'If you're guessing there's a big dirty secret, you're right. This isn't it, but let's start with this.' He pointed at the sheets of paper.

'Let me go back to when I arrived at Hampton. A dump, but I knew that. I knew there was the possibility of change. But rapidly I found I was caught in a vicious circle. To make changes, I needed a budget for various things. To get a budget, in the first instance I needed donations.

'I knew I could raise donations – tens of millions, as you've seen, which we might double by the end of today. But no-one wanted to go first. Like any newly appointed CEO, I needed an early win. Well, the college needed it, if it was to fulfil its potential. I'm sure you realise that none of the money raised has been for me personally.

'I'm a practical man. Give me a problem and I'll solve it. So I asked my good friend, the chairman of First Improvident, to help me. Lend me one or two million for a couple of years, I said, and I'll easily raise the money to pay you back.

'But the money can not come directly to the college. It needs to go to some friends of mine in one of the prestigious strategy firms, McKinsey and the like – that was a world I knew very well – for them to donate to the college through their research institute. Very prestigious, everyone gawped at how a place like Hampton had pulled that off. So now that somebody had finally gone first, much bigger money started coming in.'

Connie interrupted. 'But a loan personally to you, a director, would show up in First Improvident's report and accounts, and it doesn't.'

'Yes, you're right,' Gyro replied. 'So the loan came to me from an unconnected bank in the Netherlands Antilles. I needed a bank that would let me commit the college's reserves as security without a resolution from the governors.'

'Why would they take that risk?' Ben asked.

'The magic of securitisation.' Gyro picked up one of the sheets of paper and started folding it into a dart. 'When banks securitise a loan, they take the IOU and make it into a paper dart. In fact, they usually cut the loan into small pieces and make each of those into a paper dart. Then they sell the darts to someone else. Who knows where they go.' His paper airplane soared, stalled and fell back to the carpet.

'So the bank in the Netherlands Antilles immediately securitised this loan, and sold it for face value plus a handy profit to First Improvident. Where it has been sitting unnoticed in the bank's portfolio of trading assets, waiting to fall due. I never borrowed any money from First Improvident.'

Connie looked distinctly sick. 'None of which will look good if it comes to light, but I suppose it needn't if the loan is repaid.'

'Don't look worried yet; we're still miles away from the real problem. So yes, the loan falls due at the end of this month. Nine months ago that was not a problem, I would raise the money easily. Trust me, several of the Chinese plutocracy have been consulting clients and friends of mine for many years. But something happened towards the end of last year which you will have heard about – the first run on a British bank which – can any of us remember the name of it?'

'Northern Rock,' interjected Ben. Eventually the bank was taken over by the British government.

'Here's the big dirty secret: it's not the bankruptcy of Hampton College we need to worry about, it's the bankruptcy of the global banking system.' He folded the second sheet of paper into a dart and threw it. 'Too many paper darts. Too many loans gone to too many places we don't know.

'So six months ago – I need hardly tell you how confidential this is – the board of First Improvident was in very heavy session. We re-do all our predictions. The result is grim. We need to raise more capital, big capital, billions. And we need it urgently, because we're in the time of Noah. The rains are coming.

'Banks all over the world are going to go under – famous ones. Go under or be bailed out. Either way, large parts of national economies are going to be under water with the consequences. Imagine one-third of Greece under water. One of our scenarios is a one-third collapse in Greek GDP. Spain could be as bad, Britain not as bad, but still a large part of the country financially under water *for years*.

'Once the flood comes, capital will be desperate to come by. So we need to build our ark. But we have to do it very secretly, because that's how runs on banks start. The minute you think First Improvident might go under ... So that means talking to small numbers of people with very large pockets. The

Middle East. The Chinese. Some Russians. Some pension funds. The list is quite short. We have some good links with the Chinese and decide that they are our best bet. '

Connie was the first to get the picture. 'So your friend the chairman of First Improvident comes to you for a favour. He says you're on our board, you've got excellent contacts but the trump card is you can make several trips to China without anyone suspecting.'

Gyro nodded. He glanced at Ben. 'Hence nothing in my diary.' He looked at his watch. 'Pray God it's all being signed as we speak. If it is, you'll see an announcement tonight after the markets close. Do I need to explain that if you do anything with this information in the next few hours, being prosecuted will be the least of your worries. Quite seriously, you could start the end of the world as we know it. And for obvious reasons, although he's on our guest list, the chairman of First Improvident won't be showing up tonight.'

For a minute Gyro's three guests sat in pale silence. They had gone for a walk down a country lane and now one of the horsemen of the apocalypse had thundered by. Gyro gathered up the paper darts and returned them to Sling.

'So, Roger, we've probably taken this as far as we can today, don't you agree? If things happen the way I've described, your bank will be writing off this loan as part of my fee for saving you. And if they don't, all of us are going to be out of a job very soon. We can fight over who'll be at the top of the list, but we'll be bald men fighting over a comb.'

The meeting with Sling was shocking but short. Ben consulted Vanessa's bible. The dining room was closed to prepare for the gala dinner, but he and Connie had time for a quick dose of hot bubbles from one of Hampton's dispensing machines. Whether the liquid coating the bubbles was tea or coffee was beside the point.

The end of the known world did not feel quite the right topic for verbal respite, so Ben told Connie his next appointment was in 20 minutes with Cardew McCarthy in the tower – a run-through of Wilson Junior's speech.

'The tower does look spectacular. Despite everything, I'm really looking forward to this evening.'

'Me too. What are you wearing?'

'That's a surprise! Which reminds me, I'll pick up the car after this and go over to Frank's – collect the painting and change.' Connie clinked the spare keys to Frank's house in her pocket.

'Why don't you leave your stuff locked there? We'll probably go back there tonight.'

'Better than a single bed, you mean?' Connie grinned.

'He did have a point. Oh! I meant to tell you, but that meeting put it right out of my mind. I bumped into Bakhtin, literally, this morning.'

'I hope you gave him what for.'

'What for and then some. He's such an unbelievable shitbag.' Ben gave her a quick update on his encounter with Bakhtin. 'He's supposed to be at the dinner, but with any luck he'll have found someone who needs shagging at the Kings Arms.'

Which was how the thought came to Ben that Noah's Ark was all very well, but time might still be left to teach Bakhtin a thoroughly deserved lesson. As he walked towards the tower he withheld his own number while he dialled the one Vanessa had given him. As befitting the personal number of someone in religious silence, the call went straight through to voicemail.

'Your lucky night, your Holiness. Three of my finest ladies will be waiting in your suite at the Kings Arms at 11pm tonight. They are totally stunning and discreet, my personal selection. But if you have any problems, I am at your service twenty-four seven. Call me. My name is Alex. And this is my number.' Alex Bakhtin's mobile number was one Ben had no difficulty remembering.

MONDAY 9 JULY (LUNCHTIME)

BEN

By the time Connie and I have recounted the meeting with Gyro and Sling (confident that Amelia has already interviewed both of them, probably more than once), it's lunchtime. I want some fresh air, perhaps to confirm that we really can walk past the doorman back into the outside world. We can, and stride briskly towards Blackfriars.

We pass an EAT, a Pret, an expense-account wine bar and a café where the ready-to-microwave spaghetti and English factory sausages may, like its décor, date from the 1970s. I shake my head. Instead we buy day-old cheese-and-tomato and egg mayo sandwiches on the Thames river bus. The catamaran hits 28 knots during its 20-minute journey to Canary Wharf, and the noise from the twin engines is particularly loud by the outdoor seats at the stern. So Connie and I sit there. We're still shocked at having heard Frank's voice and want to talk without eavesdroppers.

Connie is agitated. In the next session she will have to talk about what happened when she went back to Frank's house to change. 'When I agreed to do this I didn't know they had the place bugged,' she says.

'So whatever you're worried about they already know,' I point out. 'Of course it's not an enjoyable experience, but I don't see anything to stress about.' A thought occurs to me. 'Look, I'll say we want them to play the audio recording at the beginning. It's upsetting to hear Frank's voice, and now there's no point in Amelia playing the game of pretending not to have a recording. Anyway, we should challenge her a bit. Throw her off her stride. We're not toys for her to play with.' Watching Connie's expression I add, 'Without making her angry. Just push back a bit.'

'A bit would be good,' Connie agrees, but she remains agitated until we have changed boats in front of the skyscrapers at Canary Wharf. She grabs my arm suddenly and hisses, 'They haven't got an audio recording of the afternoon.'

'Of course they have – what are you thinking?'

'That's what I've been doing – thinking. If they had bugged Frank's house in the afternoon, they would have realised that either he hadn't left by noon or that he had got back in. And they would have heard about the battery. They would have had enough warning to stop the whole thing. And they would have arrested me.'

I am silent. The afternoon has turned sunny and the catamaran is packed with French teenagers returning from the O2 millennium dome. You're exaggerating; I want to say that so desperately. But she's right about being arrested.

A crew member announces, 'London Bridge pier, passengers will disembark from the front of the boat.' A few minutes later

Blackfriars and Wren's cathedral building at St Paul's come back into view.

I glance at my watch. We will have taken quarter of an hour longer than we had agreed; maybe Amelia will think we've absconded. But if she has Connie and Frank on tape, Amelia knows we'll return. We need the immunity from prosecution.

In the room with Amelia I start the push-back. I say, 'You're pretty picky with your words. You didn't tell me when we were reviewing security on Wednesday that you were going to arrest students the next day.'

'I'm paid to be pretty picky and not just with words,' replies Amelia. 'We reviewed the college's lists of who would be on site. I told you that we would make appropriate inquiries and that's what we did. In the case of three students and one member of the catering team, those inquiries were made using our powers under anti-terrorism legislation. Everyone was released by Saturday.'

'Implying they should be grateful that you didn't hold them for twenty-eight days?'

Amelia looks me in the eye. 'Implying that I took the precautions I considered appropriate. Precautions which, at the end of the day, were not enough. Shall we get on? Connie's Thursday afternoon rendezvous with Frank is one of the things we most need to understand better.'

Connie says, '"Rendezvous" makes it sound arranged, but I had no idea Frank was going to be there. As far as I was concerned, I was picking up a painting and changing my clothes in an empty house.'

Amelia apologises. 'I didn't mean to imply anything different. The arranging was all Frank's.'

I lay out for Amelia the approach that Connie and I have discussed. 'We want you to play the audio recording first, then Connie will answer questions. What you did this morning wasn't very friendly.'

'If this is the time for embarrassing secrets,' Amelia says, 'here's mine. We don't have any recordings from Thursday afternoon.' She's not surprised by our disbelief. 'Call it a combination of my threat assessment and an administrative bungle. Greg kept bending my ear that all hell would break loose at the tower opening, but I had to look at the facts. Frank was a lone operator with no suspicious track record or connections.

'Suspicions about explosives had been tested and found wrong. And Frank was going to be off-site by noon, with the place crawling with police all afternoon. So Frank's house was being recorded but on a morning-after basis. That means conversations are scanned by computer at the time of recording for trigger words, threat words. This is reviewed in the morning by a specialist analyst with a fast-forward button. The analyst decides whether to continue, upgrade the surveillance or let it lapse. We simply don't have the manpower to listen to everybody in real time.

'The dinner on Wednesday evening didn't include any threat words – none of you joked about bombs or al-Qaeda. The morning after, an analyst should have picked up Frank persuading you to come back to the house in the afternoon, on the pretext of having wrapped up the painting you wanted. Bearing in mind that it was now the day of the opening, a higher level of surveillance would have been justified. We should have had live ears in Frank's house all Thursday afternoon.

But on Thursday morning two of the team called in sick and we bungled our procedures. No-one listened to the dinner conversation, and the monitoring lapsed at noon.' Amelia gives a thin smile. 'You can imagine what explaining that to the Prime Minister was like.'

'So that's why we're here, with these immunities and everything. If you had everything on tape, you wouldn't need us.'

'In part,' Amelia agrees. 'But as I said, even if we had it all on tape, we would still want to learn everything we can. Especially about the Thursday afternoon meeting. Because it's not about the painting, is it?'

'No it isn't,' Connie agrees. She sits up and pulls her shoulders back, and I have no idea which way she's going to jump.

CONNIE

Sometimes you jump the way you jump because you just do, which makes it sound like chance. It's the opposite of chance, it's the deepest possible intent, but coming from a place beyond any ability to explain. That's what happened when Frank asked me the question, and it's what happens right now, long before the questions come which I will answer with a lie.

I jump now because unless I tell the whole story in a certain way, my lie is going to stall on my tongue at the moment when I need the words to take wing. I don't lie well. If the lie is too much of a stretch then the image I'm projecting out there – the celluloid of my self-belief – snaps.

I'm thinking about the turquoise clip-on earrings that I bought one Saturday when I was nine. I bought them with a five-pound note stolen from my father's wallet. He had gone down the pub to watch rugby so he was sound asleep by mid-afternoon. The downside was that his wallet was as light as air; the crumpled five pounds was the only banknote in it.

For seven months Alisha had let me look at the earrings in her shop, but again and again my father wouldn't hear of me having them. Once Alisha had let me try them on. They were £7.99 until one day they were in clearance at £3.99. I was petrified that someone would buy them; Alisha was keeping an eye on them for me but sometimes her cousin minded the shop.

Afterwards, my father created a commotion because he thought he was missing some money. He said he was going to call the police, but I knew he had drunk too much to be sure. Of course I could never wear the earrings, my father would have hit the roof, but I kept them safe. For about a year I took them out every few weeks to admire under the bed-covers. That's what I'm doing now. I'm focussing on another time when I absolutely had to lie convincingly, and I succeeded.

I explain to Amelia that since the meeting with the bank manager had finished early, it may have been about a quarter to three when I parked outside Frank's house and let myself in with the spare key. The four-wheel drive had gone. All the curtains were drawn. The hallway and living room should have been bare, maybe with sacks of rubbish. Instead, they were unchanged from dinner. The only visible packing was the painting, swaddled in plain-brown wrapping paper and heavy tape.

'I was confused. It was a bit spooky. I called out a couple of times, but there was no answer. The front door had a clothes hook, and I was carrying my evening gown on a hanger in a long plastic zip-bag. So I hung it up and carried the painting to the car. Then I screamed "Frank!" and ran up the stairs.'

Amelia says, 'Take your time.'

'For a moment it came to me that he had committed suicide. Everything about the whole dinner, the way he had called it "the last supper", the not packing. But he was waiting in the bedroom, in a T-shirt and sweatpants, as calm as anything. I went into the bathroom to throw up, but nothing doing. I remember noticing that he'd shaved his arms.

'For a couple of minutes we had quite a banal conversation, something like me saying "I thought you're supposed to be gone", and him replying, "I will be shortly". After all, finding him had been a shock. But then he got to the point.

'He had realised during dinner that Ben hadn't told me the truth about his role at Bakhtin.' I glance at Ben. 'That he hadn't been in a backroom job, instead he'd been running a business – the plastic packaging business that had screwed mine. The exact one. He had thought up the dirty stuff, he had carried out the dirty stuff and he had got his reward – the promotion of his career.'

'Dirty stuff?' Amelia asks.

'You tell her,' I say to Ben. So he does – the honest version this time. Amelia is hard to read, but I'm guessing she's not very interested. Presumably her idea of dirty stuff is drugs or arms or human trafficking.

Amelia is puzzled. 'Why did it matter to Frank? Was he warning you?'

'I think he hoped the two of us would get together. He thought we were good for each other. But he thought it couldn't work out if we started with a lie. Frank hated lies.'

Ben is nodding. 'He was right. I was already slipping into thinking of course I'd tell you, but at the right time. And the only right time was at the beginning.'

'So you were pretty angry?'

'Angry? Volcanic.' I look at Ben. 'You were going to be toast. Frank did his best to talk me out of it, but I couldn't get my head round what a bastard you'd been – then and now. The biggest bastard I could imagine, and I had started falling for you.'

'What did Frank do?' asks Amelia.

'He said he'd slip off after I've gone. I tell him there are police everywhere. He said, "That's all right, I feel very safe." He gives me a kiss.'

Amelia leans forward. 'And what does the kiss mean, do you think? I mean, what did you think at the time? Did you think it was something like, "See you next week"? '

I lean back in my chair and close my eyes. 'I can't remember. Of course now I know it was "Goodbye", and I keep thinking I must have known then – but I didn't. Don't forget – what I am thinking about is tearing Ben Stillman apart limb by limb.

'The curtains are drawn so I change downstairs into the clothes I've brought for the dinner.'

Amelia looks up from her notebook. 'So you were still going to the dinner?'

I laugh. 'It seems so, at that point anyway! Bear in mind I was invited as a governor. But once I found Ben all of that goes right out of the window. So I set off.'

'Your car was outside Frank's, though?'

'Because the battery had gone flat. It had been playing up, but how typical is that? Talk about going at the worst possible time. I thought about calling the rescue service, but then I realised they wouldn't get in until the next day – the college was locked down for the opening. So I start walking, all dressed up in my silver *cheong sam* – how crazy is that? Fortunately I had some trainers in the car.'

My story hangs in the air for an age, enough time that I wonder not once but 10 times whether the police checked my car at some point early Friday morning. They had plenty of time before Ben drove me back with a new battery. But it seems they were preoccupied with other things.

Amelia wants to go through again about possible accomplices – surely, surely there were hints, clues, that Frank had people or had been consulting with people somewhere else in the world. His emails have been scanned, decrypted and generally spun-dry without revealing anything, but perhaps, she wonders aloud, he had an email identity and a mobile device for accessing the web which they haven't found yet … However I can't help them, because so far as I know, he only needed the one accomplice. Me. In my mind I'm holding my £3.99 earrings tight, like this.

BEN

Connie's holding up so well. I know she's a strong woman but this is very hard for her. I've been working at not looking at her too much, but not looking out of the window too much either; it's hard to think which might look more suspicious. She doesn't need me making things harder.

I hadn't a clue which way she would jump. I'd done my best to explain that she could just let it all out there, after all we were protected.

As I try to look sufficiently but not overly interested, I muse about Frank being so determined to tell Connie about me and Alex. What a risk, and it wasn't even his business, was it? Part of me is still angry, jumping up and down wanting to know why he couldn't trust me to tell Connie at an appropriate time.

But I know the answer to that. Anyone putting money on it would have bet on me trying to get away without telling her at all. It's the truth, even though I don't like it. And now Frank has hundreds of thousands of fans all over the world (someone set up a page for him on Facebook), because he was more committed to the truth than the rest of us.

To judge by the way Amelia's focus is now the opening evening itself, Connie's done the trick.

Oh, Frank – it's ironic, isn't it? What I'm doing now, being more than a little economical with *la vérité* when you made 'indefatigable for truth' your middle name. But I think you understand. Or would understand. We're only human, even you. That's what I remember seeing in your eyes. You had done your best to stop me going to put an axe into Ben's scalp and then you said, 'There's something else, Connie. I'm so sorry.' And when you saw my face you added very quickly, 'Not about Ben.'

You asked me to sit next to you. 'I didn't know this last night – I swear to God I didn't. I never wanted to involve you. But I need your car battery. One of mine has gone flat.'

Mine in the plural, I thought. 'You're talking about car batteries, but they're not for a car.'

You nodded.

'Are they for a bomb?'

'Never. Nothing that's going to do anything bad; only something good that I've tried to do all my life. No-one's even going to bleed.'

You were a bit careless with *la vérité* yourself there, Mr Shining Paragon. It happens to us all. So there is the longest silence, both of us sitting there, and yet again I've got a jump to make – one I had never expected in a million years.

'Is it that important, Frank? Really?'

'It's my life's work.'

'I can't give you the battery. But I'll leave the car with the bonnet unlocked.

They are the oddest things, principles, aren't they?

THURSDAY 21 JUNE (EARLY EVENING)

THURSDAY 21 JUNE (EARLY EVENING)

On each side the gown of silver silk was slit to her hips but Ben did not have much chance to enjoy the view. Connie had found him in his bedroom changing into his dinner jacket. After a 15-minute brisk walk in her trainers she was breathing hard but Ben had no chance of starting the conversation, not if she had anything to do with it.

'Bakhtin, remind me – what did you call him?'

'A shitbag – why? Have you bumped into him?' Ben was trying to tuck the coiled wire of his police ear-piece inside a clean shirt.

'I may have done. You called him "an unbelievable shitbag", to be precise. Because when he fired you, he told you a white lie.' Connie let her words hang in the air. 'Just a little white lie to spare your feelings.'

'It was more than that, but Alex is a shitbag through and through. I think we agree on that.'

'We did. We do. So what has this shitbag done that's really bad? Really, really terrible? Give me an example.'

'Connie, I don't understand.'

'Yes you do. A simple word: an example. Anything you can remember from all those years you were collecting cars and bonuses and pats on the back from your friend.'

'Well, what he did to your business.'

'Hallelujah, a great example! That was evil, wasn't it?'

She watched the colour drain from Ben's face. 'It wasn't good.'

'Come on, try harder than that. I was the head of HR, remember? When that business went to the wall I had to make everyone redundant. Your eleven-year-old who was doing so well at a special school, that's over now. Your house that you planned to extend for your dad who's getting frail – forget it. The MBA you're half-way through – sorry about that.

'A couple of hundred people suddenly looking and no decent jobs for miles. Bakhtin pulled the trigger but I watched the bullets hit between the eyes. No wonder that speech on selfless leadership made me sick. Of course, *you* wrote that, didn't you. But tell me, Ben, what else were your sticky fingers all over?'

'Whatever Bakhtin's said to you, he's just said it to upset you and get at me.' Ben was looking as sick as Connie had been in Frank's bathroom earlier, but she saw no need to correct his mistaken impression. In any case, where she had got the truth from did not matter.

'Do you remember telling me, Mr Backroom Boy, that Bakhtin's businesses ran themselves? You're the unbelievable shitbag, and I'm the unbelievable idiot who believed you. You weren't just cheering from the sidelines or warming up on the substitutes' bench – you were the manager, team captain and centre forward of Team Shitbag rolled into one. You put the ball into the back of the net, and my business was the net. It wasn't Bakhtin's idea, it was yours.'

'Connie –'

'Stick your excuses. I'm right, aren't I?'

'Yes. But –'

'So look at you. First you screwed my business and then you screwed me.' Connie leaned forward and slapped Ben's face. Hard. 'What do you get for that – a double bonus?' She stormed out of the room.

Connie walked towards the lake, trying to gather her thoughts. She could see where they had celebrated her birthday on Sunday, and wished she could mouse over the memory and click 'delete'. Was she sure she wished to delete this memory permanently? Yes! Then she tried to change the memory, editing it to show how Ben had come onto her. Of course it had been the other way around.

Not far away were a couple of police Land Rovers and a large square staked out with orange tape – the landing zone for the Prime Minister's helicopter, she surmised. Any idea of staying for the opening was mad. Although her anger at herself as much as at Ben was now beginning to plateau, she did not want to be where she would have to see him or Alex Bakhtin.

Moreover, the sight of so many sub-machine guns had enlivened a fear that she might have done something alarming in letting Frank have the car battery which he had unexpectedly – and without explanation – needed. Hampton's grounds, which he was supposed to have quit by noon, were increasingly crawling with private security hired by the college as well as with police. So Connie could not begin to conceive how Frank could move around.

Presumably he was up to some kind of academic jape, a protest stunt like Monday morning's masturbatory fist, but orchestrated somehow from his house. Frank was no terrorist, of that Connie was certain, but viscerally she wanted to get out of the place. She was dressed like a hostess in an Asian millionaires' casino but going back to where her day clothes were, parked outside Frank's house, was out of the question. She got out her mobile phone and got some numbers for local cab firms.

The firms' blithe promises soon evaporated. The cabs could not get past the armed checkpoints. So having been kept at a scalding simmer for nearly an hour, in the end Connie arranged for one firm to pick her up at 6.30pm on the far side of the Pynbal's Ridge checkpoint and take her to catch a train from Alderley. She reckoned she could walk to the checkpoint in an hour and a half. The flow of arriving VIPs watched the glistening of Connie's sweat compete for attention with her diamond earrings and silver threads as she strode past them without acknowledgement.

Halfway up Pynbal's Ridge Connie passed a Bentley the colour of burgundy, chauffeur-driven like most of the other arriving cars. This one had two passengers. The Bentley – licence place MST1 – stopped and reversed. The younger of two South Asian males of different ages but the same tailor stepped out and clasped his hands together. 'The feet of virtue are always calloused.'

Connie hesitated. 'I'm sorry?'

'Good evening. His Holiness the Maharishi Swami Tandoori is observing religious silence, but has the pleasure of offering you a lift.'

Connie looked inside. 'I'm sure that's very, ah, Maharswishy of him, but I'm going the other way.'

'Would you care to join His Holiness for dinner?'

'No offence, but I've given up men for Lent. Or whatever it is right now.'

'Perhaps some spiritual exercises after dinner.'

'No.'

'Afterwards, his driver would be pleased to take you wherever you wish.'

'Another time.'

'His Holiness believes that we must encounter ourselves in the now, or risk eternal non-being.'

Connie opened the Bentley's front passenger door. She leant inside. 'Listen up, Mr Tikka Masala. Have yourself a top evening at the college and raise tons of money. Then you can have two twerps to run around for you instead of one. Just fucking remember to get one who can listen as well as one who can speak.'

Of course the taxi was late to the checkpoint but it came eventually and dropped Connie at Alderley station. 'Station' is a term used in Britain to describe an occasional railway timetable and two stone strips connected by a footbridge. The lack of any toilet is a key part of this design. At Alderley, the experience of waiting was fully digitised. An electronic indicator showed that it was 7.05pm and that the next train, which was headed to Slough, would arrive at 7.28.

An old man with a cap and a walking stick occupied the platform's only bench. Clutching a small Union Jack, he looked as if he had been sitting there since Prince Charles' and Princess Diana's wedding, or possibly VE Day. The other sign of life was no more promising – a pub across the car park, named 'The Railway'. As Connie approached she could see that it offered a warm welcome and cups of hot chocolate for all the refugee apostrophes from the Kings Arms. The day's special was burger and chip's with garden pea's. She ordered a mineral water and found the ladies' toilet.

Opening the door of this facility temporarily relieved Connie of the desire which had brought her there. With her feet numb from her forced march from the college she composed herself as if she were a Thursday evening regular, down to watch the footy in her silver *cheong-sam*.

The three young males sprawled around the pub's pool table were following a long tradition in Western philosophy, classifying all of existence into fundamental dualisms, in this case 'sweet' and 'shite'. Connie told herself that trains had toilets – usually – and checked for phone messages. Any distraction to take away the pressure on her bladder would do, but there weren't any messages. She left her phone switched on in hope. Sitting was worse than standing, so she walked back to the station platform.

Ben was boiling over. How could one man, even if he was as rich as Bakhtin, do him so much damage? If he had to greet this Toad of Toad Hall the chances were he would punch his teeth out. But of course (Ben suddenly realised) Bakhtin was not going to be in the tower, but by the lake greeting the Prime Minister. Still, there would be an opportunity over dinner.

But why did he give a shit about dinner? He was in no mood to smarm his way around a collection of the world's largest egos, hoping to impress and land a job. Once the opening was done, his job at Hampton was done. Somehow it had not turned out at all as he had expected. As soon as the glass spaceship and vertical phallus was opened he would head back to his bedroom, collect his few belongings, jump in his Audi with LED running lights and get back to breathing the air of normal England.

But before that, there was an hour more of this. At 5.25pm the early guests, such as Casey Pinnacle, had been up in the tower for 20 minutes but the main flow of arrivals was now beginning. They were mostly in evening dress, some in an interpretation of national costume. Ben's job was to perform a dance between Dean Gyro and the auditorium. The dance was performed like this:

Sir Alastair Mecklenburgh, chairman of Atlantic Pensions, arrived. Atlantic Pensions (slogan: 'Don't spend your golden years on the rocks') managed more assets not only than most British pension funds but also than the Mafia. As Sir Alastair would remind you, this puts it truly in the premier league. He was 69.

The £145,000 annual honorarium which he drew for one day a week (was it Tuesdays or Wednesdays? – no, Tuesday was golf) helped him make sure that his own golden years were not rocky ones. He arrived with a young woman. A member of the security team checked for lapel pins of an acceptable colour. These were dispensed at the vehicle checkpoint, where IDs were checked against the guest list.

Dean Gyro's crimson doctoral robes matched the carpet laid over the grass to the foot of the tower. To begin the dance, Ben stood slightly behind Gyro on his left.

'Alastair! How marvellous of you to come.' Repetition was beginning to make Gyro sound English.

'Gyro, very good of you to ask us. My daughter, Clara. Goodness, isn't it extraordinary!' At this point an adulatory reference to the tower was obligatory.

'We're very proud of it, I must say. But go up. What you see from here is nothing compared with what you'll see from there. Ben, will you? Alastair, let's make sure to catch up over drinks. I was fascinated to see that Atlantic's changed its bond strategy.'

'Of course.'

Ben led the guests to the glass doughnut where the digital Californian *maître d'* intoned, 'The elevator doors are opening.'

This was the moment for one of the guests to say, 'Goodness, it's all glass! Do people get vertigo?'

'The elevator doors are closing.'

Mecklenburgh asked, 'Have you been with Professor Gyro long?'

'Long enough to be his number one fan. In fact, I did my MBA here.'

'Oh, how splendid.'

The doughnut rose into the centre of the auditorium where a waiter was poised with a tray of champagne flutes and glasses of sparkling water and Virgin Marys. The view was indeed breathtaking. The pre-speech entertainment was a flautist and cellist (one thing that couldn't fit into the lift was a grand piano). The doors opened and closed with their announcements as Ben returned to ground level to begin the dance again.

Donald Vane, 38, was arriving. He was the senior managing director for Europe, the Middle East and Africa of Profit Extraction, widely regarded (especially by themselves) as the world's top consultants to the drilling and exploration sectors. His company's skill was advising drilling companies how to make a fortune entirely from rocks (slogan: put your bit between our teeth). This meant he would have plenty to talk about with Alastair Mecklenburgh.

Also, Donald has sailed twice across the Atlantic backwards, which was interesting and masculine, so he did not need to arrive with a woman. In any case his private life went in another direction. The bit which Donald most frequently found between his own teeth was the moist probing tool of a Belgian dentist.

Casey descended in the lift almost on the stroke of six. As one of the Pinnacle family Casey knew most of the detail of the evening's timetable. 'The party's beginning to hum,' was his offering to the dean. His cufflinks showed $3.3 billion –

down quite a bit. The traders' screens had been bleeding a lot of red in the last few days.

Within seconds of schedule, a white-stretch limo that would have been at home in Las Vegas turned the corner of the administration block. How had it negotiated the twists and bends of Pynbal's Ridge? It pulled to a stop with the rear passenger door opposite the red carpet and the front somewhere in Buckinghamshire. Had a bus come at the right time the driver could have caught it for two stops to come and open the passenger door, but Gyro beat him to it. Junior stepped out in a grey suit with wide lapels, a blue-check tie and a pearl tie-pin, followed by a genteel woman in lavender, 30 years younger and dressed for Ascot.

'Dad! Laura!' Casey's exclamation disappeared into embraces.

Gyro did a handshake for Junior and kisses for Laura. Ben disgusted himself with an involuntary half-bow, the pseudo-royal nature of the occasion overcoming him. The whole party squeezed into the doughnut.

'Happy one-hundredth birthday to Virtual Savings and Trust!' The wonderfulness of the occasion was even getting to Casey.

The Californian *maître d'* said, 'The singing of the elevator is beginning,' and for a moment no-one noticed. Then the lift began singing 'Happy birthday to you.' Junior congratulated Gyro, who looked at Ben. Ben went white until Casey whispered in his ear, 'I bought Proximity Communications over the weekend. It's a fun business.'

'The singing of the elevator is ending.'

In the auditorium, applause engulfed the guest of honour. Gyro led Junior and his female companion on a perambulation among the lesser arrivals while Ben headed back down to greet late-comers. The lift said, 'Welcome to Voice 2.1. The orderliness of the announcements is ending. The creativeness of the announcements is beginning.'

Ben felt queasy; Casey's sense of humour might not prove universal. Nevertheless, the late-comers by and large enjoyed the short solemnities which accompanied them on their ascents. Ben thanked God that the Prime Minister would be staying by the lakeside and would not hear them.

The Maharishi Swami Tandoori and his speaking assistant arrived at 6.35pm, just as the speeches were about to begin. 'Welcome Your Holiness,' Ben offered, holding out his right hand.

'His Holiness is in silence,' the assistant replied, 'but He thanks you for your greeting.'

'The opening of elevator doors is an illusion.' Presumably the lift's sensors detected a spiritual aura. 'The closing of elevator doors is also an illusion.'

The Maharishi applauded impishly. 'His Holiness would esteem your lift's insight,' explained his assistant, 'but unfortunately insight is also an illusion.'

Wearing her academic gown, Dianne had arranged the guests
by the lake in order of protocol: herself first, representing the
college; then Mark Topley, local MP and Minister for Health;
and finally the donor and newly-ennobled moneybags, Alex
Bakhtin. Greg positioned himself to one side, near the two
police officers with submachine-guns. The other two present
were the TV cameraman and the interviewer, the latter so
young that even Greg was shocked. Presumably he was a
local since the fleeting visit merited only a couple of softball
questions. Greg got a big kick out of playing on the team
with ear-pieces, or 'whisperers' as Greg called them: himself,
the police and the TV crew – the people who really made
things happen.

Greg had been on-site and ready for more than an hour; he
knew better than all of them how to wait. The others fidgeted
but did not move around. They could not hear the speeches in
the tower, but they all felt conspicuous in front of the many
eyes packing the glass spaceship as they stood on parade where
Dianne had put them.

Greg had gone for a young executive look with a
pin-striped suit, charcoal shirt, white shirt collar and a
restrained tie. His yellow-topped lapel pin was prominent. He

---

[6] *A New Earth: Awakening To Your Life's Purpose,* op. cit.

had not seen Henderson all day. She had said Haddrill would be in charge, but Greg had assumed that was talk to show what an empowering boss she was.

With the Prime Minister coming he had been certain that she would show, but it seemed that he was wrong. If she had shown, the whisperers would have said, so everyone knew who was in charge. Well, any minute now all the cards on the table would get turned over, and who had been right about possible threats would no longer be a matter for judgement or discussion.

For Greg had not made the mistake of relaxing his vigilance. Forcing the primary suspect to be off-site from noon had been a big win, and he would not let Henderson forget who had won it. But there was still the sorcerer's apprentice, Ben, and the mysteriously prescient queen, Dianne. Perhaps the target was more billionaires than any of them had ever seen before; if so, Ben was the main threat and the Prime Minister was unplanned icing on the cake.

But if the Prime Minister was the target, all eyes needed to be on the woman who had known he was coming far ahead of anyone else. And Greg's eyes were on her. She had put herself next to where the Prime Minister would stand. She was showing too much expensively tanned flesh to be wearing a bomb, even one made in a Paris couture house, but a stiletto could be almost as quick. So from Greg's point of view MP-5 machine-pistols with a full auto fire rate of 800 rounds per minute, which the two officers carried, were not overkill at all.

The police whisperers said something and an officer motioned everyone away from the landing area. Greg was the first to see the dot in the eastern sky and said, 'Over there'. The cameraman tucked his pony-tail under his slate-leather jacket and hoisted his camera to his shoulder. The interviewer pointlessly combed his hair as the wind picked up.

The arrangements with Number Ten were for an exclusive interview of a few minutes to go out as lead item on the channel's 7.30pm news, with a 60-second clip on the main nightly news and made available to competing channels. Where each of them would stand had been marked by golf tees, making sure that the tower was in shot.

Dianne looked over to Greg and mouthed, 'OK?'

Greg nodded.

The flying chariot approached. For once the winking red light on the top of the tower seemed prudent rather than fanciful. The helicopter shot over them twice, first in navy-blue substance and then in muddy brown shadow from the evening sun. The downdraught gave Dianne trouble with her hood. Alex helped her hold it in place. The rotor beat out circular arcs in the lake.

The roar dropped to a whine and then declined towards silence. One of the police officers opened the passenger door and saluted. The Prime Minister stepped out, followed by Ed Lens. As he emerged the Prime Minister's impression of a human was not bad; presumably he had turned to grin at Ed before the door opened.

Dianne did the introductions. The longest was between the Prime Minister and Lord Bakhtin. The introduction did not take long as both knew how many pounds make £4 millon.

Greg glanced at his watch. A voice in his ear told him that the speeches and the musical tribute in the tower were finishing on time, and everyone would be ready to watch the Prime Minister in the flesh and on TV screens.

The cameraman and interviewer took their positions. Dianne invited the Prime Minister and the other guests to stand at their marks. Since the Prime Minister had not been here for the rehearsal, the camera angle had to be checked. Also in the last half hour the angle of the sun had shifted, eliciting different reflections from the tower. Ed Lens handed the Prime Minister his prompt card. The Prime Minister glanced at it, put it in his pocket and nodded to the interviewer. Ed stood back near Greg and the police officers, out of shot.

The interviewer started a voice check and then stopped. The cameraman needed to readjust. A white light like very bright moonlight had started to flood the valley from the tower. Everyone had acquired a second shadow and turned to look. The tower had become like Columbia's torch on the cinema screen: a spectacular start to the festivities for the tower's opening.

The Prime Minister congratulated Dianne. 'Most impressive. It will look even better on the television news.'

Mark and Alex added their congratulations.

'It does show off the tower stunningly well,' agreed Dianne coyly. 'I hadn't realised it was in the plan.'

Once again the cameraman was ready to go.

(NOON꘍ꓤꓷꓵꓱ) ꓘꓵꓝ 6 ꓔꓥꓷꓕꓳꓲ

CONNIE

Is it remembering how utterly, stupidly, crazily I let Frank have the car battery that makes me nauseous, or something else? I stand up in the middle of Amelia speaking and mutter something about a stomach upset. 'It's nothing, I just need a few minutes,' I say to Ben.

When you're fine tile aesthetic doesn't matter and when you're sick you don't care, but there is a zone in between in which bathroom vibe is important – is it clean or a germ safari park, graffiti central or lounge music, that kind of thing. I'm unreasonably grateful that this one is what I need now – comforting and solid. The toilet stalls have been designed for human beings – you can use them without having your arms surgically repositioned – and the walls and cubicle locks haven't been borrowed from a doll's house. I don't doubt it's bugged, but that doesn't bother me. My spasmodic dry heaves aren't fake.

How can we be so organised and logical, and then suddenly do something so impulsive, flying without or in the face of any reason? Part of me wants to say that I knew, I really did know, here in the place from which I'm throwing up air, that Frank couldn't harm a fly.

And part of me knows in the same sick place that I knew nothing of the kind. In the world of data I didn't know enough about the man to tell you where he last went on holiday. Had his partner left him with a broken heart? Did he attend the psychiatric department at Alderley hospital every month on Wednesday afternoons? I had no clue. Yet out of a dank crevice in our mind comes the water of intuition, and we drink.

After the spasms pass I wash my face and rejoin our strange inquisition. Amelia and Ben have re-arranged the chairs so all three face the large screen. Strangely, I find I'm quite excited to see for the first time what happened. Amelia can probably describe in her sleep what I'm about to see, image by image, and of course Ben was there. Still, something has altered the energy level in the room because the animation of Amelia and Ben's conversation when I enter surprises me. Just for a second I wonder whether Amelia has put something in my tea.

BEN

'Are you OK?' I say.

Connie assures me that she is, putting one hand briefly on my knee as she sits down. 'I think it was something I had at lunch, but I'm fine now. I'm sorry to have kept you waiting.'

Amelia smiles and taps the remote control. 'Not at all, you gave me time to line up the two videos. The first set of images was shot in the tower by the cameraman recording for

Virtual Savings and Trust, and they are covered by the Official Secrets Act.'

Connie and I nod.

'Then I'll show you the images from the television camera outside. You've seen them before, on television or on the internet.'

'28,014,000 views as of yesterday,' I say.

Amelia rolls her eyes. 'Beyond those two videos, the technicians were able to recover one or two pieces of audio from the tower. However, for obvious reasons it was chaos and we lost vision. So I'm counting on watching what happens now to jog your memory, Ben.'

I don't think it needs jogging. 'You impounded the video, didn't you?'

'Everything that we could. That was one of the things that went right. Of course, what the BBC sent round the world from the TV camera ...' Amelia shrugs.

'Finally just to remind both of you, don't worry about whether you're remembering something relevant; that's my job. So just raise a hand and we'll pause.'

I confess I'm excited now. These are my home movies, even though this is the only time I will be allowed to watch them.

The VST camera pans over the glass auditorium, which is full and then some. Everyone is standing. Those not in the front rows are watching on widescreen monitors. Amid the suits and evening gowns the camera briefly catches in peripheral vision the orange-and-purple hair of Luscious, the singer, before focusing on the lectern (glass, of course), and next to it Gyro and Junior and Casey. Laura is standing in the front row but isn't part of the podium party.

I pause the action to point out where I'm standing in my dinner jacket and ungainly earpiece. To be honest I'm a little podgier than I had imagined. I have positioned myself at the lakeside end of the second row, close enough to the glass wall to look down vertically and towards the lakeside where the Prime Minister will land.

'Ladies and gentlemen!' Gyro raises both hands like a presidential candidate and calls out.

A memory comes to me. 'I remember checking my watch with a huge sigh of relief. We were starting the speeches on time. Dianne had laid into Gyro about punctuality because of the Prime Minister's helicopter. I was thinking it was such incredibly good news to be on time after all I'd been through in the last week.'

The auditorium does have outstanding acoustics and Gyro does not need notes: for him inaugurating the tower is the culmination of three years' passion. He recites the various welcomes and then moves on to the symbolism of the tower. The tower will be a unique model of leadership for the 21st century and an unforgettable learning space from which generations of future leaders will draw lifelong inspiration. I remember what comes next, and it does – the Sistine Chapel of leadership. There are cheers from the audience.

Gyro introduces Junior. The auditorium quietens. Junior holds the lectern briefly before unfolding sheets of square notepaper from his breast pocket. He has written this speech with a fountain pen and without Cardew. A tribute to a 100-year-old global business; a son's report to his dead father;

a father's hopes for an only son less than half his age; a quiet man's bid for history. Junior is speaking all these things.

Connie snorts, 'Why doesn't he just say, I paid for all this, so there!' But the light-hearted poke falls a bit awkwardly. Money talks but Junior himself is no longer alive to answer.

In the tower it is 6.55pm. Junior is due to wind up. Remarkably, he is going to add something impromptu. He folds away his notes, turns to Gyro and takes the dean's hand.

'Bill,' he says. 'When you first outlined to me what this tower could be, I will tell you frankly that I did not imagine the half of it.'

Appreciative laughter and applause.

'At that time we agreed that I would now name this unique space the Pinnacle Strategic Leadership Auditorium.'

More applause. Junior is holding Gyro's hand quite tightly. In the distance, a low-flying dot is becoming visible over the hills.

'But going around it with you today, I have to say, Bill, you have created so much more than an auditorium. It isn't just a place for listening, it's an unforgettable and all-encompassing visual environment.'

Deafening applause. On the periphery of the screen I am holding up three fingers – signalling to the dean that there are three minutes to landing, I explain to Amelia.

'So on the centenary of the finest bank in the world, Virtual Savings and Trust, what greater privilege could I have than to name this tower, a pinnacle not just in name but in conception and design, the Pinnacle Strategic Leadership Auditorium and Visual Environment.'

Connie sniggers. This isn't like her, I think, but realise that it's her nerves, because of what's coming up in – what? – about six and a half minutes.

Ecstatic applause. Gyro breaks Junior's grip and joins in. Then Gyro resumes the lectern.

'Now, Junior, Casey, members and friends of the Pinnacle family, ladies and gentlemen, Hampton has a small surprise for you. An entirely fitting surprise given Junior's standing among forward-thinking global business leaders. A surprise for which Junior has kindly given his permission, but which for security reasons we did not broadcast to the rest of you. If you look down towards the lake behind me, or on the monitor screens, we are greatly honoured to receive a short visit from the Prime Minister, who is going to make a televised announcement.

Delirious applause. For a moment Casey looks flummoxed. For security reasons the visit had not been included in his schedule. The VST camera swings briefly to an outside view. The downdraught of the helicopter's landing sends Dianne's academic robes into a wild dance.

The VST camera pans back to Gyro. 'In just a few minutes, we shall be able to follow the Prime Minister's announcement on these monitors. But as we wait, we will bring forward one of the musical items with which we were going to close.'

A ripple of orange-and-purple hair. Luscious moves to a point on the glass wall at about 90 degrees to the lectern. She is tall and as she moves, to the extent it can, the crowd parts in front of her. She is carrying the glass Bakhtin chair which she places between two waist-high speakers. Good God,

I'd forgotten that … while it is not really a £4 million chair, in one sense it is.

Gyro addresses his guest directly. 'Junior, your family have told us about some of the songs which have truly inspired you. For you they epitomise the principles of leadership. And of these songs, one has said it better for you than any other. If this tower can mean for others even one percent of what this song has meant for you, what an incredible force for good it will be in the world. Junior, we love you.'

Junior puts his hands up to his temple. His tears are few, but more than he has ever shed in public before. Laura beams. Casey cheers, having recovered from his discomfiture. Gyro beams at Junior.

Luscious is wearing a jewelled hair clasp, a full-length, long-sleeved orange sequin gown and elbow-length white gloves. We see these things because Luscious has climbed onto Alex's chair. I remember now – because of the crush of bodies it is the only chair in the auditorium. We can't watch her on the monitors because they are showing us the scene at the lakeside, where the Prime Minister is shaking the hands of his greeting party.

Luscious' voice surges out in a gorgeous contralto and everyone turns to look. It is mercury, liquid power, filling any space for vibration in people's souls as well as their bodies. By the final chorus everyone in the auditorium is joining in:

Climb ev'ry mountain
Ford ev'ry stream
Follow ev'ry by-way
Till you find your dream!

The Prime Minister is positioning himself to speak but in the auditorium he is unnoticed, the place now fully alive with whistles and cat-calls. Luscious is bowing deeply from the waist, both arms flung down in self-abasement, her hair tumbling forwards like Niagara. Or perhaps like Viagra, I remember thinking, wondering about the age of the audience and their reaction to a slightly ridiculous singer singing a more than slightly ridiculous song. Come on people, I remember thinking, a little proportion – this isn't Tina Turner.

Luscious uncoils from her bow, her arms now up and triumphant, acknowledging the crowd or perhaps blessing them, holding microphones. Obviously she is moved by the feelings of the moment, sweating a little, even crying. Even the roots of her hair have been moved by the moment, coming forward over her forehead and to her left. She looks at the camera with hope, or even love.

Oh people, dear people, this isn't Tina Turner, I remember thinking. This isn't even a woman.

Amelia has paused the video at the moment when we can just see that it is Frank. But it's Connie who's asking me if I can remember what I was thinking right then. I know why she's asking: this is my death moment, and her own will be coming up later.

'I'm thinking those aren't two microphones, the auditorium has exemplary acoustics. If those aren't microphones, then what they're wired up to aren't loudspeakers. I'm thinking, did Frank assume that the Prime Minister would be in the tower or perhaps he had only ever been after the fat cats all along? But today I stand with those fat cats – me, a thin and confused cat, a cat who never did any harm at all. Even if I did harm others – all right, I did harm others – you are going to kill me. What about Gandhi? What about non-violence?' I realise I'm yelling the last words.

Amelia presses the remote. Frank brings his hands together. What his hands hold touch each other. There is a flash beyond vision, a flash beyond pain, beyond noise and beyond understanding. The blind camera shows us nothing any more but nothing can stop me re-living the memory: Frank's 45-year-old male womb is ripped open and a new body is born, both heavenly and deformed. A crumpled, wilting, collapsing body of brilliantly different, sword-white light, accompanied by the smell of charred flesh and a poisonous umbilical cord of flame, burning from a plastic wig.

CONNIE

Ben has described it to me but of course it's indescribable. It's agony to look into Frank's eyes for the last time, but there is also glory. The nausea has gone, but it will take days to work through what I'm feeling in its place. I wonder if I'm hallucinating. Ben looks almost luminous.

Amelia is pushing on with the television clip, although these are images we have seen countless times on our TV screens – as news, as investigative journalism, as mystery, as the time the Martians landed. Starting that evening, Downing Street claimed that hackers got into the BBC's computers and introduced 'patently ludicrous' words and images into the Prime Minister's announcement. I ask Amelia about that.

'Hackers is less embarrassing than North Korea. North Korea would be less embarrassing than the truth,' she replies. 'It saves face, doesn't it?'

Speaking of face, the screen flickers and of course it's Quincey Parcha's, the tower glowing like a jubilee beacon in the background. We all know about Quincey Parcha, the 20-year old journalism student on a summer placement with BBC South who asks the question that goes round the world in less than an hour. Of course he doesn't know that yet; he's standing in for a sick colleague and about to do his first broadcast interview ever.

'Welcome to Hampton College, where we are with the Prime Minister for a significant announcement about the National Health Service. Prime Minister, good evening.'

'Good evening.'

Parcha stutters slightly. 'Prime Minister, what is your announcement?'

'I'm delighted to be here with Mark Topley, who is Hampton's outstanding MP as well as Minister for Health in the government. In Hampton we have a world-class business school, supported by outstanding global business leaders such as Wilson Pinnacle and, beside me, Alex Bakhtin.

'The college's tower which has just been opened is an outstanding example of cutting-edge British design. As leaders we should always be looking ahead to the next frontier. My government has no more serious responsibility than to do precisely this for the NHS.

'We need an NHS fit for the future. Already, we have world-class doctors, nurses and other clinicians: I say today that we need NHS managers to make the same grade. And so I am announcing the investment of one hundred and twenty million pounds by government and business to make management education in the British NHS the best in the world. We will double the number of doctors in the NHS.'

Parcha says, 'Will the new doctors from this one hundred and twenty million pound investment be doctors of medicine?'

The Prime Minister grins. 'They will be doctors of healthcare management excellence, graduating from business schools like Hampton. We are moving beyond MBAs and master's degrees, useful though these have been. Having a doctorate means being at the cutting edge of research in your field. You may know that a long time ago I gained one myself. We are pledging, and this is the first time that any British government has pledged this, that NHS management will be as cutting-edge as NHS medicine. Why should British patients accept less?'

The interviewer says, 'Prime Minister, but why Hampton? Why not London or Manchester, where there are strong business and medical schools side by side?'

The Prime Minister says, 'Well, Hampton is a marginal constituency, isn't it? We need to keep Hampton at the next election. I am very confident that this investment in Hampton will bring the appropriate return. And that will be the return of Mark Topley as Member of Parliament.'

Mark Topley's agreement is emphatic. 'I couldn't agree with the Prime Minister more. This is outstanding news for

Hampton and outstanding news for the college. And what has really helped bring the two together is that Dianne and I sleep together from time to time.'

The interviewer stalls before following his script. 'Lord Bakhtin, you have donated four million pounds to this programme. Why?'

Alex puts his arm round Dianne. 'Dianne is a very sexy lady, and Mr Topley is not the only man who can testify to that.'

Behind the camera a violent coughing fit strikes.

Dr Peach-Gyro says, 'But please don't put it all down to me. I mean, Alex, you got a peerage out of it.'

The Prime Minister nods.

Studio voices are whispering manically in the interviewer's ear. He nods decisively and turns back to the Prime Minister. 'Prime Minister, you have emphasised the international perspective tonight. So let me ask, why did Britain invade Iraq?'

A figure – Ed Lens – flies across the screen, punching the Prime Minister in the jaw so that he cannot answer. The camera is the next to fly, ending up upside down on the grass. Bedlam erupts. For a couple of minutes the screen is filled with sky and upside-down shoes and police boots. Two voices shout, 'Stop! Armed police!' Something is bleeped out.

'Decompression,' Amelia explains. 'When an undercover police officer suddenly needs to identify themselves to uniformed colleagues. Like the bends, dangerous, painful and best avoided.'

Ben says, 'Greg, I assume? You've blanked out a code word?'

Amelia nods. 'He's a detective now. Worldwide publicity

and undercover careers don't mix.' She clicks the remote control. 'You'll see more if I turn the image the right way up.'

Someone (presumably the cameraman) leaves the camera lying on the ground but nudges it to point towards the action. Off-screen, Lens is shouting his innocence but the starting of the helicopter rotor drowns him out. Greg races the Prime Minister towards the helicopter and pushes him inside. Circular agitation disturbs the lake as the helicopter lifts off.

In the foreground a Land Rover with flashing blue lights brakes abruptly. Now we see Lens, dragged by two armed officers. He is still shouting. As the helicopter recedes I can make out more of the words: 'Get Number Ten. Get a news blackout …' He screams as the barrel of a sub-machine gun smashes into his spine.

Suddenly the helicopter shudders as if with unspeakable fear and swoops back towards the water. The side door opens, and you can just make out the Prime Minister's immortal grin before he is shoved out. Two figures tumble towards the water as the helicopter rockets upwards. Two white splashes, and ten seconds later the screen shows us the picture of the Prime Minister that is on the front page of every national newspaper the next morning. In three cases the headline is identical:

NOT WAVING, BUT DROWNING

Then the screen goes black. 'A police boot, I'm afraid,' says Amelia. She pushes five sheets of paper towards me and Connie. 'At this point we've lost video inside the tower, obviously. The camera's microphone is still giving us an audio feed but what's happening is utter chaos – shouting, screaming and crying. The technical experts were able to pull out some phrases and voices. So we can identify Junior shouting, 'Casey, are you all right?' and Casey yelling, 'Dad, Dad, Dad!'. I thought if we wrote them down rather than played you a racket of noise, you'd more likely remember things.'

That makes sense. I scan the phrases, the script of a play with very short lines, most of them missing. A digital timeline runs down the left-hand margin from the detonation at 19:09:21 until 19:18:30, when I finish announcing the evacuation.

'Can you remember how it was for you, immediately after the flash?' Amelia asks me.

Amelia and Connie are leaning forward equally. Yes, with the script in front of me it's easy to remember. I tell them.

I remember that the blindness lifts slowly, although the brilliant light doesn't. Even if you are shielded from the light by others you cannot look towards it. Hands cling to eyes or ears. Those who can, look to see if they are hurt. I remember so many people crying out, 'Am I hurt? Am I hurt?'

You have to look yourself to see whether you are blind. That's scary. I remember saying to myself, 'Look at the monitor! You're not blind!' The monitor is showing figures by the lake. Not only am I not blind, but the world hasn't come to an end.

I hear, 'Welcome to Pinnacle College at Hampton, where we are with the Prime Minister … ''

My abiding memory of that first two minutes is the odour of charred flesh and burning plastic. A fire extinguisher is passed through the crowd and someone – maybe Cardew McCarthy – sprays foam into the vortex of light. The smell diminishes but not the light. A realisation passes among us like guilt – we're all all right. Except Frank Jones.

I look at Gyro. He is wondering how to take charge, but then the surreality overcomes him. It transfixes even the police officers on the terrace. I hear on the monitor the wheeze I came up with about doubling the number of doctors in the NHS. But something is very wrong.

The Prime Minister says, 'Well, Hampton is a marginal constituency, isn't it? We need to keep Hampton at the next election. I am very confident that this investment in Hampton will bring the appropriate return. And that will be the return of Mark Topley as Member of Parliament.'

Mark Topley says. 'I couldn't agree with the Prime Minister more. This is outstanding news for Hampton and outstanding news for the college. And what has really helped bring the two together is that Dianne and I sleep together from time to time.'

In the auditorium we are doing what it says on the tin – listening.

On screen, Alex puts his arm round Dianne. 'Dianne is a very sexy lady, and Mr Topley is not the only man who can testify to that.'

Gyro faints.

Dianne says, 'But please don't put it all down to me. I mean, Alex, you got a peerage out of it.'

Gyro isn't the only one. Junior collapses. McCarthy runs forward and starts pumping Junior's chest. I'm thinking *what is going on*? What is going on is that people are telling the truth. As if this was perfectly normal.

'Which is when I get it,' I say to Amelia and Connie. 'Suddenly I understand Frank's project. He cared more for truth and honesty than for anything else, and he went back to physics to try to get there. He started searching two years ago for a different way up the mountain. He found a way to make a different kind of light. He found a way to tear the veil of our human world.'

Back in the auditorium I realise everyone has stopped listening and wants leading. It's strange to see: every big-wig's face – even Alex's – is pleading, lead me! Someone lead me! It's a spaceship full of emperors with no clothes.

Clearly, the someone to lead them will not be Gyro. He has passed out, his flagship event in tatters. Someone has died in his beloved tower, and two heart-stopping doses of marital news will be going out on national television.

And the leader will not be the Pinnacles either, father or son. The shock has killed Junior. 'Casey realises that his father is dead when the amount on his cufflinks suddenly jumps to $50 billion dollars,' I explain. Casey has inherited.

I realise one of the voices screaming in my ear is Haddrill, from the command centre. Stillman, he says, take charge please. Orderly evacuation in groups of ten by the lift. Use the lift because many of the guests are elderly and in shock. Everyone is to muster in the car park. Once the tower is clear, he will cut the power and hopefully the light.

I push the pages back towards Amelia. 'So that's what I do. I go to the lectern, I get everybody organised. I go down in the lift with the first group. Except I do one thing before all that. I find the set of keys to the Lexus which Gyro keeps in his jacket.

'Then I jump in the Lexus and race out of the college like a bat out of hell. And I call you.' I'm looking at Connie. 'Thank God you were in the called numbers on my phone.'

CONNIE

It seems Amelia's questions will never end, but around six o'clock they do – although neither of us can imagine what all that effort of inquiry will produce. Ben and I walk across the Millennium Bridge from St Paul's to the Tate Modern. It used to wobble but no more. Downstream from the Tate is Shakespeare's Globe Theatre, where Ben has booked us to have dinner in the theatre restaurant. Is that what we have been telling – tales told by idiots, full of sound and fury, signifying nothing? I hope not.

The drizzle has stopped and it's a spectacular summer evening. We pause to watch a dozen tourists in waterproofs be flung from side to side on the surface of the Thames in a high-speed inflatable boat. They have paid for that experience. The two of us have had quite enough of being flung from side to side as it is.

We say to each other that we both want to build normal lives, possibly together, but it will have to be some kind of 'new normal'. For one thing, Ben needs to decide on a job. He has had some offers from those fat cats who see him as the hero of the tower.

However, so far 23 of those fat cats have given interviews somewhere in the world media in which their own role in saving world capitalism is centre stage. (I don't normally read *Private Eye* but the satirical magazine is keeping score. Seth Carter showed me.)

Most of the offers he's told me about, however, are Bakhtin 2.0 – more or less money, no life and for a terminal bonus they turn you into an arsehole. To put it another way, everything (which includes any question of 'us') depends on what the two of us have learned from this extraordinary circus. I'm glad Ben's sticking to not making any on-the-spot decisions.

Ben asks me about tomorrow.

'Tomorrow is my second governors' meeting. It's in the evening, but to do what I've decided to do about Gyro I will have to go early, in the afternoon.'

'What you have decided to do is?'

'I checked with Sling – the bank have written off the loan as Gyro said, to pay him off for saving them. So, on the plus side, Hampton has no immediate nightmare scenario.'

'But you want the rules tightened up so it can never happen again.'

'I do. But the more I've thought about it, that doesn't work. First of all, I'm the newbie youngster on the board. I couldn't get the board seriously to tighten up the rules unless I came clean about how Gyro evaded them. So that would push us straight into the him-or-me scenario, who's telling the truth and what's my evidence.'

Ben muses, 'That's what Frank would have wanted you to do.'

'Yes, you're right. But I reckon I lose that fight.'

Ben protests, 'Even if someone leans on Sling to shut up, don't forget I was a witness. There'll be records on the systems of that bank in the Netherlands Antilles, you can't wipe computers that easily. A court could subpoena them.'

I wave my hands. 'A legal nightmare. I don't want my life ruined.'

'Our life.'

'I'm waiting to see what you decide, remember? Anyway, there are still two problems. So what if the rules are tightened up? What does that really achieve? Gyro knew what he was doing wasn't allowed. Rules can be got round if someone wants to badly enough. And Gyro isn't all bad. He isn't even mostly bad.

'Both of us admire what he's done for the school, far more than any other dean by a long shot. Gyro's better placed than anyone to spend the next year turning our new-found fame around the world into the income and high-paying students that Hampton badly needs.'

'That's a dilemma.'

'Which I've solved.'

'Really?'

'Tomorrow afternoon I'll tell him his secret is safe with me provided he does four things. One, spend the next twelve months getting our income up – converting our fame into cash. Two, propose me as a member of the audit committee and support a tightening up of the rules over the next six months – it's not sufficient but it's necessary. And three, give in his notice in twelve months' time so we can look for a new dean. At the end of the day, he sailed too close to the wind. Changing the rules isn't enough.'

Ben's eyebrows rise and rise. 'Wow. That's a heavy-duty play. I don't know what you've been learning, but it's some potent stuff. So, do you think Gyro will say yes?'

'If he doesn't, I'll blow the whistle.'

Ben is quiet. 'Well, he'll need something to keep him occupied over the next year. Did you see he and Dianne have separated?'

'Yes, but how much time did they spend together anyway?'

Ben puts his hand on my arm. 'You've only listed three things.'

'Number four: a memorial for Frank – and a promise never, ever, ever to slag him off.'

(THGIN) ƎNUႱ ⇂Ɛ YAᗡꙄЯUHT

BEWARE THE CANDIRU. This minute, almost-transparent Amazonian catfish, about 2.5cm (1 in) long, is reported to be able to swim up the urethra of a person urinating in the water – where it gets stuck by the dorsal spine. The chance of this happening is remote, but don't take the risk. Cover your genitals and don't urinate in the water.

JOHN WISEMAN[7]

As soon as the light had flooded from the tower, Greg's neurones and hormones had gone to DEFCON 1. He had known something would happen, and it was happening – but what was it? The moment to burst from the chrysalis of waiting and nonentity to claim his destiny by surprise and storm had arrived; every tissue of his body knew that. Well, unfortunately, not the pulmonary and oesophageal tissues: he fought to suppress a coughing fit that arrived from nowhere. Superheroes didn't cough, that was one of their lesser-known superpowers. Besides, the Prime Minister was on television. But the fit defeated him.

'Why did Britain invade Iraq?'

Et tu, Brute? was Greg's final thought as Lens punched the Prime Minister in the jaw and then turned on the cameraman. He had not seen Lens coming. But from that moment, Greg was pure action.

The two armed police officers jumped Lens, who went down on the grass. In his ear-piece Greg heard them call the back-up team for assistance.

Lens screamed until a punch broke his nose. 'The evening news ... in 10 minutes ...'

'PORCUPINE TITTY!' shouted Greg, like the devil bellowing for his lawyer.

The words came from a list computer-generated after extensive research. They had been calculated to offer the optimal combination of audibility, memorability, unlikelihood of arising for any accidental reason as well as generating immediate attention from male and female workforces. Greg had never expected to use them and the police officers had never expected to hear them, but they worked. Decompression: the emergency identification by an undercover officer of himself to the uniformed branch.

Greg's body weight propelled the Prime Minister towards the helicopter. The pilot started the rotor. Greg shoved his precious cargo in and followed, slamming the door shut. The pilot looked blank, so when he repeated the phrase Greg threw in 'Undercover police!' for good measure.

As they climbed, the scene below turned into an explosive incident in Toytown. The back-up car arrived and all the figures pumping adrenaline and guns receded into miniatures. Greg followed the pilot's gesture and put on the headset hanging above his seat, happy to discard his once-adored ear-piece. The latter had gone mental and was stopping Greg from thinking. Lens? So the conspiracy extended *inside* Downing Street? In which case the helicopter might not be safe.

The involuntary passenger stared out of the opposite window like a sack of potatoes, all eyes and no comprehension. And no seatbelt either. Reaching over to buckle the Prime Minister in flitted into Greg's mind and out again: it was too much trouble. Instead Greg glared suspiciously down at the lake, looking for new hidden enemies. But the lake was toying with him: the secret of the pain which it would inflict on his groin in a few hours' time remained hidden.

At 400 feet, the Prime Minister and Greg began to regain their breathing. They were climbing away from the sun, so towards the east. The pilot spoke on a channel Greg could not hear, two or three words at first and then rapid-fire. From the movement of the pilot's lips, something had just changed. Abruptly they banked, reversed direction and dived hard towards the lake. Cabin roof 3; passengers' skulls 0. The Prime Minister put his hand up to dab a rivulet of blood. The tower made their skin and bones glow as they passed over.

Greg's headphones purred into life as the pilot addressed him. 'Two unidentified incoming from the west, ultra-low altitude.'

Greg thought, fuck me. And then: so why have we turned towards them? 'Incoming?' he blurted.

'Jets. Or missiles,' the pilot explained.

We who are about to die might as well act the part. 'Life jackets!' barked the pilot. 'Grab him! Get ready to jump!'

The violent dive left Greg feeling sick. Being a superhero was over-rated. Surely he had done enough, unmasking at least part of the conspiracy and taking the Prime Minister to safety, or what had seemed like safety at the time. But with one hand he groped for a life jacket, while with the other he hung on for dear life. The plunging cabin stopped about ten feet above a stormy lake. Spray soaked him as, at the pilot's press of a lever, the door was jettisoned and tumbled away in a gale. The pilot tilted the cabin toward the wet void and held up five fingers. 'Impact in five,' he said, and began counting down.

Embracing fate in both arms, in one case in the form of the Prime Minister and in the other case in the form of a life jacket, Greg jumped into the lake.

The Slough train was due in eight minutes.

'Nice evening,' said the old man with the Union Jack but Connie ignored him, pacing the length of the platform and back. All men were the same and she was not in the mood to forgive any of them – whether the tattooed youngsters in the pub, this barnacle on the railway bench, the fat cat, the slick misogynist, the weird scientist or, no better than any of them, the apprentice shitbag.

The human race had been betrayed by its priapic half, and several of them had betrayed her personally. On another day she might have felt more kindly towards the pensioner but her bladder wasn't having any of it. Whoever fixed the wanking hand to the lift had called it right.

She told herself again and again that all Ben needed to have done was own up to his role at Bakhtin on the Sunday afternoon of her birthday. What could have been easier? She would have shouted for a bit but forgiven him (she liked to think). Probably they would still have slept together, but without a lie growing like a weed in between all the words they said to each other.

Without that lie, Frank would not have decided during Wednesday's dinner to get Connie back to his house this afternoon. Without going back she wouldn't have been confronted by his need of her car battery. Without giving up her car battery, she would have had no reason to feel the soft curds of fear welling up inside her which she was covering over with a hard blow-torch of anger.

Still, from what she remembered from Ben's timetable, the tower was open by now and the Prime Minister's announcement made. In a few minutes she would be on her way to Slough and could begin to calm down. Of all towns, Slough was the epitome of tedious normality, although the poet laureate Sir John Betjeman had wanted to obliterate it from the sky. Connie has fixed the horizon with eyes like red lasers, as if in a minute two smudges of smouldering ash four inches apart might appear on the celestial dome.

Which, a minute later, they did. Connie pinched herself. The approaching roar, horrendously loud, caught her by surprise. Standing a few feet from the man on the park bench, the vibrations in her bones turned her blood to ice. Two cigar tubes about six metres long with stubby wings flew overhead.

She ducked. Waving his Union Jack, the old man has spoken to her but she heard nothing. 'What did you say?'

'Tomahawks,' he repeated matter-of-factly, waving his flag as if at a military exhibition. 'Cruise missiles. Turbofan engines. 1,500-mile range. Nuclear capable.'

Connie's thought was run! Run, either from the firestorm of a tactical nuclear explosion or from police hunting for Frank's accomplice! But either would be useless. Even if all of the checkpoint police were killed in the blast, she would die, too. And if for some reason she did not, Alderley station, like all public places in modern England, had closed-circuit surveillance. She could not have chosen a more visible dress if she tried.

She forgave Ben. He only betrayed her. She had murdered hundreds, perhaps thousands, of innocent people. Frank must have needed the batteries to operate some sort of homing device for the missiles.

Connie remembered the mobile networks going down on 7/7 and the calls made from hell on 9/11, but reached for her phone anyway. She would leave a message for one of her brothers. She crouched behind the stone hut on the platform that housed engineering equipment; she knew it would not shelter her from the blast, but did it anyway. Out of sight she heard the whine of the missiles' engines going up as they approached their target, the change in sound destroying any possibility, however remote, that the instruments of death were en route to somewhere far away.

It was 7.28 but the indicator has changed to predict the train's arrival at 7.32. Connie knew this was a train that would never arrive, and fainted as her phone began to ring. The number that was calling was not one she had stored in the phone's memory.

Ben's all-access lapel pin got him through the police checkpoint but at the price of a near-heart attack. He crested Pynbal's Ridge as two cruise missiles, hugging the ground with their terrain-following radar, blasted out of nowhere singeing the Lexus with exhaust. He stopped in total confusion. Five minutes ago he thought he had worked out what Frank had done, but now …

The missiles headed down the lake where Ben saw two people swimming. One of them waved, and suddenly the missiles arced up, parting company to make the arms of a 'V'. Two maelstroms appeared in the water. Trails of orange-and-gold smoke shot upwards, creating the logo of Virtual Savings & Trust several thousand feet high.

'Casey,' Ben said, understanding it all. Casey could not get the Red Arrows so … sadly Junior had died before seeing the surprise. Ben jumped back in the Lexus and dialled Connie's number. She answered on the fifth attempt, badly dazed. 'Connie, where are you?' he asked.

'Alderley station. There's a train here. I don't know if it's mine.'

'Stay there. I'll be less than five minutes.'

'Ben.' Her tone was like a glass of tap water, neither cold

nor warm, not happy or angry, yet potentially offering the conditions for life. 'I think it's my train.'

'Stay there. I can't explain. It's terrible, and it's amazing. He finally did it, Connie. Frank finally did it. You need to come and see.'

'Is Frank dead?'

'I think so.' Pause. 'No, Connie, I'm sure he's dead. I can't lie. But don't go. He wanted you to see what he's done, you know that. Afterwards, I'll drive you home.'

Over the phone Connie could tell a bend was being rounded in alarmingly stunt-man style.

'Slow down, Ben! All right. But on one condition.'

'Anything.'

'Take me to the ladies' at the Kings Arms first.'

For four hours they had been parked at the lookout on Crassock hill, where they had walked on Sunday night. Ben had driven there after securing Connie's urgent relief at the Kings Arms and then sausage and chips twice, bought from the take-away next door with both of them in evening dress.

At first like moths they had simply looked, and had been excited by the looking. The valley was bathed in the light of an impostor moon, and they were bathed with it. This moon was fixed several floors high on a titanium column while ants scurried beneath it and inside it. The scene transfixed them, all the more because the intensity of the light was palpably fading.

The radial night-shadows cast by themselves, by the trees, by the college buildings and by the occasional car moving up Pynbal's Ridge were becoming less defined than they had been two or three hours ago. As the light declined, its reflection in the lake mingled with the flashing blue necklace caused by the glow of innumerable police cars. They would stay until the light had gone, in memory of Frank.

By 8.40pm some of the police cars had moved halfway up their side of the valley and towards Frank's house. Ben recounted two or three times what he had seen, sifting fragments to try to expand what he had deduced. But it was Connie who recalled Frank's words best, piecing together things which he had said to the two of them over dinner, things intended to be understood afterwards. Frank, the crusader for truth, had lit for a few hours an enchanted light in whose beam it was impossible to lie. He had almost succeeded in getting to the bottom of the Iraq War. Almost, but not quite.

At about 9.30 Ben took Connie to stand at the lip of the lookout. 'I don't know how much more time we've got,' he said simply. 'I brought you here for a reason.'

She was curious. 'What reason?'

'To be in the light, the two of us. And then I say, I want to marry you. Will you marry me?'

'Why do you want to marry me?'

'Because I love you.' Ben seized Connie's hand. 'You see it, don't you Connie? This is Frank's present to us. When I say I love you, I can't lie. In all of history it may never happen again that a man asks a woman to marry him when he cannot lie.'

'You're crazy.'

'I'm not.'

'I'm ten years older than you. Do you worry about that?'

'Yes. But women live longer than men anyway. Though if we want to have kids we shouldn't waste time.'

'Having kids is one thing, being a dad is another. Do you want to be a dad?'

Ben looked up at the moon and then at its impostor. He was as curious as Connie to see what he said. 'I want it very much. I want to be a good dad.' Then he added, as if it was part of the same thought, 'I want a good job, but it doesn't have to be a top job.'

Connie was quiet for centuries. Then she said, 'Am I beautiful?'

'Very.'

'Just to you?'

'To many people.' Ben smiled and pointed at the tower. 'Frank is keeping me honest. I thought about saying "everyone", but I couldn't.' A pause, again. 'So will you marry me?'

'You realise that I can't lie either? Silly me, of course you do. The answer is no.' She kept hold of his hand. 'Or not yet. I feel something for you, something very strong. I have done ever since you were sprawled across the dean's desk.' Both of them laughed. 'But it's too soon to know if it's love, and it's definitely too soon for you to know what you want. You only started growing up earlier this evening.'

Around them were silver birch trees. All of the words they had spoken hung pegged out on invisible clotheslines between the branches, and they walked round inspecting them, gleaming and wet in their honesty. Not even a preposition slipped away forgotten.

'You might be right,' Ben said finally. And then, 'I suppose we will find out if I stick around.'

'We will.'

'If this had been a fairy-tale, you would have said yes and I would have produced a ring.' He put his hand in his pocket and turned it inside out, producing nothing. They collapsed laughing and sat on the grass holding each other tightly.

Later he asked her, 'What is it we have, if it isn't love?'

'It is what it is,' she replied.

When it was cooler, nearly midnight, the tower light had become quite dim. Connie and Ben sat on the back seat of the Lexus watching the car's television with the sound turned low and the doors closed. Ben's arm was around Connie's shoulders. The news cycle had been continuous. The announcers were simply repeating the same film clip of the Prime Minister's interview, mixing it with so-called expert opinions and fanciful speculations.

The spokesman at Number Ten: 'Obviously we need the details from the forensic examination of the incident at Hampton College. But so far as the interview is concerned, this is quite a simple, although certainly a spectacular, piece of hacking. Completely false sounds and images created in an animation studio were hacked into the BBC's news feed. The Prime Minister, who is entirely safe, has insisted on a full inquiry, but at no stage has there been any risk to national security, and at no stage did the Prime Minister say any of the ridiculous things attributed to him.'

The reporter on the scene: 'Well, Carol, here at the tower the police have confirmed the death of one 45-year-old male, a member of the college faculty. Apart from shock, we know now that there were no other injuries, although there is one unconfirmed report of a heart attack. It is important to emphasise that no-one here sees any risk to the public whatsoever.

'That said, the police are offering no explanation at this time either for this man's death or for the light which continues to shine, even though the tower's power supply was cut off at 7.45pm. Scientists from the National Physical Laboratory are arriving as we speak, with some urgency because the light is fading. Indeed, from the amount by which it has faded just in the last two hours, the prediction is that it will be totally extinguished by 4am.'

The newsreader in the studio: 'Meanwhile, this unusual story is continuing to spread around the world, with the clip which may be the Prime Minister and a bodyguard jumping into the lake stirring enormous interest on Japanese breakfast television.'

Connie whistled. A new headline started running across the bottom of the screen. 'First Improvident poised to expand with £10 billion capital injection from the China Financial and Monetary Corporation.'

Connie reached across to unbuckle Ben's belt. He lay back. She bent over him. Then, above her head the rear window shattered under a blow that rocked the car on its suspension. Covered in glass, they both screamed and drops of blood fell onto Ben's shirt from Connie's cheek.

Whatever it lacked in consistency, 'Stop fucking swearing or I'll leave you to drown' made up for in effect. The Prime Minister stopped taking water into his lungs and Greg made more progress lugging his catch to shore, where two sets of flashing lights raced to meet them. As soon as the Prime Minister was out of earshot Haddrill scowled, 'Help me. Should we shoot you or give you a medal?'

After 20 minutes inside, Greg's shivering became less frenetic. After another 20, his feet were still in the puddles of water called his shoes but other parts of his body were starting to believe in the possibility of getting dry. Henderson remained unreachable and Greg had given up trying to explain the glaringly obvious, the classic one-two. He had worked it out as soon as he had discovered Ben's rapid departure from the scene. Even on a good day, Vanish had had the disposition of a rabbit with a weak bladder – it would have been a piece of cake for Frank to push him over the edge a few weeks before the big event and switch Ben into the crucial vacant space.

Clearly, Ben had tipped Frank off to empty the boathouse, and authorised the ludicrous woman singer. God alone knew how Ed Lens fitted in, but the scorched tyre marks behind the departing Lexus (Greg's Lexus!) with Ben at the wheel spelled out the truth in neon lights. Those with eyes to see, could see. Unfortunately, Greg counted their number on the thumbs of one hand.

Greg headed to his place to lick his wounds. He lived on campus in a studio flat – well, a cupboard with a balcony in the janitorial block. On the balcony he lit neroli incense for the aroma of bitter oranges, and pondered the way modern uses of 'incense' overlooked its meaning – to make angry. He changed out of his sopping clothes and showered. His laundry had not come back so his only clean underpants were lilac, which was hardly fit for purpose. He chose a dark cotton sweatshirt and – after a moment's hesitation – black leather trousers. He touched them and they felt like revenge.

Like any luxury car the Lexus had a satellite tracker to monitor its location in the event of theft. By entering a 10-digit identifier and a password into the manufacturer's website, Greg would be able to access the car's location over the web. But first there were security procedures. Lexus would not hand out the whereabouts of their cars lightly. They would call and verify identity over the phone, but on a Thursday evening after 8pm there was a skeleton staff. As the incense burned, Greg listened to Wagner's *Siegfried*, the young hero who grows to manhood without knowing fear and sets off to kill the evil Fafner.

Lexus called back an hour later, after which Greg could locate the car on his computer screen. Oh the happiness, oh the deepest sense of righteousness, once he saw where the Lexus was! According to the tracker it had been motionless for nearly two hours. He pondered whether the car could have been abandoned – but abandoned within the college grounds, at a lookout point where it would easily be seen in the morning? No. Even now the culprit was betraying his guilt. Ben's sick and impudent mind had returned to the scene of the crime to survey his handiwork.

Through the windows of the maintenance workshop came more than enough of the tower's light for Greg to find a crowbar and a length of rope. He blacked up his face, his hands and his trainers with boot polish. Just before he slipped into the shadows between the college buildings and the woods on Crassock hill, for a few seconds Greg caught sight of himself in a mirror. Erotic in moonlit war-paint, he felt a stiffening in his pants. Tonight the spirits were with him and he would triumph.

As he climbed, his eyes got worse. The last milligrammes of antihistamine gave up, turned tail and bolted after half an hour spent crouching and crawling with his face in the night grass. Even as the leaves reached out to touch him like admiring fans, perfidiously they stabbed his eyeballs. So his eyes wept, making the shoe polish on his cheeks run.

It was well into his climb when Greg noticed that the stiffening in his pants was his pants. Then the hardening had got worse and spread, beginning to cramp his right leg. He tried to take off the offending garment, but had no luck; slowly it was turning into a mediaeval torturer's vice. He had first put on Ben's spare pair of SmartPants a week previously, but had never logged on to register them. Thus the lake wreaked its harm: if Greg had not had to jump in, he would not have had to change underpants.

By the time he glimpsed the Lexus Greg was unable to walk and barely able to see, gritting his teeth together against the increasing pain. But he pushed on and then deployed his most practised skill, waiting.

He was lying on the ground on his side about 10 paces behind the car. Ben and Connie had closed the doors and he was taking advantage of this, his chest beating out a strenuous rhythm while twigs and small stones were crushed underneath. He left behind a wake of black smears, like an irregular tyre track. Despite cramping pain in his right hamstring, he pushed forward. With each push, the crowbar clipped to his belt above his left hip slid off and got in his way again.

In the three-quarters night, the light of the moon was contending strongly with the fading light from the tower. The light of the television inside the car went out and the silver Lexus was completely dark. From it an occasional noise escaped, an indistinguishable word or the car moving on its suspension.

Greg's line of approach had the car's exhaust coming up directly in his eyeline. But this was not a problem because the engine was off. Earlier, while he had still been able to walk, he had heard the hooting of a pair of owls excited about prey. Now he was as excited about his own prey.

On his iPod Touch Greg selected the track which Wagner wrote for the actions which he now had to perform – when Siegfried's hammer blows forge anew the sword which will defeat Fafner. Now was the hour for revenge. Now was the hour when he would be unstoppable. He forced himself to his feet, resolved to overcome all possible resistance. He smashed the crowbar down on the back window above the courting couple. He would tie them up and drive them to Alderley police station to heroic acclaim. Now was the moment when Greg screamed and fell to the ground, clutching his groin in agony.

The agony could have been avoided had Greg complied with the instructions on the SmartPants card and registered them online within one week of first use. But to a right-thinking person, such things served only to confirm life's inexcusable and lamentable unfairness.

AFTERWORD
AFTERWORD

(three years later, in November)

BEN

Pearl says 'Boo', addressing her balloon on a stick. Connie reckons she'll be all right for 10 minutes and then I'll take her downstairs.

Pearl is our joy, our 18-month-old bundle of trouble and smiles. She fiddles with my silver neck chain. The grey clouds are light, high and skidding by fast, and the winter afternoon sun visits from time to time. But it's too blustery to walk by the lake. So when the big people get talking, Pearl and I will head for a corner of reception where there is plenty of furniture to cling onto while she stands up and bumps around.

Connie wants me to say hello to people but I'm here for the views. It's my first time in the tower since the opening. How creepy to hear the lift announcements, now voiced by a poor man's Hugh Grant but working fine. Carrying Pearl, I thread my way through the thickening crowd to enjoy the range of views from different spots.

This month's storms have been vicious and a dozen trees lie flattened, but the main newcomer is the new Frank Jones student accommodation block (Gyro is no slouch at re-positioning: in *The Sunday Times* three days after the opening, the exit pay-off Frank had given to his brother had become 'an exceptional bonus').

With three floors laid out in a 120-degree arc, each studio bedroom has a view of the tower. Since the arc is centred where I am standing, I can see into the lives of 60 MBA students at a glance. When I was one, my fellow students were mostly British; now the chances are I'm looking at posters, photographs and travel bags from three or four continents.

Not that I would be accepted now: the average GMAT test score to get into Hampton has risen more than 90 points. Hampton is a much more luminous star in the firmament, its light firing up the dreams of new crabs in new rockpools. This is the light that remains after the fading of Frank's fierce incandescence.

Did Frank mean to propel Hampton into the top global division of capitalist *madrassas*? I imagine not. *Madrassa* is an even more apt term now that Hampton is synonymous around the world for uncompromising truth and honesty. The competition has also been busy manufacturing and marketing their own versions of extra ethical vitamins – values, integrity, sustainability, even an MBA oath from Harvard.

Seeing the lectern makes me do an abrupt 360-degree swivel but there's no singer today, no amplification system.

We find a small space and I crouch down beside Pearl on the glass floor. 'Look,' I say, pointing downwards. 'Birds. Down there.'

She's mildly curious but no more, which on reflection hits the nail on the head. 'Boo!' she says.

'No wonder we couldn't see you down there! Say hello to Dorothy!' Connie pulls me up. She's with Dorothy Lines, the deputy dean. Dorothy didn't throw her hat into the ring for the top job when (slightly to my surprise) Gyro handed in his resignation bang on Connie's private schedule. His successor arrived the same week as Pearl. He is a full-time academic, a scholar in the best sense (so they say): a Malaysian whose route to Hampton came via Stanford and Shanghai. According to Connie he has much of Gyro's energy and ambition but is house-trained, organisationally and academically, which lets the governors sleep at night.

Of course the main factor affecting the quality of their sleep is rocketing student numbers and fees, which mean that Hampton can afford a dean who costs 285,000 a year (pounds or dollars, whichever has the greater value – he is the head of a *business* school, after all).

Who would say boo to that? Pearl, naturally.

Dorothy is beaming. 'It's wonderful to see you again, Ben!' Dorothy has already met Pearl because these days Connie is a big cheese. She was the driving force on the governors' committee which found the new dean. 'Did you know that this will be Gyro's first speech back at the school since leaving? And it's particularly good that you're here because we've got a writer wandering around with a recorder. I need to send him in your direction. Did Connie tell you about the book?'

If I needed another reason to skedaddle downstairs, I've just got one.

'What business are you doing these days?' Lines asks. ' I see a lot of your wife but I feel embarrassingly out of touch with one of Hampton's most celebrated alumni.'

'I did get a few offers three years ago, but in the end I set up a small management consultancy with two friends – not writing reports but getting hands-on with small businesses which are scaling up. Talk about shit timing with the economy! We joke that we're a private equity fund without any money.'

'How is it working out?'

'So-so. Often it's been more hours and more worry for less money than a corporate job. But we get to choose our clients and our business practices. We could eventually make a reasonable whack if the economy can get over its hangover.'

Connie looks over my Pearl-free shoulder and grins. 'If there's one man who can get the economy to do that, he's here.'

'Ben!' William C Gyro CBE, deputy governor of the Bank of England, comes up all effusive. I appear to be a long-lost buddy with no personal space needs. 'And this must be?'

Pearl hovers on the edge of boo but decides to spit in Gyro's eye instead. Connie is all 'Oh Pearl!' and tissues to the rescue, while giving me a sly wink. After all, Connie insisted Gyro move on because of a dodgy loan, so it's only reasonable that he becomes deputy governor of the Bank of England. Gyro's role is a new one, specially created to make sure that we learn the right lessons from the financial crisis.

'Welcome back, Professor,' says Lines. 'We miss you.'

Gyro frowns. 'Now then, Dorothy – don't get any smudges on Hampton's untouchable reputation for truth and honesty.'

The perfect opportunity to take my daughter in the lift back down to sanity approaches, in the form of the writer with a digital recorder trying to catch Gyro's eye.

'But we should see more of you,' Lines continues. 'Don't forget you're a professor here – the inaugural Julia Bakhtin Professor of Selfless Leadership, no less.' Then her face crumples like the rear bumper of a resprayed car wreck.

Connie giggles. I busy myself with a health-and-safety check on Pearl's balloon.

Then everyone including Lines is laughing like a gang of teenage girls trying to walk in stilettos, doubled up and falling over. Give him credit, Gyro is laughing by far the loudest, and he doesn't appear to be faking it.

The chair in question is the first anywhere in the world to renominate automatically each time Bakhtin acquires a new wife. So while Lines described Gyro's title correctly at the point it was bestowed, William C Gyro CBE is now the Dianne, Lady Bakhtin Professor of Selfless Leadership. As I have good reason to remember, the award comes complete with a very splendid glass chair.

Acknowledgements

Diana Nyad was the first person to swim from Cuba to Florida. She did it aged 64. Her TED talk 'Never, ever give up' hammers home this point: solo long-distance swimming is not something to do alone. As night followed day followed night, Diana's crew were there for her in a boat. Since then I've constantly asked clients who face the difficult and apparently solitary challenge of changing careers, 'Who's in your boat?'

In my boat for *MBA* were Rosemary and Peter Drew, Guy Meredith, C M (Craig) Taylor and the crew at EyeStorm Media and Lightning Books: editor Martha Ellen Zenfell, co-publisher Dan Hiscocks and collaborator Kathy Jones. Thank you for the feeding, the navigation, the encouragement and the correction. Thanks, Trish, for so much love and inspiration. If in some way, at some time, my late father and my nephew Ben accept the dedication made herewith to them, I will be delighted. The inadequacies which remain after so much help are exclusively mine.

There is a scholarly critique of business schools and their role in financial capitalism, originating in part from business schools themselves. In 2004 Henry Mintzberg wrote *Managers Not MBAs*[8]. In 2005 Sumantra Ghoshal argued that 'by propagating ideologically inspired amoral theories, business schools have actively freed their students from any sense of moral responsibility'[9]. In 2007 Rakesh Khurana delivered his highly readable and thorough critical history of business schools in the land of their birth, the United States[10]. Ralph Stacey[11] has offered an essential post-crisis perspective. I owe Ralph, Doug Griffin and my other doctoral faculty and fellow students special thanks.

The aims of this book are different, but I hope kindred.

[8] *Managers Not MBAs: A Hard Look at the Soft Practice of Managing and Management Development,* Barrett-Koehler, San Francisco CA (2004)

[9] *Bad Management Theories are Destroying Good Management Practices, Academy of Management Learning and Education,* (2005), vol. 4 no. 1

[10] *From Higher Aims to Hired Hands:: The Social Transformation of American Business Schools and the Unfulfilled Promise of Management as a Profession,* Princeton University Press, Princeton NJ (2007)

[11] *Complexity and Organizational Reality: Uncertainty and the Need to Rethink Management after the Collapse of Investment Capitalism,* Routledge, Abingdon UK (2010)

Lightning Books

Lightning Books is a new way for authors and publishers to work together. The publishing industry has changed, and unknown authors find it hard to get a hearing, let alone a publishing deal.

Our company has responded to this challenge by giving publishers a new way of nurturing new talent, and giving authors a chance to succeed. Lightning Books is founded on an equal relationship between author and publisher. We work equally hard. We take equal risks and share equal rewards. We are collaborators. We are co-publishers.

Our small team collectively has over 50 years' experience covering every aspect of publishing – from editorial, design and production to marketing and global sales. We put our experience to work as we work. For our authors. For ourselves. For each other. Lightning Books publishes novels with cracking endings. If you've written one, then why not submit it to us to see if together we can introduce your manuscript to the audience it deserves?

Visit us at: **www.lightning-books.com**

MBA · Lightning Books
ISBN 978-1-78563-005-7
9 781785 630057 >
90pcfree.com · Pub Date: 7 Sept 2015

This is a new concept for getting good books into readers' hands. It allows you to try 90% of a book for free. It allows you to share this 90% with whoever you like and as many times as you like. It also allows authors and publishers to ask, having offered 90% for free, that readers who buy the book pay the price set by the publisher.

Competing on price is healthy but only until it compromises quality. With low-cost products, the people who produce the goods end up having to cut corners, which often impacts on parts of the creative process. It is the detail in these processes that can often add real value to what is being published. Without these, the reader's experience can be compromised.

We want to be able to invest fully in the process to produce books that stand the 90pcfree test and which people are then willing to pay a fair price for. While there are books being sold at 99 pence, this is difficult to do.

We want to live in a world where there are books worth paying more than 99p for. Go for 90pcfree.com, not 99p.

Look out for 90pcfree

The logo and logo bar at the top of the page are the way to recognise being able to get 90% of a book downloaded and shared for free.

The logo bar will not only house the logo, but will give the title of the book (top left), the publisher (top right), the website from where you can download 90% free (bottom left), and the publication date of the full version of the book (bottom right). The barcode in the centre is the barcode and isbn of the full version of the book.

With thanks

It always amazes us at Lightning Books just how many people
– each with different skills and many years of experience in
their field – are involved in publishing a book. They rarely get
any mention, as for instance those involved in films do.

In a world where value often drives purchasing decisions, we
feel that by showing those involved we are not only recognising
them but also demonstrating the real value that the book holds.

Douglas Board
Dan Hiscocks
Martha Ellen Zenfell
Kathy Jones
Jenny Orr
Simon Fenton
Georgina Sylvester
Anna Torborg
Darren Mead
Sue Rendell
Jackie Coglan
Gavin Reed
Stehen West
Toni Sawyer
Julia Evans
Ruth Goodman
Paul Wood
Alan Cooper
Brooke O'Donnell
Bridget Costin
Pam Harcourt
Elizabeth Kepsel
Mallori Bontrager
Laura Di Giovine

Ed Shamwana
Joe Roche
Andrew Easton
Natalie Fox
Fiona Incledon
Theodore James
Ian Gibson
Joan McGowan
Jenny Keating
Vincent Henchion
Elenor Pigg
Adam Petros
Joshua Arthur
Oran Michaels
Calum Nile
Facility Wood
Nikki Hird
Josef Lentsch
Fiona Bradley
Tobias Stead
Eva Swan
Bea Carvalho
Matthew Bates
Mike Roberts

Izumi Chavez
Sam Leo
Bridget Radnedge
Matt Wright
Lisa Leaver
Ethan Walles
Candace Hays
Lauren Klouda
Cara Sample
Robin Rainer
Jillian Tsui
Clark Matthews
Jill Hughes
Simon Blacklock
Ainsley Boe
Christian Forder
Robert Mitchell
Martin Ellis
Randall Northam
Grace Griffin
Annabel Bennett
Emma Routh
George Palmer
Vanessa Oloughlin

The Author

Douglas Board is co-head of Coachmatch Career Management and an honorary senior visiting fellow at Cass Business School, City University London. After growing up in Hong Kong and receiving degrees from Cambridge and Harvard, he worked for the UK Treasury and then as a headhunter. In 2010 he received a doctorate on how leaders are selected. He was treasurer of the Diana, Princess of Wales Memorial Fund and chair of the British Refugee Council. He is married to Tricia Sibbons; they live in London and Johannesburg.

Douglas is also the author of *Choosing Leaders and Choosing to Lead: Science, Politics and Intuition in Executive Selection* (Gower 2012) and (with Robert Warwick) *The Social Development of Leadership and Knowledge: A Reflexive Inquiry into Research and Practice* (Palgrave Macmillan 2013).